the Jezebel

The Jezebel

SASKIA WALKER

HARLEQUIN® HQN™

Recycling programs
for this product may
not exist in your area.

ISBN-13: 978-0-373-77744-0

THE JEZEBEL

Printed in U.S.A.

For my wonderful agent, Roberta Brown.
For my exceptionally talented editor, Susan Swinwood.
For my rock, the man who supports me every step of the way, Mark Walker.

chapter One

Billingsgate Docks, London, September 1715

Captain Roderick Cameron had just been forced to abandon his plan to procure a woman for the night, when one thrust herself upon him.

"Pardon me, sire." Throaty and alluring, the woman's voice called to him from the misty dockyard gantry under which she sheltered.

As much as he wanted some female company, Roderick Cameron pressed on. He couldn't afford to dally. His intention had been to oversee delivery of the bespoke goods they carried, imbibe some decent ale, then seek a woman's company for the night. The delivery was done, but from then on his plans had gone awry. He was currently hastening back to his ship with an excise man and a navy officer on his trail, and he was not eager to be waylaid. He'd already sent his crew back to ready the *Libertas* for departure on the turn of the tide.

"Are you Captain Cameron of the ship known as the *Libertas?*"

Roderick frowned. Something about the woman's voice stating his name aloud halted him in his tracks, despite the threat of imminent arrest that loomed at his back. It was as if she had touched him to the quick. Bemused, he peered into the shadows. "What do you want with Captain Cameron?"

The woman stepped out of her hiding place and into the moonlight. "I've been told that his ship sets sail for Dundee this evening."

Heavily cloaked as she was, and with her hood drawn low, it was impossible for Roderick to distinguish the woman's features. Was she a penny whore with a pretty voice who had agreed to waylay him and call him out? Excise officers were in pursuit because of a prior dispute about the goods the *Libertas* carried. Roderick grimaced. The navy had a network of informants and collaborators down here at Billingsgate docks, where so many ships came and went.

If it were a trap he would have been jumped by now. Nevertheless, he sensed trouble and quickly pressed on, striding toward the docks. He had no intention of confirming or denying his identity. His vessel still concealed French wine that was destined for the lairds in the Scottish Lowlands. It was cleverly hidden between two false walls behind his private quarters. If the navy found out what he was carrying and where he was headed, his troubles would be doubled. Nevertheless, the woman had caught his attention, and now it seemed as if she intended to pursue him.

"I need to speak with the captain most urgently." She hastened along at his side. "I need to know if he truly is bound for Scotland."

"What is it to you where any ship docked here is bound?" He shot the question back over his shoulder.

"Please, sire, I seek passage to Dundee."

It was uncanny. Her voice beckoned to him, reaching into him far deeper than words alone ever would. Roderick turned back and peered down at her. From what little he could see of the woman she did not look like someone he might expect to find here on the dockside, where only drunks and whores and lust-fueled seamen passed by this late in the evening. Her face was still hidden by her hood, but upon closer inspection he could see by the quality of her clothing that she was no dockside whore. Her dark blue velvet cloak and the gown beneath it looked costly, with a jeweled bodice and sumptuous fabric. In one hand she clasped a small bundle, partially hidden beneath her cloak.

It felt like a trap, but Roderick found he had to know and understand it before he sidestepped it. "The *Libertas* does not take passengers. Besides, why would a fine English lady such as yourself want to travel to Dundee...alone?"

She lowered the hood of her cloak, finally revealing her face.

Roderick stared at her. Her appearance defied him to do otherwise. She was a beauty, with silken black hair that cascaded over her shoulders. Delicately defined eyebrows arched over eyes that glinted brightly in the moonlight. Her lips—still parted on her plea—were exceedingly kissable.

She gave a quick and rather forced smile. "I am as Scottish as you are, Captain Cameron."

Roderick lifted his brows in surprise. She'd not only decided that he was indeed the captain, she also claimed to be a Scot. His curiosity flared, as did his wariness. "If it's true, we're both far from home. But I hear little trace of Scotland in your voice."

Her hands twisted together over her bundle. "I have lived in London since I was a bairn. I am a grown woman now and I wish to return to my kin."

The woman's strange request compelled him to listen. Her body, so feminine and so close to his, bewitched him, which was dangerous. A woman who held sway with a man of the sea was capable of breaking his bond with it. He'd seen that happen often enough, but it was not for him. Perhaps he was intrigued by her because his earlier plan to seek a whore's company for the night had been thwarted. It had to be the reason why she made him pause on the journey back to his ship, a journey that should have been stealthy and fast.

Glancing back over his shoulder, he saw figures moving in the distance. Seamen on their way to the port, but it kept his senses keen nonetheless. "I'm afraid you must seek assistance elsewhere."

When he met her gaze Roderick found that the oddly solemn look in her eyes stalled him yet again.

"Please, Captain." Reaching out with her free hand, she clutched at his coat sleeve. "You would do me a great service if you helped me." Her tone grew pleading. "I must leave London tonight."

Roderick indulged himself a moment as he contemplated making her comfortable in his cabin, imagining her there. His desire to assist her increased, as did a more basic desire.

He'd planned to bed a woman that night, and a tryst with this strange beauty would be quite something, he was sure. He attempted to force the base urge away. They had rules aboard the ship and he had to be on his way. "We do not carry passengers," he repeated. "Neither do we allow women on board the ship."

"I cannot go back there."

Roderick's attention shifted. The woman had attempted to shield her emotions, but now he could see that she was afraid. It was not his concern, but he did not like to see a woman with fear in her eyes.

Shouts sounded in the distance. Unease crept up his spine.

Her eyes flickered. She seemed to sense that he was torn. "Please, sire, I must leave this very night, for my liberty is at stake."

Liberty? It could be a tactic meant to sway him, and yet Roderick knew he would not rest easy if he sent her back to whatever it was she feared, without knowing the truth of the matter. His sense of honor on such matters would not allow it. His shipmen would not be happy having a woman aboard, but it was not a long voyage. They would be in Dundee before the week was out.

The scent of her made him hanker to get closer, while her rosebud lips seemed to beckon him to taste.

"I do not have much to offer you in payment," she whispered, stepping closer still, "but I can offer you several trinkets."

Her eyelids lowered and Roderick noticed that she was assessing him from beneath her lashes. Her hand on his arm tightened.

That touch ignited him.

When her black lashes lifted there was an altogether different look in her eyes. It was determined and alluring both.

"And there is something else I can offer you," she added.

Roderick cocked his head to one side while he waited to hear what it was.

Her gaze held his and her lips—as soft and tempting as a ripe berry—parted as she spoke, her voice scarcely above a whisper. "My virginity."

Roderick stared at her, then laughed. A woman so wily and forthright was no innocent virgin, but her brazen offer fired his loins nonetheless. Could he resist having her? He'd have to deal with a barrel load of trouble if he took her on board ship, but when he looked down at her upturned face he also knew he would forever be haunted with regret and curiosity if he did not.

He cupped her jaw in one hand, admiring her strange beauty, imagining how she might look while he claimed his reward between her thighs. Heat built in his loins, his cock hardening.

Her eyes flashed. "I am yours to plunder as you wish, Captain Cameron of the *Libertas*," she said, and that voice of hers seemed to reach all the way into his innards and hold him to her, "in return for safe passage to Dundee."

chapter Two

Maisie Taskill was tempted to influence the captain by means of magic, even though she knew it would complicate matters further into their acquaintance. She would do it if she had to, but only if it was absolutely necessary. It was, however, essential that she depart from London that night. She was overdue at The King's Theatre, where she was expected to watch a performance of an opera by Handel with her guardian, her master. Her absence would be noted soon enough, if it had not already raised suspicion. The thought of her master's reaction chilled her. Icy fingers encircled her heart, clenching it in a grip so tight she could scarcely breathe.

Please take me with you, help me escape this treacherous web I am caught in.

The captain grumbled low in his chest as he assessed her. It was a strange sound, rough and manly. It made her want to press her hand to his chest to experience the occurrence through touch as well as sound. Maisie Taskill was always curious about such things.

She could not see him well, for his hat was low on his brow and his face was cast in shadow. Occasionally he lifted his head to look about, and when he did she caught sight of his eyes in the moonlight and saw reluctant interest there. Her offer of a carnal exchange had definitely secured his attention. Desire was there in his expression, but for a moment she still thought he was going to shake his head and turn away.

Instinctively, she clutched at his coat to stop him from doing so. Before she had even made contact his gaze sharpened, following the movement of her fingers, intent and watchful. When her hand rested close to his chest he gave another low grumble, but this time it sounded different to Maisie. Less disgruntled. Seductive, almost. His chest felt broad and strong beneath his coat and she almost pulled away, so unfamiliar was she with a man such as he—a burly man who worked with both brawn and brain. A sturdy, honest man.

At least that was what Maisie hoped Captain Cameron was. One could never tell, and men could turn on a woman—as she knew too well—but right at that moment she didn't have any choice. She parted her lips, about to plead again.

In the distance a whistle sounded, cutting through the thickening mist with a warning of trouble.

The captain grabbed her hand in his. "You will have your passage to Dundee if your feet are fast enough to carry you to my ship."

Before she had a chance to respond, he set off, drawing her along in his wake as he broke into a run through the gloomy dockyards of Billingsgate. It was dark and mist clung in patches. She could barely see, and yet the path he forged was not straight, which was apparently his intent. Maisie wondered how he knew this place so well, but she was glad he did. It was also a mercy that the whistle had made him take action. The sound had set his deliberations to short shrift. Could it be that she would truly be on her way to Dundee that night? Hope lit in her heart.

The captain's stride was long and fast, and even though she lifted her skirts and hurried along behind him, still clinging tightly to his large, callused hand, her breath was soon labored. She rued the tightness of her corset. It had been appropriately laced for sitting in a theater box, but not for such a vigorous activity as this.

The captain made a sharp left turn, pausing briefly as he did so. The moonlight broke through the clouds and she saw the dark looming shape of a ship up ahead. He glanced down at her. "I'm sorry, but the haste is necessary."

Maisie realized that he, too, was fleeing. "Why is it that *you* must run?"

The captain grabbed her bundle with his free hand and urged her forward again even while he answered her question. "There are those in London who will pay highly for the best French wine. My men have delivered several cases under cover of darkness and risked their neck in doing so. The excise men have been alerted. I was on my way back to my vessel when you called to me."

Maisie silently corrected her previous assumption about his honesty. Not entirely honest in matters of commerce. With some trepidation she hoped that he was an honorable man, and not brutal by nature. Many traders sidestepped the excise man. Earlier that day she had ascertained that Captain

Cameron was in charge of a free trade vessel, a merchant ship. She had no idea he might be hunted down for his dealings, but she would have had to approach him anyway, for his was the only ship bound for Scotland that night or in the days following, and she didn't have much time to make her escape. It did make her feel a mite less uneasy about the fact she was tricking him into taking her, for in all likelihood she was every bit as dangerous to him as a bout of smuggling, if not more so.

Lurid laughter emerged from a shack to one side, and when she glanced in as they passed, she saw a woman ensconced with two men. One held a lantern aloft as she lifted her skirts for them. Shocked, Maisie stumbled on.

"Tread carefully," her guide urged, and pulled her away from a tangle of net and rope.

They drew nearer to a ship and she thought their hasty dash was at an end, but he went beyond it, to another vessel. The closer they got, the more it seemed to loom above them.

Three figures perched on upturned crates close to the dockside were engaged in a huddled conversation. They lifted their heads as she and her guide approached. One, a scrawny lad, rose to his feet and saluted the gentleman at her side. "Captain."

Just as she had expected, this was indeed Captain Roderick Cameron.

"On board at once, Adam," he said in reply. "We are ready to set sail. Pass the order below deck."

The young man picked up a flagon and looped one finger through the handle at its neck. Then he turned on his heel and launched himself at a large rope net that hung down from the side of the ship to the dock. Maisie watched in astonishment as he climbed it with one hand, the toes of his bare feet gripping the rope with easy agility, his other hand holding tight to his flagon as he went.

Surely she and the captain would not have to board the vessel that way? Maisie swallowed down a fresh wave of anxious emotion.

"You appear to have company, Roderick," one of the other men said in a wary tone, and nodded at her.

"The lady has to get to Dundee."

The man shook his head, grumbled to himself and turned away. He crossed to the ship on a wooden plank that had been placed from the quayside to the vessel. When he got to the top he vaulted over the ship's railing. The third man, who was elderly, with a pronounced stoop, followed the first, clambering up the rope net like a bird flitting from branch to branch, despite his apparent age.

"Make haste," the captain urged Maisie. He glanced over his shoulder once more, then waved up at a man perched near one end of the ship. The man on deck signaled back, and she heard shouting, as if he was rousing others. Sure enough, several sailors came to the rail and started hauling up ropes attached to bags of sand that sat upon the quay.

"You go ahead of me," the captain said. "I'll bring up the rear and then we must be off." He nodded toward the plank and smacked her on the behind, urging her along.

Maisie gasped at the sudden contact. Swallowing, she reminded herself she was amongst workingmen now, who did not behave the way she was used to gentlemen acting. When Cameron slapped her rump a second time and pointed, she realized that he meant for her to board his ship by walking up the plank. She put her hand on the place where he had stimulated her flesh through her gown and petticoats, and stared at the wooden walkway in disbelief. It was perilously narrow, and didn't seem to be well secured. Rubbing her hip, she took a few tentative steps, urged on by the captain. The wooden board sagged and shifted as she moved sideways along its length.

Beneath her, the flash of moonlight on the murky waters seemed an ominous warning. An unsavory stench rose from the dockside, invading her nostrils—the odors of rotting vegetables and excrement. Her stomach turned, and Maisie bit back the urge to shake her head and flee. Swaying unsteadily, she berated herself for being so weak, well aware this swooning attitude wouldn't get her to Scotland. Why, the captain and his men surely tramped up and down this wooden plank all the time, and she was making a fool of herself. Suitably emboldened by that notion, she forced herself on. She couldn't turn back. With a wry sense of her own unhappy situation, she silently admitted that she'd rather end up in the filthy waters below than have to go back where she'd come from.

With that grim thought as motivation, she made it to the boat. Clamping her hands over the rough wood rail, she wilted with relief and gasped for breath.

As she wondered how she was supposed to mount the railing, the board beneath her feet began to bounce heavily as the captain approached. Without further ado—and hoping that no one was in the vicinity to see her unladylike actions— she hauled up her skirts and flung herself over the barrier.

Staggering, she clung to the railing again and stood upright on the deck. The smell of wood and tar was heavy in the air. Voices called out all around her—the shipmen in action.

"Well mounted, my lady," the captain said with some amusement as he vaulted easily over the railing behind her. He tossed her bundle to her, then bent to pull the plank onto the ship.

Maisie attempted to get her bearings. Farther along the railing, the men had finished hauling the sandbags onto the deck. Beyond them a fearful rattling sounded as a sailor cranked a wheel. "Anchors aweigh, Captain," he shouted over his shoulder.

Captain Cameron shoved Maisie on ahead when he noticed one of the men who had pulled up the sandbags peering over at her, a hand on his hip. She couldn't see the sailor's expression, but supposed her unexpected arrival made him curious.

"Stay here in the shadows," the captain instructed, leading her to a sheltered spot beside a ladder up to another level. He jerked his head, nodding down to what looked like a doorway in the surface of the deck. "As soon as we're on our way and out to sea, I'll take you below deck to my quarters."

With that, he was gone, climbing up the wooden ladder quickly and shouting instructions as he went.

Maisie pressed back against the boards behind her and held her precious bundle to her chest, for the ship's movement on the water took her by surprise. She peered over at the odd hatch in the floor he had indicated, and wondered what he meant by 'below deck.' Was his cabin down there?

Reference to his cabin alerted her to the fact that he intended to accept the offer of her virginity. Perhaps there was nowhere else to house her, if they did not usually take passengers. Either way, her virginity was something she had to be rid of, and the sooner the better. If she were returned to her master, he would claim it, and then she would never be free of him. It had to be a man of her choosing—a man who knew nothing of her secret nature and could not gain from it, unless she deemed it possible. Nevertheless, the impending event made her nervous. She tried to control her emotions. It was important that the coupling was done the right way, that she be the one who gained from the undertaking and became empowered by it, for it would take her abilities into a higher realm. If she was to escape and to survive, she would need every ounce of her potential power to do so.

A bleating cry, like that of a child, made her jump and pulled her back from her thoughts. When she turned her head to seek out the source, she saw two young goats tethered nearby, their hooves planted widely on the boards for balance.

Startled, she watched as men emerged from another hatch at the far end of the ship, scrambling out and darting about the deck. She pressed farther back into the shadows. At first it seemed chaotic, but she soon realized they were all set upon a particular task. Three of the men ran toward the tall wooden poles that rose high above the ship, and began to clamber up them, their legs and arms wrapped around the masts as they inched rapidly upward. Maisie stared, fascinated, as they untied the sails. The great swathes of material unfurled, dropping down with almost majestic grace. The sound of the sailors' shouts was all but lost in the flapping of the canvas.

She caught the captain's voice from beyond. He was somewhere above and behind her, and she struggled to remember what little she knew of ships. The vessel's wheel must be there. She strained to hear the content of the bellowed instructions.

"Make haste!" It was his voice.

"The tide is barely on the turn, Captain," a man replied.

"There's no wind," another added. "It is not a good time to sail."

"We must away," the captain replied. "I was followed, I'm sure of it. I saw a man lurking and watching as we came aboard ship."

Maisie's right hand went to the silver clasp on her cloak and she clutched it for comfort. *Followed.* The captain thought it was him that was being followed, because of the goods he carried. But what if he was wrong and it was she who was being pursued? She pressed her eyes tightly shut and hoped that the captain was wrong and that no one had seen them depart.

Another shout from above made her look up. The men who had undone the sails were busy clambering down, but one of them signaled to the captain and then shook his head. The sails fell flat. They needed wind to fill them.

Maisie heard the captain grumbling. She felt a sense of danger as the vessel floated close to the dock, barely tipping in the turn of the tide. That had to change.

This would not do. She pulled her hood low over her face, concealing it in case anyone noticed as she whispered a spell to encourage the wind to fill the sails and aid them in their escape. An echo of her magic, when she drew on it, often shone in her eyes, the depth and color reflecting the emotional nature of her quest. However, in the gloom of this overcast night, she might not draw the attention of the men around her. It was worth the risk.

Inhaling deeply, Maisie readied herself. With one hand still clutching her bundle to her, she drew her free hand over her heart and then opened her fingers to the sky, whispering an enchantment. Breathing deeply, she pictured the clouds shifting faster, willed the air to swirl in around them and push them out to sea.

"Captain!" A startled voice rang out.

The ship lurched, and Maisie gasped in alarm at the sudden, vigorous motion, pressing into the corner where she was hidden, and clutching the wall. When she glanced up she saw the sails flap, then bow out, filled with a steady gust of wind. Relieved, she smiled, thanking her lineage for her gift.

A cheer rang out behind her.

"You have the luck of the devil on your side tonight, Captain," the same voice commented, with a disbelieving tone.

Maisie's smile faded.

The luck of the devil. That's what they thought it was.

It was crucial they didn't discover she had aided them by magic, for they would think her one of the devil's own. Just as the villagers had thought her mother evil when they'd stoned her, forced her to the gallows then burned her corpse.

Maisie shivered as the memory ran ice through her veins, reminding her of the pain, as well as the constant danger of discovery. She was alone now, no longer protected by her keeper. It was the way it had to be. She could not regret leaving, but danger abounded for a woman like her.

chapter Three

The captain's quarters were surprisingly comfortable for the cabin had the look of a small parlor. The only difference was that the room also contained a bed, a wood-framed affair secured to the wall and the floor by solid carved plinths. The walls were lined with shelves and cabinets filled with goods. There was also a large table that took up a good quarter of the space, maps and tools set out upon it. Maisie noticed that the maps were anchored with weights. Would the roll of the ship increase when they were farther out at sea? It was already rather dramatic and had set her belly in a quandary. She took a deep, steadying breath, sensing she would soon find out whether she liked it or not.

"Make yourself comfortable," the captain said, and cast off his hat. "You'll be accommodated here for the journey."

Maisie got her first good look at his face, illuminated by the glow of a glass-covered lantern fixed on a shelf at his side. Thick red-brown hair fell over his forehead. He was a robust seafaring man, largely built, with an attractive mouth, stub–

bled jaw and brown eyes. He would not be considered handsome, Maisie decided, not by the young ladies of London,
but there was a rugged quality to his features that drew her
attention. It made her think of her birthplace, the Highlands.
Perhaps because he was a Scot, and she had not been in close
quarters with a gentleman from her homeland since she was a
child. It stirred her in a way she had never thought it might.

When she nodded at him, he studied her with a brazen
stare, his gaze raking over her appreciatively. "What is your
name?"

"Margaret," she answered, cautiously. The less he knew
the better.

"Margaret, eh? And what do they call you? Meg? Maggie?"

His voice, a deep rumble with a Scottish burr that took
her back to her childhood, appealed to her senses immensely.
It also made her respond by giving the name her kin would
call her. "Maisie."

"Maisie." He broke into a grin. "You *are* a Scot."

"That I am." Despite her wariness toward him, something
unfurled inside her: the tight fist of concern that surrounded
her escape. Now that she was truly on her way, she thought
of the destination instead. Scotland. It was a journey she
should have undertaken many years before. But her master
had promised to take her himself, telling her she would enjoy
a reunion with her siblings—and she had believed him. Once
she found out how many lies he had told her, she knew that
a reunion would happen only if she were to pursue it herself.

"Come now, take off your cloak." The captain nodded at
her, then turned to his table. He was so broad and tall that
he seemed to fill the space, yet he managed to move around

it easily. Familiarity, she supposed. He exchanged the map that was currently laid out with a different one, swapping the sheet of parchment for one he retrieved from a stack of rolls in a recess above.

Maisie set down her bundle and reached for the clasp on her cloak. As she took it off and folded it neatly, she had an odd feeling, sensed an echo of familiarity with her surroundings—which could not be the case. Looking about, she frowned. She ran her fingers along the sideboard, and something touched her mind, like a memory trapped within. When she laid her hands upon various objects in the cabin, the connection grew stronger. It was as if she knew someone who had traveled here before.

For a moment, she was aware of her twin sister, Jessie. Maisie sensed her in a way that she had not for many years. It was rather like times when they were children and they would turn to each other, state the same thing and chuckle. Maisie had felt that connection rarely in the years they had been apart, but when it happened, she could sense Jessie thinking of her, too. Could it be her sister had also traveled aboard this vessel at some time? Was that it? "Have you carried a woman aboard before?"

The captain was busy disrobing. He'd thrown off his greatcoat and set about unbuttoning the waistcoat beneath. Maisie stared at him as he shrugged off the garment, revealing the broad expanse of his chest when he stretched. Surely he did not mean to undress fully and claim his fee from her right at this moment?

He glanced her way, and as he replied, reached for a cloak that was tucked in a gloomy corner of the cabin. A momentary sense of relief passed through her as she realized he was changing his shore garb for this odd dark cloak, coated in some thick substance akin to oil pigment. The odor of linseed came from the garment, along with something else that smelled like sap or tar, Maisie observed with curiosity.

"We carried a female passenger once before. My men vowed they would mutiny if I tried it again." His stare raked over her, the implication heavy in his sensual smile. He had risked the wrath of his men taking her on board, and he meant to be well rewarded.

The hungry look in his eyes sent a shiver through her. It was a clear statement of intent. He meant to have her. That in itself was no surprise; it was what she had arranged. But the *way* he looked at her, with his mouth pursed, as if he was thinking lewd thoughts… The very intimate and suggestive nature of it made her wonder what it would be like to be bedded by a rogue such as this—a man who thought nothing of giving her a sound slap on the rump if he chose to. It made her heart beat faster and let loose a flutter of anticipation between her thighs. She would experience his passion, and soon, by the eager look of him. That made the tingle in her intimate places grow wilder still. Heat flooded into her face.

Forcing herself to ask, she pursued that strange echo in her mind. "Did your passenger look like me?"

He shook his head. "Not in the least. She was a grumpy dowager who ordered my men about as if she were queen and captain both."

His expression indicated the extent of the trouble the woman had caused, and Maisie found she could not help being amused. "Now I see why you were reluctant to take me."

"You'd better not cause me as much grief as she did."

Maisie lifted her chin. "I will endeavor not to."

She thought he was about to leave. Instead, he approached her, and again there was hunger in his eyes.

Maisie felt her nerves flutter. Anticipation pulled deep within her, for she'd been thoroughly prepared for the moment her deepest, most powerful magic would be unleashed through carnal congress. This man would be her lover. He would make her both woman fulfilled and witch empowered.

"In fact, you must stay here, safe in my quarters and out of the men's way, or there'll be trouble aplenty."

Maisie did not like the sound of that. She could not survive long without seeing the sky. "How many days will the journey take?"

"We'll dock in Dundee inside a week. We break at Lowestoft, where the first officer must visit with his family for the night, but we'll be gone with the tide in the morning. The pause will not hamper us much." Captain Cameron nodded at the bed. "Rest awhile."

"You must go back to your men now?" she asked, finding herself eager to know her host a little better, keen to listen to his gruff voice and have it stir her deepest memories and her anticipation both.

"Alas, I must, although I would rather stay and bed you now."

Inhaling sharply, Maisie reflected that it would take time to get used to his frank manner. He gave a low laugh in response, the rumbling sound vibrating through her.

"Let me look at you, so that I may relish the thought of

returning to your side." He put one hand on her waist and pulled her body closer to his.

He leaned into her, his face so close to hers that she could feel his warm breath on her forehead. His large figure looming over her all but shrouded her in darkness, making her instantly aware of his male strength and power. She could scarcely control her erratic breathing, for his proximity and boldness overwhelmed her and made her feel light-headed.

His stubbled jaw brushed against her cheek, a gesture brusque, but oddly tender.

"You smell good," he whispered, breathing against her hair, his hands moving over her as if measuring her outline. From arms to waist and then up they went, his thumbs moving toward her breastbone, while his palms cupped her breasts through the barrier of her bodice, corset and under things. Squeezing her flesh through the hindersome garments, he murmured approvingly.

Then his hands moved around her back and down. Cupping her bottom, he drew her against him. With effortless strength he lifted her feet from the floor, and she was barely on her tiptoes as he fondled her flesh through her skirts. So determined was his touch that Maisie gasped in astonishment.

"Oh, yes, I will enjoy mounting you, my lady," he said, a wicked smile on his face.

Looking down at her with heavily lidded eyes, he appeared to her the embodiment of male prowess, sheer animal lust spilling from him as he arrogantly stated his intention. His comment teased, as if he were touching her all over, making every part of her tingle with awareness, and deep between her thighs she grew hot and slick. Nevertheless, Maisie was overwhelmed by his basic, arrogant ways, and even while her body responded to his advances, she trembled.

His eyes glinted, and she knew that he had felt her shiver in his arms.

Maisie swallowed. She did not want to annoy him in any way. Would he find her gaucheness unappealing?

It seemed to have the opposite effect. A wry smile lit his expression. He put one hand around the back of her head. Grasping a fistful of her hair, he looped it around his fingers and used it to draw her head back. With his other hand on her waist, he held her tightly against him.

Seduction was his aim, and she wanted that. The nervousness she felt subsided somewhat but did not ebb away entirely.

"Do not look so afeared, Maisie from Scotland," he said with a chuckle. "I will use you well, but I will not break you. You have my word on that." He sealed the promise with a kiss, his hard mouth on hers relentless.

Instinctively, Maisie put her hands to his chest to push him away. Then his mouth moved and the sensual brush of his lips took the strength from her entire body, melting her. Moments later, she found that instead of pushing him away, her hands clutched at his strange oily cloak and her lips parted under his. So sensual, so arousing… Maisie had never experienced anything like it. When his tongue touched hers and thrust into the heat of her mouth, her groin flooded with sensation again, arousal swamping her.

Unbidden, a low moan rose inside her, escaping into sound as the kiss broke. Instantly, she was aware of what her deflowering would bring to her magic, for her spirit flared within.

When he freed her mouth, the captain still held her by the

skein of hair looped in his hand. It didn't hurt, but his grip was tight enough to show that he meant to master her. Why did that make her legs falter? Maisie could scarcely breathe. The layers of clothing between them did nothing to hide his intention, for his hips were pressed firmly against her and the hard rod of his erection was all too apparent.

"Rest now," he murmured gruffly, "for you will get little rest later, when I return for my reward." His brows lifted, humor flashing in his eyes. "I mean to ride you until dawn, Maisie from Scotland, by which time you will be so thoroughly used and sated that you will beg me for respite."

With that provocative pronouncement, he let her go.

Maisie wilted, staggering backward until a chair halted her. Grasping at it with both hands, she held herself upright. Her entire body was hot and unsteady, a fever of nerves and longing assailing her as she thought on his words.

She remained in that place for several long moments after he had gone, staring across at the door he had tugged closed behind him. Captain Cameron was a force of nature, no doubt about it. Her passage into womanhood at his hands would be memorable, she was sure. The kiss he had bestowed on her had left her feeling quite exalted, but there was no telling how events might unfold.

Hastening to the bedside, she set her velvet bundle on the floor, close by. It contained her most prized possessions, and items she needed to ready herself for the moment. Alongside her training in the knowledge of witchcraft, she had been preparing for her initiation into full carnal congress for several years. It had to be done right, and it was crucial that the man who had nurtured and hidden her as a young witch did not claim her for himself now. Maisie still wasn't sure that choosing a lover by chance would free her of her obligation to her master, but she had to do everything she could to break away from him.

Perching on the edge of the bed, she was grateful for the moment to herself.

Everything had happened so quickly. Inside the turn of one day she had learned the full truth of her situation, and had taken flight. Now she was on her way to her true home in Scotland. So often she had dreamed of returning, but it was hard to break with the life she had become used to. In many ways it had been a good one, and she had felt protected and valued for several long years.

That was no longer the case.

But she had broken free, and now—as she recalled the image of the captain in the lamplight, and her body still vibrated from his touch—she found the anticipation helped to quell any doubts she might have about her actions. Captain Roderick Cameron had given her his word he would not break her. It had been a lucky encounter, she knew, when the manner of selecting him for the task had been so random and fraught with untold dangers. He would make a fine lover, she decided, one who would make no claim on her when the deed was done. It would be a simple exchange, and when she left his ship she would easily be able to make the onward journey alone because of it.

For a moment she reflected on how resourceful she'd been, buying her voyage with her virginity. Escaping from London as soon as she could had been essential, but so, too, was the small matter of ridding herself of that prize that was so valued by her master—for he wanted to be the one to have her.

The strange echo suddenly came over her again—drifting around the cabin like a forgotten memory, or a tale as yet untold—and it stimulated a question. Were her siblings even alive? Resting her head in her hands, Maisie faced her deepest fear. Now that she was going back to the land where her mother had been put to death, she had to acknowledge it. The heady rush that accompanied her escape dimmed momentarily as she thought of the reality that had haunted her kind for so long: persecution and death.

She lay down on the bed, as her emotions dipped and churned like the waves beneath the ship. The uncertainty of her journey was quickly overtaken by the imminent unleashing of her most powerful magic. Hope fluttered inside her.

I will find a path home to my kind. I will forge it.

For years she hadn't wanted to return to Dundee, after witnessing the horror of her own mother's death. Nevertheless, Scotland called to her—called to the purest part of her soul, reminding her that she could be free and whole in the far north of the Highlands.

The journey had begun. Exhaling, she felt the tension in her body begin to unravel.

She would seek out her kin—her twin sister, Jessie, and her beloved brother, Lennox. Homeward bound, she was on her way. As she drifted into sleep, she thought of them as she'd known them years before, children running barefoot in the forest, picking flowers and herbs for their mother, who used those gifts to teach them her craft, rooting the ancient ways in them. Maisie pictured Lennox as a wily, rebellious lad who cared for his sisters nonetheless. And her fey twin, who was wilder even than she. Had they thought of her as she had of them?

Let them be safe and free in our birthplace, she wished as she drifted toward sleep, hoping that she would find them there. So many years had passed since they'd been torn apart. Too long. Pain twisted inside her as she remembered the day.

On the day her mother was put to death on a charge of witchcraft, Cyrus Lafayette and his wife, Beth, claimed Maisie Taskill.

Maisie and her sister had been forced to watch their mother stoned until she was close to death, before the villagers forced her upright to stagger to the gallows, where she could see her own funeral pyre as the rope went around her neck. The villagers decided the lad, Lennox, was too far under the devil's influence to be saved. They said he should be destroyed.

Maisie heard every word they spoke about her and her kin, and a deep part of her became locked in a prison of fear and horror in response.

The villagers decided the two girl children were young enough to be redeemed, if they were taught the wrongness and evil of their mother's ways. So it was that Maisie had been placed on a pillar at the kirk gates alongside her twin. With the church at their backs and the persecution of their mother before their eyes, they were supposed to learn what was wrong and what was right. Both girls learned what was wrong, because they balked at what the villagers said was right.

Maisie had struggled to stand upright on the stone pillar, but had kept her silence as she had been ordered to do by the people gathered there. Her brother had already been dragged away, lashing out and cursing the villagers. Jessie had whimpered and flailed, and Maisie wanted to go to her sister and help her, but could not.

Instead, the two of them were made to watch, made to suffer every wound and insult as their mother suffered. When she tried to turn her face away and close her eyes, Maisie was prodded by the man stationed nearby, his task to force her to observe.

Maisie had all but fainted from the horror unfolding before her when a man in coachman's livery pushed through the crowd and lifted her down from the pillar. The villagers did not stop him.

Maisie could not even attempt to break free, for she was in shock, petrified by what she had witnessed. The coachman had a scowl on his face and a whip in his hand, and she'd believed she was about to meet the same fate as her mother. However, the man held her tightly to him, with both arms around her, as he made his way back through the crowd. He did not speak, and Maisie had been so afraid, she could scarcely understand what was going on around her.

He took her to a coach, and a grand coach it was. When the door opened, she was taken from the coachman's arms by another man. He stood her on her feet in the interior and examined her before indicating the coachman should close the door.

The din of the crowd grew muffled once the door shut. Maisie trembled violently, her legs buckling under her.

The man put his hands beneath her elbows, easily holding

her slight form in place. Then he forced her to look at him directly by putting a finger under her chin.

Maisie's first glimpse of Cyrus Lafayette was not reassuring, for he was an imposing man with dark hair and intense green eyes.

"Your name is Margaret?"

She nodded.

Interest flickered in his eyes. He seemed to approve of what he saw. Instinct warned her that he knew what she was. Maisie could see it in his eyes and she shied back. But he smiled, and his eyes glittered, as if he was pleased.

"Poor child," a woman's voice behind her said, and Maisie found herself drawn backward into a comforting embrace. Shivering with fear and shock, she barely felt the woman's touch and could not fight it. Lifted onto the woman's lap, she was rocked to and fro. "We have saved you, child. You will come and live with us, and no harm will befall you."

The coach had set off, and Maisie remembered hearing the coachman ordering people out of his path, shouting and bellowing and urging his team to a faster pace. Was it true? Was she really safe? She turned to look at the woman who held her.

Beth Lafayette smiled. With pale blond hair and a gentle smile, she seemed kindly.

Eventually, Maisie reacted, speaking for the first time in several hours. "My brother and sister, Lennox and Jessie, are they coming with us?"

"They will find guardians, too, never fear," said the austere man, who sat opposite. "But your life is with us now."

"I have always wanted a beautiful girl child like you to call my own," the woman told her, and tears shone in her eyes. "Even though you are not of my blood, I would be greatly pleased if you would call me Mama Beth."

Feeling the woman's emotion and gratitude, Maisie closed her eyes, attempting to blot out the images she had seen, and gradually taking the comfort Beth Lafayette offered.

And at first it was good and it was safe.

But Cyrus had not collected her simply to fulfill his wife's wish for a daughter.

Cyrus Lafayette had plans of his own for Maisie Taskill.

chapter Four

Cyrus Lafayette meshed his fingers together as he paced up and down the polished wood floor of the drawing room. He had to keep his hands that way in order not to throttle the young coachman who cowered before him. The urge to snap the servant's neck was far too tempting.

The coachman shifted uneasily. "Please, sire. With your permission I will go back and ask again, see what I might find out."

"No." Cyrus paused and examined the man again, looking deep into his eyes. Was there something he was hiding, something else that he knew about Margaret that he was not sharing? Cyrus saw only fear, dim wit and incompetence.

The fear that shone in the coachman's eyes branded him a fool, in Cyrus's opinion. If the man had any sense of self-preservation he would speak more confidently, offer to lead Cyrus to the scene of Margaret's disappearance, instead of looking as if he was about to turn on his heel and run.

Pain needled Cyrus's eyes, the result of his barely withheld rage. He had to keep a rigid hold on it. He couldn't afford to let it overcome him, not now. "Tell me again what you witnessed, from the beginning. Salient details only. Do not embellish."

The coachman swallowed and then cleared his throat. "I was waiting to escort Miss Margaret to the theater, as instructed. At the appointed time I went inside, announced that the carriage was ready and inquired her whereabouts from the housekeeper. Miss Margaret was said to have dressed for the theater, but was nowhere to be found. When I stepped outside I believe I caught sight of her climbing into a carriage at the corner of the street. I wondered if she had forgotten I was there to take her to the opera. I thought that perhaps she'd hired a passing carriage instead, when she didn't see me. I quickly followed. My concern grew when I realized the direction the carriage had taken was away from the theater."

Cyrus interrupted the coachman. "You intended to stop the carriage?"

That's what he'd said on the first telling of the story. Cyrus's levels of suspicion and mistrust were so acute that he was ready to string the lad up and beat the truth out of him if even one detail differed from before.

The coachman nodded. "Unfortunately, I lost it in the maze of streets in Billingsgate. I secured the coach and then went by foot, but could find no trace of the carriage I'd seen. However, there was a mighty commotion down there by the dockside. Navy men and soldiers were everywhere, so I followed them to see what it was about."

"You say they were after the captain of a merchant ship?"

The coachman nodded. He clung tightly to the hat he held

in his hands as if it were a shield and he would be safe behind it. "I asked one of them, who said it was a ship by the name of the *Libertas*. But he knew nothing of a young lady who might be lost down there. In the chaos there seemed no hope of anyone having caught sight of her, alone or otherwise."

Cyrus frowned. Alone or otherwise. Why would she be down there alone? Did Margaret have a secret rendezvous? He could scarcely believe it. No, that could not be the case. He gave her no time in which to nurture friendships that were not conducted under his watchful eye.

The coachman rattled on. "But I wended my way through the place, looking for her, and I was about to give up when I thought I saw her crossing onto a ship, with a man close behind her."

Cyrus ground his teeth. The darkest question of all reared its ugly head again. Had she run into the night to a secret friend? Or worse still, a lover? The raw anger he felt doubled in response to that thought. For years he had nurtured that girl. *She is mine and mine alone.*

"I will return to Billingsgate," the coachman offered, glancing at the doorway, eager to be on his way.

"No." Cyrus glared at him. "I will send others. Men who are more adept at seeking out information."

The man lowered his gaze to the floor. "Forgive me, sire. I know that my task was to watch over Miss Margaret when you were not doing so yourself. If you forgive me for saying so—" he dared to lift his gaze, cautiously "—it was as if she slipped away into the night."

Cyrus lifted his brows in query. He was starting to detest the sight of this inept young man, a worker whom he'd been assured was reliable and astute when he was hired as third coachman to the household the year before.

The man stumbled on. "Perhaps Miss Margaret did not want to go to the theater."

Cyrus gave a harsh laugh.

The coachman recoiled, his hands tightening on the brim of his hat.

"If Miss Margaret had not wanted to attend the theater she was at liberty to say so. I am not a tyrant."

The coachman gave him a wary stare.

Cyrus twitched. "Did she give you any reason to suspect she might run away tonight, or at any other time during your employment here?"

The coachman shook his head.

"She has never slipped away from you before?"

Again he shook his head. Then he frowned. "She went for a walk earlier today. I heard of her intention and readied the carriage, but she insisted she needed no companion other than her lady's maid."

Cyrus lit upon that. Mayhap he would have more success gaining information from the maid. This dolt appeared useless. He wanted to dismiss him immediately and have him thrown into the gutter, but he could not rule out the possibility that the young man might as yet furnish them with something useful. It was necessary to get someone else to deal with it, however. The urge to make the young man suffer some part of what he himself was feeling was growing too great.

Cyrus snatched the man's hat from his grasp and threw it aside, then pointed at a nearby chair, into which the coachman slumped.

Standing over him, Cyrus forbade the man to move. "Miss Margaret is the most valuable thing in my life," he said, lowering his voice in an effort to convey the importance of his comment. "You will stay here and be prepared to repeat the details of your sorry story to anyone who enters this room tonight. There may be many, for I intend to hire all the best men I can find. I will raze London to the ground to find her if I have to, and you might hold the only information that can stop that from happening."

The coachman looked suitably rooted to the spot.

Cyrus headed for the door. As he approached, it sprang open and the housekeeper entered.

"Master Lafayette, it is Mistress Beth. I fear she is near the end."

Cyrus grimaced. He had nothing left to say to Beth, who had been near her end for days now. He nodded briefly. "Make her as comfortable as you can. I have other matters to attend to."

The housekeeper looked at him in dismay, disapproval flickering at the back of her eyes. "Begging your pardon, sire, but she is scarcely breathing."

Cyrus gave the servant a warning stare.

The woman dropped her eyelids.

Rightly so, and heaven help anyone else who stood between him and Margaret. Pushing past the housekeeper without further ceremony, Cyrus left.

Under limited sail the *Libertas* passed out of the Thames estuary and into open seas. Only then did Roderick breathe easy. It had been a near miss back there at Billingsgate.

They'd had similar scrapes many times before, of course, but it was essential they were not stopped now. They were due in Dundee to meet with Gregor Ramsay, the fellow shipman with whom he owned the *Libertas*. Roderick had been ready, though. If he'd been arrested back in London the men were under strict instructions to sail with the tide without him.

"Full sail," Roderick instructed.

Clyde relayed his orders, scurrying about as fast as any of the younger men, despite his hunched form and his advanced years. The man refused to rest. He also refused to make his home on land, swearing he would end his days at sea.

Men leaped at Roderick's command, climbing the rigging. More sails unfurled, quickly capturing the wind. He turned the wheel hand over hand, held course and inhaled the salt on the air. The creak of the boards and the snap of spar and sail reassured him, for they were a heartbeat that raced in concert with his own. Married to the sea, he was, and it was where he felt at peace. He directed the wheel awhile longer, then handed it over to Brady, the first officer. "Bear northeast awhile longer, then we turn full north."

Brady took the wheel, but stared at him, making it obvious he had something on his mind. Roderick could already guess what it was. Brady was waiting until they were in open waters before he confronted him, but the leaden stare had already conveyed enough.

"Do you intend to inform us about your passenger," the officer eventually said, with sarcasm, "or are we supposed to pretend we did not see the woman you brought aboard?"

Roderick frowned. He and Brady often held each other to account in Gregor's absence, but he did not appreciate the challenge in the seaman's tone. "The woman needed passage to return to her family home in Scotland. Would you have me leave her alone in London?"

"We take no passengers, especially not a woman."

Roderick bristled. "I am the captain of this ship, and if I deem it necessary on occasion, you will accept that and act accordingly."

Brady shook his head. "Since when has a woman swayed you so easily, Roderick Cameron?"

Again he frowned. Brady's comments needled him, for Roderick was determined his captainship would be a resounding success. In the six months since Gregor had been away from the ship the men had answered well to him, yet only days from reuniting with Gregor he now risked having the crew turn against him.

"What a spectacle you made, arriving with a slip of a girl in tow and God knows how many men after you."

"Enough!" Roderick barked. "Think on this. What if she was your sister, desperate to find her way home?"

Brady left that hanging in the air between them a moment. "But it was not your sister you were thinking of when you brought her aboard," he finally said with a wry smile. "I saw the way you looked at her as you took her below deck."

"It is easy for you to judge, when you have a night with your wife to look forward to."

"A fair point, I'll allow," Brady said with a mock bow. "As long as she gives the men no trouble, I will back you up and remind them of...what was it?" He gave a sharp laugh. "Oh, yes, their *sisters*."

Roderick was about to reply when Clyde appeared at their side.

"I gather from the raised voices that you quizzed him about the Jezebel." He directed his question to Brady, and followed it up with a chortle.

The Jezebel. Roderick gave an internal groan. It was what Clyde called all women, but it only served to implicate Roderick.

"I did, and he said he was thinking of his sister."

Clyde chortled again. "That Jezebel is a whole lot prettier than any sister of yours would be," he said to Roderick. "Lord help any woman saddled with your looks."

"I was concerned for her safety," Roderick insisted, "and she is a Scot."

Clyde rubbed at his beard. "Concerned for a warm bed tonight, I wager."

"How is it you have survived so long at sea, when you show such cheek toward your captain?" Roderick snatched the eyeglass from Clyde's hand and turned away to scan the waters behind them, straining his eyes in the darkness. There was no sign of lights on the water, no flash of a navy flag in the moonlight.

Still he stared into the darkness.

Beyond him the two men continued to whisper and chuckle, making lewd remarks about the captain's intentions.

Why in God's name had he brought a woman aboard? He hadn't been thinking straight. He'd been won over by her plea and the promise of a lusty tumble in bed with a lady such as her. It had been too long that he'd been without a woman's touch, for Roderick Cameron was not used to seeking them out alone. In fact it had been his fellow shipman, Gregor Ramsay, who had been the brazen carouser when they docked at ports near and far. Roderick did not consider himself a man of finesse, especially when it came to women. He was not gifted with charm and the necessary skills of seduction. Since his cohort, Gregor, had taken time away from the ship, Roderick's sole task was to keep the crew aboard the *Libertas* safe, no matter what dangerous task they undertook, and to keep his men content. He had dreamed of captaining a ship since he was a lad watching the vessels come and go down at the docks in Dundee, and he wasn't going to let anything threaten his leadership, least of all a woman.

They were trouble, no good for anything but a quick roll before you were on your way again. If you got a taste for it they could break your bond with the sea and hold you to the land. Brady was in a position to warn them of it, for he was saddled with a woman and bairns, too. Brady's lot was a warning to them all. He had a family he had to provide for even though he was a man of the sea. It tore the sorry man in two directions.

Roderick had longed for a woman that night, though, and she had appeared. Maisie from Scotland. What red-blooded man could have resisted? Surely it would do no harm to keep her below deck and deposit her in Dundee.

A cold wind whistled in over the water.

He thought of his bed, and the woman who was warming it.

"She's aboard now," he said, returning Clyde's eyeglass to him, "and you'd be wise to get used to the idea, because I intend to put her down on Scottish soil myself."

"What a gentleman you are," Brady said. "But you do intend to bed her, don't you?"

Roderick nodded. "Oh, aye. The men may grumble about her presence, but they would respect me even less if I didn't bed her."

Brady grinned. "Now I am reminded why you have their loyalty. You've a canny knack of sounding as if you're talking sense, no matter what fix you've got us all in."

Roderick laughed, but talk of getting them in a fix still niggled at him. There would be no fix, if he didn't let his curiosity about her circumstances get the better of him.

Much later that night, Roderick strode across the boards and climbed down the ladder below deck. He made his way along the narrow corridor to his quarters with his plan in mind. He would claim her, then arrange for her to be accommodated elsewhere until they docked in Dundee. He could not afford to be distracted by a woman. Assuring himself that it was possible to bed her and be gone, he opened the door and entered the cabin.

He'd been about to speak when he noticed she was slumbering on the bed. The sight pulled him up short and he stood by the door, staring across at her.

What a picture she made.

He'd been correct in his assumption she was no penny whore, for the gown she wore was now fully revealed, spread out on the bed as she was. It was a fine gown, made for a fine lady. How was it that a man such as he had the task of carrying her to Scotland, let alone bedding her?

Roderick relished the prospect. It would be a pleasure

indeed. His cock was already roused, hardening inside his breeches.

His gaze ran her length and he saw a flash of ankle between boot and skirts. Soon enough he would be lifting those skirts and shoving them out of his path. What he could see of her stockings indicated they might be the finest he had ever touched, and he looked forward to stroking them down her lovely legs. The cloak she had worn was folded neatly beneath her head. The fact she had used her own garment as a pillow made him smile. His pillows were clearly unworthy. She was a woman of some wealth, and yet she had no coin to pay for her passage. It made him curious, which was unfortunate, because it distracted him, when his intention was not to be distracted by any woman.

Maisie had settled enough on his bed to fall asleep. She had unlaced her bodice before doing so, and her breasts swelled enticingly from the silk corset beneath. One hand rested at her collarbone, the other was partly folded at her side, clutching her unraveled laces.

A true beauty she was. A princess dozing on his humble bed. Roderick found himself glad that she was asleep while he observed her silently from just inside the door. He wanted to wake her, but he savored the vision before him, and the fact she was there at all.

Easing off his cloak, he set it aside and moved closer to the bedside.

In her sleep, her brow seemed softly troubled. Roderick felt the urge to smooth that frown away, but held back his callused hand from the task. That was a delicate endeavor for which he was not best qualified. Instead, he sat on the edge of the bed and wrapped his fingers around those of hers that held her laces, lowering his head to breathe in her scent. The aroma of her femininity—both floral and fecund—intoxicated him. The alabaster skin of her throat and breast had him humbled and yet aroused. The women he had been with in previous trysts had been basic sorts, and now he felt cursed in his blind lust, uncouth and unskilled.

A woman, a beautiful woman at that, had offered herself to him. Desire pumped within him.

How easy it would be to pounce and plunder her. But what Roderick Cameron wanted most of all was to have her welcome him aboard. He rested a kiss on the elegant bump of her collarbone, holding himself back from diving down into her luscious cleavage.

Wake up, my beauty.

She stirred, her head rolling from one side to the other on her makeshift pillow. Roderick could not help but notice her delicate earlobes, and the soft, enticing skin behind them. Instinctively, he ducked his head and kissed her there, behind her right ear. The silken skin enticed him closer. He nuzzled her.

Oh, but you are precious and beautiful.

It was only when she jolted under him that Roderick realized he might have said that aloud, and woken her.

chapter Five

Maisie leaped awake.

Captain Cameron hovered over her.

Frozen to the spot where she lay on his bed, she met his stare as levelly as she could, her heart pounding, her mind filled with wonder about the fate she had designed for herself.

For an achingly long moment he seemed to search her deepest soul, looming over her with curiosity and fire in his eyes. How his gaze burned. It made her want to squirm, for she knew what it meant—that he wanted to possess her. And yet she felt caution in him. Had he sensed something about her? Her witchcraft, perhaps?

He lifted his head, then gave a broad smile. "You are the most beautiful woman I have ever had the prospect of bedding."

Maisie replied quickly, following her instinct. "I have been called pleasing, but you are a captain who has conquered many oceans. I am sure you have known many women and are merely flattering me."

He gave a husky chortle, then stepped away, unfastening his cloak and casting it aside.

She felt regret for her curt response. She was not normally so forthright. Her master had encouraged her to speak her mind only to him, for it was safest that way.

She shifted, sitting up and turning on the bed so that she could put her feet on the floor. Even though it was not the lush and fertile earth beneath her feet, doing so gave her some of the strength she would have drawn, had she been on land.

"I have known enough." He glanced back over his shoulder. "You are not like other women."

Her stomach knotted. What he said was true, although she could not let him believe it for longer than necessary. "I am but a woman," she insisted, "a woman at your mercy."

He turned back, closing in on her. Reaching out with one hand, he slipped it around her neck, his thumb stroking the skin of her collarbone. "At my mercy, eh?"

Maisie suppressed the shiver of anticipation that ran through her. How easily he could hold her. There was hunger in him. With her master such an action would have disturbed her greatly. With this man it only made her hope she had made a good choice. She forced herself to negotiate, to make the best of what she had given him in exchange for her passage to Scotland. "It has to be done a certain way."

"Oh. I know exactly how it has to be done, lassie, trust me on that point." He dropped to his knees, sliding his hands beneath her skirts to push her legs apart.

Maisie gasped. That was not what she meant. For her this moment was more sacred even than it would be for a normal woman. Her magic would be enriched and enhanced, her power unleashed.

However, the way he had opened her thighs, and his obvious desire for her, was overwhelming. Her curiosity about the carnal act made her anticipate the event, but she had not realized she would be so thoroughly affected by a lover's touch and eagerness. His actions made her feel as if she was sinking and rising all at once, her body responding with fervor. *I am aroused by him.*

Maisie had not reckoned for that in her carefully laid plans of how she would rid herself of her virginity—the gem that was so deeply coveted by her master.

"Are you ready for me?" The captain stroked a palm between her thighs, edging her skirts higher.

The touch of his rough hands above her stockings, where the skin was bare and sensitive, set her nerves alight. "Please... please allow me a moment, sire."

Maisie scanned the room. Her bundle was on the floor nearby. There were items that she needed, lodestones that would bind her unleashed carnal powers to her forever.

"A moment? It is yours. Not much longer, though." He chuckled as he stood and began to undress. "You are too enticing to a man."

Maisie had to act fast, yet she could scarcely drag her attention away from the sight of the captain removing his clothes. He did it so easily, tugging off his boots and tossing them aside. Mustering herself, she reached for her bundle and pulled it closer. Opening it, she made sure the lodestones were close to the top, then placed it as discreetly as she could beneath the bed, positioning it to sit directly below her center while she lay there.

Captain Cameron turned back to face her just as she straightened.

He pulled the loose shirt he wore up and over his head, revealing his chest. Maisie had scarcely taken in that sight when he moved his hands to the lace on his breeches. Her gaze was drawn in that direction. There was a bulky swelling within. Inhaling sharply, she looked away, thinking herself unable to observe as he shed his remaining clothing. It was too compelling a prospect. From the corner of her eye she caught glimpses of him as he undressed. The breadth of his chest seemed even more impressive unclothed, and his upper arms were surprisingly large. The way he moved, his body rippling with male strength, enthralled her. When he shoved his breeches off and his manhood was revealed she could not stop herself from staring openly. It rose from his groin as sturdy as the bough of a tree, its state of arousal undeniable. The prospect of it invading her left her breathless. She knew it was possible, for she'd had access to illustrations in the course of her education, but for a moment she doubted it. Even so, her blood raced.

While she was trying to decide whether she should disrobe herself, he strode over and lifted her bodily onto the mattress, then lay beside her. The heat and presence of his naked form made her move her hand to her chest in an attempt to quiet her nerves.

"It is not a large bunk," he said, "but it will take us both if we stay close together, which I warrant we will." His laugh was husky and he looked her over with undisguised interest.

His proximity was a seduction in itself. Peering up at him, she felt unsure what to do. She didn't have to fret upon it for long. He bent to place a kiss against the skin of her throat while he pulled her skirts up and bunched them at her waist, revealing everything beneath.

"Lord, what a sight," he murmured, when he drew back to take a look.

Maisie swallowed down the nerves that threatened to get the better of her, and forced herself to study his expression. He looked different with his eyes so alight with desire. Just then he traced his fingers around her exposed hip, sending a skittering sensation beneath her skin. Between her thighs, molten heat built, her body reacting to his blatant stare.

His expression had grown dark and he looked down at her with possessive eyes. "You will be well ridden tonight, my lady," he whispered.

The promise sent a delicious ripple through her. Her breathing felt increasingly constricted. Tentatively, she slipped one hand around the back of his neck. The other she locked on his shoulder. She wanted to couple with a man, had desired to for a long while. Her body ached to know how it felt, to feel his thrust as he filled her. She lifted her chin as the captain's mouth lowered toward hers. His arms went around her as their lips met.

Her eyes closed, her body melting in submission. His mouth made hers open beneath his touch, the kiss enmeshing her in a web of sensations. A feeling of great need bloomed within her, and she pressed closer to him. The totality of his strength and maleness enveloped her. Her skin prickled. She felt feverish. His tongue thrust into her mouth and she relished the experience, a moan of longing escaping her even as they kissed.

He encouraged her to open her legs, easing them apart with his hands, and then he broke the kiss and climbed between her thighs, giving her no option but to receive him there. The moment was almost upon her. Maisie quickly thought of the precious lodestones ensconced beneath the bed, and willed the event to strengthen her in every way.

The captain cursed under his breath at the very moment he settled his rigid manhood against her damp folds. Maisie gasped at the sudden contact. His shaft was both hard and hot, and it made her want to wriggle against it. Would that be wrong? she wondered. A trickle of moisture seeped from inside her, dampening her thighs. Heat flushed her face.

"Ah, but you are lush down there, my lady." His hips were hard against hers, his erection pressing against her seam, holding her folds open.

It was so hard, and the size of his member evoked a renewed sense of doubt. Again she stared down at it, marveling at its length, for when she lifted her head she could see the head of it poking up between them, despite the bunched skirts now wedged above her waist.

"You seem surprised," he said teasingly, and nodded down at his shaft. Shifting his hips, he rode it up and down against her folds, which made her moan aloud. "You like the look of it enough to receive it?"

Maisie wasn't quite sure if she liked the look of it or not as yet. She'd seen drawings of women receiving an erect member inside their body, but she suspected this one was far too large for her to manage.

"It arouses you to see a woman startled at your size?" she retorted defensively.

He stared down at her, his expression heavy with lust. "It arouses me to see you eager to welcome it. Are you ready?"

Whether it hurt or not, it had to be done. She nodded. "Yes, I am ready to...to welcome it."

That seemed to please him immensely. He paused to look down at the place where her breasts swelled up from her corset, and she realized her nipples had ridden above the edge of her bodice. It looked lewd to her, but the captain only grinned and bent to run his tongue over the hard pink tips that had been revealed. It felt achingly good—not only in her breasts, but all through her, from her nipples to the pit of her belly.

"I cannot wait long enough to undress you, but I will, before the second turn."

The second turn?

With that pronouncement he rearranged his position, then reached down and moved his fingers into her folds, stroking them into her entrance. With a deeply satisfied sigh, he nodded. "I want to be inside you badly. It must be done and now."

She closed her eyes a moment when he directed his rigid manhood to that place, pressing it against her. He coaxed the head of his erection up and down over her entrance, coating it in her juices. That only made her want it more. No matter how big, she had to have him inside her. "The way you touch me..." She rolled her head and then stared at him, captured by the desire in his expression. Her own body echoed it, craving him. "Use me, make me yours."

He growled at her words.

That triggered something between them, something that felt untamed and right. Every part of her clamored for him.

With one hand he stroked up and down the length of his shaft, squeezing a drop of dew from its tip. She swore and closed her eyes when she caught sight of its size again, her body clenching. It was too large, too hard. Surely it would injure her! But she did not have time to deny it, for he eased it into her opening.

The sudden push, stretch and fullness at her entrance captured her senses fully. "Oh!"

He pressed on.

Stretching her to capacity, he plundered her in ways she could not have imagined. Pain flashed through her and she felt hot fluids running onto the bed. She cried out. Her innermost flesh contracted and she tried to pull away.

The captain lifted his head and stared at her in surprise. "It was true, you really have not...?"

"Of course it was true," she blurted, her vision misting.

He paused, but did not withdraw. Instead, his jaw turned to rock, his hands firm on her hips as she struggled against him.

"Oh, oh!" she cried. "It is too much."

"Hush. Hold tight, my lady, it will pass." Slowly, inexorably slowly, he eased back. "You are plenty wet enough to receive me. I will go slowly for as long as I can."

With that promise he worked his length inside her again, measure by measure.

Through the pain, rapture sprang from the place where

they met. Maisie lifted her eyelids and looked at him in wonder.

"Better?"

She nodded, forcing herself to take a deep breath. The rigid bulk of his cock was hot and throbbing against her tender flesh, but she could tell he was holding back, waiting for her to get used to his presence there. Thankful for his care, she wrapped her hands around his shoulders and rocked her hips, getting the measure of him and the way they fitted together. Then she found that she could clasp his hardness within, welcoming him.

"Ah," he said, through gritted teeth, "now it is me who is nearly come apart." The muscles in his neck were rigid with restraint. "Go steady or I will not be able to hold back."

She nodded again. "Show me," she whispered, encouraging him to lead the way.

His eyes gleamed. Needing no further encouragement, he moved his hips, pulled back and then plunged deep, an action he repeated immediately, over and over again, until Maisie thought she might faint from the pressure he built there at the pit of her belly.

"Yes, oh, yes," she murmured, nearly delirious under him.

Pleasure and power welled inside her, its intensity threatening to overwhelm her. "Please," she whispered, begging for something she wasn't sure of.

"Eager again now," he commented with humor. "I like that."

The need inside her was feverish and her hips rocked to meet his as she sought her release. It shocked her how it took charge, how driven by instinct they both became.

The captain pulled out almost fully, before returning again to thrust her into a frenzy of anticipation and pleasure. The muscles in his arms gleamed in the candlelight as he rose up and drove into her with fierce determination. The more she moaned, the faster he thrusted, as if trying to tip her into madness.

Sheer ecstasy poured through her. Each time he thrust she moaned aloud, the force of their joining swamping her with ebullient emotions. The well of her magic was full to overflowing, and soon it would be visibly reflected in her eyes. To avert that she loosened her hands and let some of the energy escape from her fingertips into the air around them, creating a tremor in the cabin. The candle in the lantern fizzed and popped, and the captain glanced at it, but did not break his stride. He'd shifted, though, and the pressure of his body against hers—inside and out—made her grip her hands around his back again, holding tight to him, for she felt she might drown in pleasure. A garbled plea caught in her throat. Heat flamed in her groin, and her juices flowed even more readily.

"Ah, now, that is pleasure incarnate," he gasped.

His shaft seemed to get harder still, then she felt it jerk, and he pulled free. Rolling to one side, he erupted in his fist, which he continued to pump up and down for several moments after, enthralling her.

When he saw her watching, he seemed pleased.

He kissed her mouth, then rose to clean himself.

When he returned, he began to undress her.

Dizzy with pleasure, but eager to do the appropriate thing, Maisie half sat, giving him access to her laces.

"You have undressed women before?" she murmured.

"No, but it appears to be a similar mess to a tangle of rigging, and I've always had a knack with unraveling that."

That made her laugh, and when she glanced back over her shoulder at him, he smiled her way. Now that they had uncoupled she felt strangely adrift, but the way he undressed her, with care and attention, soothed her. Even so, she was embarrassed when he bared her fully.

He encouraged her to climb beneath the cover on the bed, then he carried her gown and under things to the map table, where he deposited them.

Joining her under the cover, he rested on his side, propped on one elbow to study her, observing her even more closely than he had before. Reluctant admiration shone in his eyes.

Maisie saw curiosity there, too. She had impressed him.

It hadn't been her intention. This whole endeavor was a means to an end for Maisie, her virginity a trinket that she had to be rid of, for all it was worth to her keeper. Being admired wasn't something she was unaccustomed to, however. She had spent so long being nurtured by Cyrus Lafayette, cocooned safely—or so she thought—in his worldly arena, that she had grown used to being watched and admired by a man.

When she looked at her lover she realized that what she saw in his eyes was very different. Admiration, yes. But he knew nothing of her secret talents, and he was admiring her as a woman, a woman who had apparently satisfied his lust.

That did surprise her. As much as she knew what she was doing by offering herself to him, and why, she did not expect that she would enjoy it herself—and she had, immensely. Nor did she expect the man she had chosen by default, in exchange for her passage to Dundee, to seem so thoroughly sated and pleasured by her company.

"There is one thing I do not understand." He considered her, his gaze encompassing her body, stretched upon his bunk, as he spoke. "It is true that you have not lain with a man before—that much is plain to see."

He paused and lifted the cover, the look in his eyes brooding as he considered her intimate womanly flesh at the juncture between her thighs, so freshly invaded by his rigid manhood, and the lingering streaks of blood on her inner thighs.

Maisie trembled. Every sensation she had experienced—from pleasure to pain, and back again into ecstasy—was so close in her physical memory that when he looked at her that way it ran through her flesh like myriad lightning strikes. How strange that was, that she had been so thoroughly affected by him. Maisie marveled at it, her heart racing as she contemplated the intense pleasure that had been borne out of the pain.

"How is it then," he continued as he lowered the cover, "that you seem to be so skilled, that you know so much about giving yourself willingly, and pleasuring a man?" He asked the question in a forthright manner, as seemed to be his way.

But how was she to answer? The explanation would sound strange to anyone she might offer it to, and she would not blame a man for not believing it.

A virgin who was highly educated about fornication.

It was little wonder his brow was so furrowed. Maisie could not give her answer aloud. Instead, she rose up to kiss his firm, masculine mouth, in order to distract him.

It is because I was taught everything I would ever need to know by my guardian, my keeper, and that included detailed study of the nature of physical congress and all it can bring for a woman such as I.

chapter Six

At his wife's request Cyrus Lafayette allowed "young Margaret" several weeks to grow accustomed to her new life in their Islington home before he began her education. Even though her guardian waited for her to settle in, Maisie could tell he was impatient. He wanted her instruction to begin. She soon discovered that her education was of great importance to Cyrus, although it was not until she was much older that she fully understood the reasons why.

The Lafayette house was large and overwhelming, and it took some time for Margaret to think of it as her home. The hallways were filled with sculptures and paintings, and the many rooms each had a different purpose, unlike the small croft cottage in which she had spent her infancy, and later the rented room she and her siblings had shared with their mother in the Lowlands. Maisie's favorite place was the garden, where she felt closer to nature, but also safe, because of the high walls that surrounded it and kept it private. There were mulberry and crab apple trees, and neatly planted borders either side of the path. Cyrus often reminded her that she was safe inside those walls, indicating that would not be the case if she ventured beyond.

Margaret learned that the house was located in London, close to the cabinet where Cyrus was known as an influential government orator, and near the fashionable coffeehouses where he engaged in intellectual discourse with other important men. In those ostentatious environs Cyrus discussed subject matter for many of the articles he wrote on important issues of the time, essays that were circulated far and wide in books and then pamphlets and newspapers.

The passage of time did settle her, eventually, and it helped that the Lafayette household was run with strict routine, according to the master's instructions, the servants and the mistress of the house following his orders without fail. So it was that Maisie adopted their strange but somehow comforting regimen. As the Lafayette ward, she did not want for anything, and that was strange, for it was very far from what she had known in her life before. The horrific memory of witnessing her mother's death made her lower her gaze and be grateful that she and her siblings had been spared. During this time she did not even dare to think of her magic, let alone use it, lest her saviors cast her out to face a death like her mother's.

Almost everything of a feminine nature was introduced to her life by Mama Beth. It was the master of the house who took control of her education—and through that, ultimately, took control of her.

"Young lady." He beckoned her over one evening before

Mama Beth and the upstairs maid prepared her for bed. "You must begin your classes tomorrow."

Maisie instinctively went to his side, nerves building within her as she grew concerned about his meaning.

When she stood beside his winged armchair, he took her hand in his. "If you are to become a proper young lady you must learn about the world." He looked at her with a searching gaze, his opaque eyes shrewd, his black hair shot through here and there with gray strands, drawing her attention, for he didn't wear a wig in the informal setting of his home. "Can you read?"

"No, sire." It was not a question she had been asked before, but she felt shameful, knowing she was amongst privileged people now and did not want to disappoint them.

"That can soon be remedied. Your schoolmistress arrives on the morrow. You will begin your lessons then." He tapped Margaret on the end of her nose with one finger. "She will have you reading in no time, and then we can study together." He showed great interest in that prospect, and his faith in her potential made her a little less afraid.

From then on her mornings were devoted to lessons with a schoolmistress, lessons that might be considered normal fare for a girl of her age. Under the governess's instruction her reading and writing skills quickly improved, and her mind broadened as she took on geography, history and arithmetic. Her teacher, Mistress Hinchcliffe, was a widow. She had nut-brown hair and sad eyes, and her smile was so rare and special that Maisie soon learned its immense value. Mistress Hinchcliffe was a keen teacher, and she rewarded Maisie for her enthusiasm. Sometimes with her smile.

Maisie quickly learned things that she recognized to be useful and important—things that were not often afforded to young women of her age, and especially not those of her questionable background.

Once her reading skills were addressed, Master Cyrus began to undertake some of her tutoring himself, just as he had promised. He studied with her after Mistress Hinchcliffe returned to her lodgings, and the books he shared with Margaret were very different from the ones she studied with her morning tutor. At first he kept the volumes in a locked wooden cabinet in the schoolroom. However, Mistress Hinchcliffe often looked at it with a dubious glance, and eventually it and its contents were moved back to the library, from whence they had come.

"You must not share the nature of the lessons we look at together," Master Cyrus instructed her after the cabinet was moved, "for neither Mama Beth nor your tutor would understand the precious subject matter, and it is my duty to protect you from those who would wish to harm you…the way your mother was harmed."

He told her this as he led her to his personal library.

Her grip on his hand tightened.

In those early days he didn't often refer to her mother's demise. He did not have to remind her of it, but when he did so it was always in warning.

The books they studied were never shared with his wife. Neither did Mama Beth partake in any of the special lessons.

"I want you to know and understand your beginnings," he informed Margaret. "You come from a long line of witches, and you are gifted and special. It is not my intention to quell that part of your nature. In fact, I mean to encourage it, but only in private. It is to be our secret."

"Why are you so generous to me, Master Cyrus?"

"Because I have a great interest in your skills, and if we learn about them together I can protect you, and you can perhaps help me in return, one day in the future."

"You might need me to undertake healing?"

"Perhaps."

She was innocent of his real intentions.

"We will study all the books that I have on the subject, together, and we can discuss the matters therein. Do you understand?"

Young Margaret nodded. She felt excitement at the prospect, and was humbled that he cared to encourage that part of her for which most people would persecute her.

"You will discover, when we read together, that there are people all over the world who understand the natural rhythm of life and the power inherent in nature."

"All over the world?"

Cyrus nodded and opened her first book.

They spent several weeks studying that first tome, returning to the beginning to read the important parts again, talking about it as they went. Margaret learned that people practiced magic in many faraway countries, and it wasn't something solely borne of the Scottish Highlands. The book was beautifully handwritten in painstaking script, each page illustrated with tiny drawings. The knowledge excited her, introducing her to possibilities beyond her own experience and beyond the difficult days that her family had endured after their mother led them to the Lowlands.

There were several such books, and one in particular captured Margaret's heart, for it documented Highland witchcraft. She was enthralled when she saw the old Gaelic and Pictish words written within. There were enchantments that her mother had taught them by ear, and many more besides.

"Some of these I know, but others I don't."

"Try those that are new to you, if you want to," her protector encouraged. "Only when we are alone, though."

Delighted, she nodded. "I promise. I will only make magic with you, Master Cyrus."

His lips curled.

Under his watchful eye she learned to flex her skills, growing her craft and her repertoire of spells. It was an exciting time, and one in which her loyalty to her guardian evolved.

In time he tempered this by introducing a different kind of tract, books that advocated the hunting down and killing of witches. Young Margaret, who had flourished through her learning, had come to believe that it was a terrible mistake that her mother was persecuted. When she saw what he meant for her to study next, she felt instantly afraid. Two years had passed and she felt safe at last. Now that would be undone. "Why?"

"In order to be strong you must understand the reasons why your kind are so often feared and persecuted. Be brave, for it is only through understanding such ignorance that we can hope to defeat it."

However, when he sat her down and encouraged her to read King James's book entitled *Daemonologie* it shattered her heart and put her young life into stark relief. This was the very document from which all laws about and persecution of witchcraft had spilled down in her homeland and beyond. It was a brutal indictment, one that used the justness and power of religion and royalty to seek out and kill her kind.

"This will shock you," Master Cyrus warned her, "but it is important you understand they are driven by their fear."

Margaret was only a few pages in when she began to feel sickened, tormented by the words, and the images they conjured. It took her back to that fateful day. Since then she'd had her mind opened, and she'd been excited to find that those who believed and practiced magic were everywhere. Even though she'd witnessed her own mother's persecution, it was hard for her to see how something borne of nature could offend souls and make them afraid. This document only reinforced the fact that she and others like her were in constant danger. Those in power—the monarchy and the church—feared and despised them, and turned honest workingmen against them. The more she read, the more ill she felt.

She drew back from the book, confused by it.

"Perhaps reading it aloud would be better, so that we might discuss it," Master Cyrus offered, encouraging her to turn another page.

She had hoped that he would set the book aside for another day, for it was too close to her own experience, and the words of the magistrate and the villagers who had condemned her mother were reflected in every page.

"Ask me anything," Cyrus said, forcing her on.

Why was he so determined she read it? Margaret stared at the page, faltering, yet afraid to disappoint him. "It says the witches serve one master. Who is this master?"

His eyes narrowed as he studied her. "Read on."

She read aloud, needing to do so to share her confusion with him. "The devil…it says the devil entices witches into his service. He lures them to follow him by promising them great riches." She paused, turning to the man who was her only protector, her only master. "The devil? But this is Christian belief. They said this about my mother, but I didn't understand it then and I do not understand it now. We believe in that which folds in on our lives time and again, bringing life and growth and good things. We believe in nature's way, the seasons and the rebirth of everything that is good."

He nodded. "Your people have often been unjustly accused of being evil, although I expect some turn that way."

He tapped the page, encouraging her to read on.

Reluctantly, she did so. "It says that the devil bestowed the knowledge to cure illness—" she shook her head in disbelief, for that was not her experience "—or to curse and kill via means of wax figures." She felt quite ill. "Wax figures to curse or kill? I have never heard of such a thing." Upset, confused and angered, she wanted to destroy the book and all it represented. "These are lies!"

"People believe this because it is the king's word, and the church and the lawmakers agree and act upon it. Try, if you can, to imagine you knew nothing of witchcraft, and how you might feel if you read this and believed it."

The thought sent a cold shiver through her. "Yes, it would make me afraid, and if there really are people who did such things…people who used magic for their own gain…then I can see why men believed the king's word."

Master Cyrus did not respond to that.

"And the remedy they recommend?" He seemed determined that she finish reading the king's *Daemonologie* that very night.

She read aloud again, unable to analyze the words on her own. "'What form of punishment think ye merits these magicians and witches? They ought to be put to death according to the law of God, the civil and imperial law, and municipal law of all Christian nations.'" Her voice faltered as she remembered, the tears welling. "But…but what kind of death…I pray you?"

She heard the jeers, the accusations, the thud of stones that made her mother drop and bleed. Margaret did not need to read on, for she knew what the answer was. *Fire*.

"Burn her to death," they had shouted. "Rid our village of their evil."

Tears spilled down Margaret's cheeks as the wounds reopened and she relived the pain, remembering it all.

"Hush now." Master Cyrus rested back in his chair. "You are safe, and you always will be, with me."

Crying and gulping in distress, she found her vision misting.

"I do not want to remind you of your mother's fate," he said, after some time had passed. "You know that. But it is important that you understand why it happened."

She lifted her head and looked into his eyes. "Why do they think these things about us?"

"It is ignorance and jealousy that lead people to do such things to a gifted, special one such as you." His eyes flickered thoughtfully. "Fear of the power that you might have over them." His brows lifted.

Maisie stared at him. He seemed pleased with her. Was it because she had been brave enough to read it all?

His eyes gleamed as he contemplated her. "I do not have your powers, my precious, but I respect them in you. You will not be harmed, not while I watch over you. That much I promise you."

And she believed him.

"In time these laws will be revoked," he added. "I have heard it spoken about amongst the important people, and there has been much written about the injustices that have taken place." Cyrus's mouth twitched into a smile. "And many people do not even believe witchcraft exists," he added, "which suits us rather well, don't you think?"

Margaret nodded, although deep down she wanted to disagree and state that she'd rather her kind were acknowledged. But she trusted Master Cyrus to guide and protect her. "I hope that you are right, that these laws will be altered." She pushed the book away, resisting the urge to set it alight with a choice Pictish enchantment.

The lessons were hard, but she learned.

Acceptance, knowledge, caution and experience wove together in the fabric of her soul. She had been born into a line of folk who were different than most, and who must hide their skills. She accepted that. The more she read under Master Cyrus's guidance, the more she understood, and the more wary and sheltered she became. So it was that Maisie Taskill grew into Margaret Lafayette, elegant, beautiful, educated and wary beyond her tender years, a girl who had earned her guardian's approval.

When she was considered old enough, and Master Cyrus and Mama Beth introduced her to society, she found herself much admired. It was her thoughtful expression and her resigned gaze that she heard whispered about when she sharpened her hearing by magic. Some remarked she was gifted, that her intellect was said to be as sharp as a man's, if not more so. The influence of her clever guardian, no doubt, they would surmise.

Her clever guardian watched on.

It was when she blossomed into young womanhood that Master Cyrus brought out his most precious tome on witchcraft—the book that told of the powers that could be sourced from the physical and emotional union of lovers.

As was their usual practice, they sat side by side at the heavy mahogany desk in his private library. The candlelight flickered as Master Cyrus set down the book he intended to study with her that night.

She looked at it curiously, for it was not leather bound, nor did it have a title page. Instead, the loose parchment pages were stitched together in a makeshift binding. The parchment was rough and heavy, and when Master Cyrus carefully turned the pages to the first words written, she saw they were hastily scribbled with an erratic hand.

The content startled her. It was about carnality.

She glanced at him in surprise.

"My feeling is that you are grown-up enough to study the most important subject of all, the gateway to your most powerful magic."

She felt heat rise in her face, and could not force herself to meet his gaze again. Instead, she stared down at the document before her. She felt embarrassed because he meant for them to look at this together, and yet by some deep instinct she also knew what it contained and how significant it was. Memories whispered through her mind, memories of her mother's words, and more.

"Why did you bring us here to the Lowlands?" her brother had asked their mother, when they were scorned for her pagan ways.

"Because we must find your father, for without him I am not complete," she had replied.

"He's not worth it, not if he abandoned us the way you said he did." Lennox stomped off angrily, as he often did, frustrated that he carried the burden of an errant father. It was then that their mother had turned to Maisie and her twin, and confided to them a witch's deepest secret.

"It is through our physical union with one another that magic is at its best. When you are grown women and you couple with your lover, you will become more powerful. You will learn more about these things soon, for I will tell you all you need to know."

It was not from her mother that Maisie Taskill learned, though.

It was from Cyrus Lafayette.

"Don't be embarrassed," he said. "This is your destiny. You will be a woman and a witch fulfilled, and you must know these things and be ready for them...when the time comes."

She stared down at the pages, heat burning her skin as

she read the passionate words and descriptions, and studied the drawings of lovers entwined. She saw their desire and recognized the exaltation in their expressions as their love-making unleashed a new vitality in them. It made her blood heat and her heart yearn for completion.

The words and images were intensely stimulating, and she wanted to know more, but she also dreaded meeting Master Cyrus's stare, for it embarrassed her that he was there while she read about such intimate things.

He did not leave her side, and the air became heavy with tension.

"If you wish to ask me questions, or discuss anything you read, you know you can."

"Thank you." She did not ask questions.

Thankfully he did not encourage her to read aloud, as he so often did.

Instead, she just read on silently, her emotions oddly skewed because she had been thrust into this subject matter while he observed her reactions intently, turning the pages for her as soon as she was ready.

Silently, she would lower her eyelids to the desk when she reached the end of a page, and he turned it to the next. There was no conversation, and she was glad of that, but she could feel the weight of his stare on her all the while, and her discomfort built.

When she reached the end of the document, he closed the book.

Turning her to him with his hand beneath her chin, he searched her face with blazing eyes.

Margaret could scarcely believe he looked at her that way,

and a fresh rush of embarrassment took her, flaming into her face and making her squirm in her seat.

Master Cyrus did not pass comment, but his lips curled into a knowing smile, and for some reason it chilled her to the core.

chapter Seven

Maisie watched the flex of the captain's broad back as he rose from the bed.

His naked form was breathtaking.

She had never seen a naked man before that night. In illustrations, yes. She had seen drawings of the male body as part of her studies in witchcraft, but not a real man, not in real life.

Not only that, but his build was so much larger and sturdier than anyone she'd met in the limited but privileged circles in which she moved in London society. His strength must have come from his work aboard ship, she surmised, for his muscles were big and flexed readily as he moved. Many women would find him uncouth, but he stimulated a different reaction in Maisie—an urge to touch and explore his body. The suspicion that she would feel secure wrapped in those mighty arms also flitted through her thoughts. It was not a notion she had encountered before and she wondered at it. Her master had once made her feel safe, but that was with clever, twisted words, not comforting embraces and the vague hope of genuine loyalty that came from who knew where.

Loyalty? I have made that silly notion up in my head, because I crave a protector.

Again she eyed the captain, impressed by his male strength. The rest was but a dream. How easily she had fallen for Cyrus's promises. It was a long time, too, that she had believed what turned out to be duplicity on his part. She must never allow herself such naivety again. Especially not with a man of the sea. *I mustn't,* she told herself. *This is merely a transaction of convenience for us both.*

When her gaze dropped to the taut outline of his buttocks, she found that the view affected her in a decidedly carnal manner. It made her recall how she had clutched at his back, and the deeper he pushed within her, the lower her hands had roamed, until her nails were bedded in that fine posterior. At that very moment he turned around and caught her looking.

Blushing, she glanced away, but it was too late. Not only had she been caught, she had also caught sight of his cock. Even in its current indolent state it seemed spectacularly large to her, and she could scarcely believe she had survived it.

"You are not used to seeing a naked man," he commented as he returned to the bed. In one hand he held a dish of water. In the other he had a folded cloth.

"No," she responded, watching as he dipped the cloth into the water, then wrung it out in his hands. "I have never seen a man unclothed before now."

Again her gaze was drawn to his starkly male form. What was it about his broad, shapely shoulders that made her hands ache to explore him? There was a dusting of burnished hair across his chest and it narrowed into a line that drew her eye down to his groin. The drawings she had seen in the books her guardian had given her to study about witchcraft and carnal rites never looked as enticing as the captain currently did. Seeing his potent masculinity—even in its dormant state—fascinated her. And he was unashamed. He wore his nudity like the finest cloak. Was it shipboard life that stripped him of any self-awareness or shame, or was he used to a woman admiring him the way Maisie was? Perhaps he enjoyed it.

"You are getting an eyeful now," he said, with no small amount of humor.

Blushing once again, she looked pointedly at a spot on the wall beyond his head.

Tension arose between them, but how oddly stimulating it was. Like the tug of his ship's anchor rope, it captured her attention. Peculiar though it was, it made Maisie want to spar with him. "I am curious about you. It is a natural instinct, is it not?"

He shrugged. "Look all you want."

When she met his gaze again, she did so with astonishment and curiosity.

"I intend to get my fill of looking at you during our voyage to Dundee," he clarified. "It is only fair." With that statement he set the dish of water on the floor. Turning to face her, he raised the damp cloth in his hand to her groin.

Maisie gasped aloud when she realized it was his intention to bathe her—down there, where she had been so recently plundered. She shot out her hand, intending to stop him,

but he stayed it with his free one and continued his ministrations with the other.

"Lie back. I will see to this." His eyes twinkled.

Maisie balked. "No!"

"I will enjoy the task, believe me," he promised with a
chuckle.

That only served to deepen her embarrassment. "You cannot do such a task."

"Oh, but I can."

Then the firm swipe of the cold cloth on her sensitive
mound distracted her from her argument with him, making her cry out and squirm against the surface of his bed.

He laughed again, a low rumble in his chest that both
teased and inflamed her.

A dribble of cool water ran down into her niche, arousing her. She squeezed her thighs tight together, mortified.
"I can see to it myself," she murmured, weak with sensation,
racked with embarrassment.

He shook his head.

Did he know that bathing her would affect her this way?

After dabbing at her mound, he squeezed the bunched
cloth between her locked thighs, prizing them open.

Pressing her head back into the mattress, Maisie covered
her mouth with the back of her wrist. How delicious it felt,
but how wrong. The two wildly conflicting reactions confused her, for they made her feel hot, lusty and liable to do
something she regretted.

When she dared to look at Captain Cameron again she
could see he was indeed enjoying it. His mouth was pursed
in a half smile, his eyelids lowered as he eased apart her legs

and stroked the damp cloth over her inner thighs. Maisie whimpered when she realized he was looking directly at her splayed flesh. Every part of her was on display to him, and he was studying her intently. His expression was brooding, pleasured and intense. He clearly approved of what he saw.

The fact he was looking at her that way made her chest feel tight and breathless, as if a weight pressed down upon her. Yet it was pleasurable. Again she was astonished at the effect his intimacy had on her. Not only was she rapidly aroused once again, but she felt almost dizzy because of it.

Her mind flashed to what could have happened, how different proceedings would have been if it had been Cyrus who had deflowered her. It would have been awful, of that she was sure, because she could not think of him that way, even though it was what he wanted. In contrast, mating with Captain Roderick Cameron made her feel stronger in every way. She thanked nature for playing a part, for landing her in his charge, when all she had to offer was herself.

Much to her astonishment, she realized her legs shifted farther apart of their own accord, her body responding to him without censure. She covered her eyes with her hand, unable to bear witness. Control was gone, reason, too.

The captain only took advantage of her opening legs, pushing the cloth against her plump folds and then swiping it up and down. When her body arched, then fell supine, it was because he had extended a finger beneath the cloth and probed her entrance.

Clutching at the thin blanket that covered the mattress beneath her, she tried to calm herself. It was no good. His ministrations were about to make her lose her last vestige of self-control.

"Oh, please," she begged, pleading for mercy.

"More?"

She shook her head, adamant. "No, I did not mean that."

But it was too late. He was moving his finger inside her as if testing her.

Her spirit flared. "You embarrass me, sire, and I sense you are enjoying it!"

"You think so?" With his free hand he pinned her down at the collarbone, stemming the rise and fall of her torso, and then he glanced at her hips, still moving rhythmically in response to his touch.

"You are a beast," she blurted, then instantly regretted it.

"Perhaps I am, but I am not blind. I can see you are enjoying it, no matter what you say." With that he set about stroking her with even more deliberation. Abandoning the cloth, he extended one finger inside her and then rubbed at her swollen nub with his thumb.

"Oh, oh, oh, I cannot allow it...." Her words trailed off.

The rhythmic movement of his thumb while his hard finger was inside her was a dangerous combination, one made to drive a woman mad. Maisie's body tightened at the intrusion, her hips rocking as he stroked his thumb back and forth. It was a fleeting, almost feathery touch, and it made her throb with want. His actions tormented her, yet drew her close to a rapid release.

She reached out blindly, catching at his arm while she lifted her hips to meet his hand. Pleasure washed through her in a dense, hot wave, and for a moment the clutch and spill of her release made her feel faint. Panting for breath, she felt her body grow limp. It was astonishing, and she relished the way the heat seemed to reach every part of her. Minutes later, she found she was still clutching his arm. Reluctantly, she loosened her grip.

"Apparently you can allow it," he teased.

There was humor in his expression and it reached her, warming her. Breathlessly, she accused, "You have the advantage of knowing how to touch a woman."

His expression grew more serious. "I did not believe you were a novice, for which I apologize. I'm sorry, too, for my rough handling of you, my demands."

"Did not believe?" She repeated his words, confused, barely able to speak because the sensations he had aroused in her were so oddly invigorating. Her body tingled, and the source of her magic, deep within, felt freshly stoked.

"That you truly were a virgin."

She was not offended, for her virginity had become an immense burden to her, but she did not understand his confusion. She had stated her condition quite honestly to him. "Why didn't you believe me?"

"Virgins do not appear so wise nor so wily, nor do they brazenly offer themselves to complete strangers."

Maisie considered his words. What he said was most likely true, for most young women. She was not like them, but if she had been she supposed she would have thought differently on the matter. She did not have many friends amongst her own age group, having been brought up in a very particular and controlled world, but she knew that a girl's maidenhood was what gained her a good marriage. "I had no other choice."

The captain wrapped his hand around one of her thighs. "I'm sorry for that."

"Don't be. My virginity was a burden to me." The words were out before she considered how strange they would sound to him.

He cocked his head, looking at her as if she were not in full possession of her faculties.

It seemed necessary to offer an explanation. "It was of value to someone who…who wanted to use me in ways I could not endure."

She could say no more.

He reached out and cupped her face. "You have enjoyed this?"

She knew what he was asking, and nodded. He wanted to be sure *he* was not using her in ways she could not endure. He seemed to be a decent man. No doubt he would think her a fallen woman, probably had done since the moment she approached him. It had not discouraged him, though. In fact his kindness toward her now that he knew the truth of it touched her deeply. Maisie had known the protection of a man, a guardian, but she had never been in a position such as this, where a man who knew nothing about her treated her as a lusty, desirable woman, then cared for her in the aftermath.

Was this how it was between a man and woman?

She did not want to consider such things. It had been important that a stranger take her virginity because she didn't want to be bound to someone who knew of her ways and knew how the carnal act would enrich her. Neither could she risk becoming attached to a man. She was vulnerable to that, being accustomed to a sheltered existence. She had taken her first steps along the path to independence and she would need to gird herself and be strong if she was to continue all the way to the Highlands. This man was merely someone she had done a trade with, nothing more.

"I would not enjoy it, if you did not," he whispered. Then he smiled and lowered his head to her groin, where he placed a kiss upon the cleansed flesh of her mound.

Maisie leaped at the touch, then almost fainted away.

As if that kiss was not startling enough, he then proceeded to lick and tease her sensitive folds with his tongue. She cried out, not only from surprise, but from the dizzying pleasure that his actions caused. He ran his tongue over her intimate places, licked, stroked and sucked on her exposed folds with slow deliberation, and then pushed his tongue inside, lapping at her entrance.

Maisie writhed on the bed, driven to distraction by his attentions. She felt wildly empowered, yet exposed and trapped, all at once. The way his tongue explored her had her nub swollen and pounding again. She felt hot and weak, and as if her whole body was being drawn into the spot he currently lavished with openmouthed kisses.

Never had she felt more alive than she did this night, in his bed.

"You are delicious," he said as he lifted his head to look at her.

Eyeing him with curiosity, she had to ask. "Why did you do that?"

"Because I wanted to." His mouth quirked. "You enjoyed it, did you not?"

It wasn't as if she could deny it. She nodded.

Glancing down, she saw that his cock was fully ready for her, long and hard and bowed up from his hips, the crown touching the hard, flat surface of his belly as he arched over her. Inside, her body rippled and clenched, reacting to the sight of his male virility.

"Instinct is a great thing, and when it leads to mutual plea-sure I see no reason to deny such urges."

Recognition pumped through Maisie. Whether he knew it or not he'd tapped into her true essence, because it was one of the fundamental beliefs of her kind. Passion was deeply connected to nature, and those who welcomed and explored it would be gifted with its bounty. The lingering embarrass-ment she felt was only because it was all new to her, but deep down she knew it was right and true.

Passion bound them to nature, and to each other.

Her breathing hitched.

She must not be bound to any man. That was why it had to be a stranger. The captain was a passionate man, a wor-thy man. Luck had been on her side. Meanwhile, at her center, her body ached for him again, the tenderized flesh freshly slick with wanting. Meshing her fingers in his thick hair, she did not attempt to resist calling him closer, invit-ing him to take her again. "Please," she whispered. "Let us be as one again."

He smiled roguishly. "Now that your maidenhood is gone, you find that you enjoy the bed tousle?"

Her hips rocked of their own accord, and she gripped his

hip with one hand, eager to be undone while he was inside her again. "Sire, you know I cannot deny that. You are surely jesting."

"A lusty wench you are." He gave a low chuckle. "Lady or no, you cannot deny your nature."

It was impossible to reply, because his comment said more about her than he realized. How strange it was, Maisie reflected. But it was more than empowerment. She had expected that, the enrichment of her magic. She felt it swelling within, powerful and ready. What she did not expect was the desire, the delicious desire for ravagement and completion.

"I cannot deny it, but you would not want me to, for you are also ready, are you not?" She nodded down at his engorged cock.

"Brazen, too," he responded, then wrapped his fist around his erection, moving it up and down while she watched.

The action made her wild, the longing she felt doubling instantly. Moaning aloud, she lifted one knee, resting her foot flat to the bed, exposing herself.

"Oh, yes." He ran the fingers of his free hand over her bared folds.

"Captain…" she pleaded.

His fingers stilled. "You must call me Roderick, or I will not answer."

"Roderick," she breathed. "Please."

He smiled. Moments later he obliged her.

Moving over her, he arranged himself between her open legs, then kissed her mouth passionately. Lifting her easily with his hands beneath her bottom, he eased inside and filled her again.

His cock slid against her sensitive flesh more readily this time. For a moment there was soreness and pain, then she was flooded with pleasure. Clinging to him, she had never felt more grateful. He was a good lover, and Maisie knew she'd made a lucky bargain.

When he pushed deeper still, his hard length stretching and kneading her at her deepest point, she met his gaze. He stared down at her, admiration shining in his eyes, while he stayed still for the longest moment—right there at the place where she seemed to feel most sensitive to his manhood.

Emotion welled in her. She fought it back, focusing on the act, the carnal act and the joy and enrichment it would bring.

This man is someone I have done a trade with, nothing more.

Then she flung her arms around him, and urged him on.

chapter Eight

It was not long after dawn when Cyrus Lafayette's carriage arrived in Mayfair and he requested an audience with Edward Russell, the first Earl of Orlford, a former member of the cabinet and first admiral of the British navy fleet. Cyrus and the earl were well acquainted, and Cyrus went to his London residence meaning to use that acquaintance to his advantage.

Because of the early call, he waited for almost an hour before he was granted an audience. Frustration drummed at his temples.

"I trust this is important, Lafayette," the earl said as he received Cyrus in his chambers. He was hastily dressed and scowling.

"I am most grateful for your time and attention." Cyrus bowed his head, but was unable to keep the bitterness from his tone. It was almost impossible to act appropriately, given the night he had passed, the information he had gained and the fact he'd been kept waiting. Margaret was in the hands of a lawless merchant seaman. If Cyrus didn't act quickly, she might be injured or exposed as a witch. Her precious powers might be spoiled, or worse still, aligned with someone other than Cyrus himself. "It is a matter of great urgency, and of a personal nature."

Russell gestured languidly with his hand, urging Cyrus to continue while he flapped out the full skirt of his coat and took his seat.

"There was an incident in Billingsgate last night. Your men were there together with representatives of His Majesty's revenue collectors. They were in pursuit of a merchant ship that sailed on the tide."

Russell neither confirmed nor denied the matter, which was as Cyrus would have expected. The news might appear in reports the earl looked over, but it would be a menial matter for one such as him. Cyrus hurried on. "Eyewitness accounts of the ship's departure reported that a young woman was taken on board the ship. I have reason to suspect that young woman is my ward."

Russell raised his eyebrows in surprise. "Margaret?"

"Yes. I trust you understand my concern and my reason for raising you from your bed at this ungodly hour."

"She has been kidnapped?"

Cyrus had anticipated the earl's response. "I can only assume that is the case. She has no acquaintance with disreputable people such as they must be, and neither have any of her personal belongings been taken." That was a lie. The most precious fetish items of her craft were absent from her chamber. He had discovered that himself before dawn. The knowledge had torn him asunder, for it indicated she had been prepared to go. Why? Why had she gone? Had some-one forced her? If it was a foolish whim, it was out of char-acter for her, but it could happen. His deepest concern was that she would be too afraid to protect herself by means of magic. It was his fault. He had drummed it into her often enough. Trapped aboard a ship with a bunch of superstitious, ill-educated shipmen, she would surely know it was not a wise place to unleash her magic. "She was due to meet me at the theater last night and never arrived. I can only assume she was waylaid."

"Have you received a demand?"

"Not as yet, but I am not willing to wait until I do." Cyrus took a deep breath. "I'm taking a great liberty here, but I wondered if I might request your assistance."

"In what way?"

"I know from my investigations that your men already have good cause to pursue this ship. If you were to sign an order for a British navy ship to hunt down the vessel, and I were allowed to go aboard, I might gain an advantage, and in doing so rescue my ward before she comes to any harm at their hands."

Russell reached out and rolled his blotter back and forth on his desk while he considered the request. "It is more than we would normally undertake in the matter of revenue and governing law."

"I would be most grateful, and my allegiance will be yours in your future endeavors, should you need it." The prom-ise of backing in government matters was always tempting, and Cyrus felt sure that the earl would claim his return sev-eral times over in the future. But Cyrus was willing to do anything in his pursuit of Margaret. He had to have his precious commodity returned to him. He hadn't groomed her all these years for her to slip away from him just as he was ready to reap the fullest rewards from her.

Russell cast a diminishing look in his direction. "I am the head of the admiralty. Whyever would I need your assistance?"

Cyrus twitched. It was what he might have expected, however. Russell wouldn't want to be seen to acquiesce too easily. "It is often useful to sway men by means of the written word. I am adept at offering subtle, persuasive opinion in my discourse. Should you wish to gain power, my support in the written word would be one way to achieve it." He paused, adding weight to his final comment. "On any matter, from this day on, the nature of my discourse would be yours to command."

Russell considered him at length, then rose to his feet. "I will summon one of my best captains. He will know how easily we can purloin one of the ships ready to set sail on His Majesty's business, and rearrange its voyage about this new task. While we await his arrival, we will breakfast." Russell flicked his fingers and nodded at the servant who waited by the door.

The man disappeared immediately.

"Quails eggs today, if memory serves. Does that suit you?"

Cyrus felt his patience falter. He wanted to see orders given, people leaping to action on command. That was not the way with this man, so he nodded as graciously as he could.

Russell led him to the dining room, where the table was being laid out for breakfast.

Cyrus could neither eat nor drink, and when the naval officer arrived and he, too, was encouraged to sit and dine with them, Cyrus's frustration only grew. Captain Giles Plimpton seemed a capable man, but Cyrus wished his case was being approached with more haste. Every moment that passed was squandered because it took Margaret farther from his grasp.

As the earl ate heartily, Cyrus summarized the situation for Captain Plimpton and ventured further suggestions about how the matter might be handled. "I've had several men investigating my ward's disappearance overnight. We've already established that the ship in question was bound for Scotland."

"Ah, yes," the captain responded, heaping his plate. "I recall news of a recent sighting, the ship known as the *Libertas*, yes?"

"The very one." Cyrus was relieved the officer was aware of the ship.

"The captain and crew are well-known to us." Plimpton nodded sagely. "A heinous, sully bunch they are. They slink in and out of harbor under cover of darkness and without even a nod to the harbormaster or the customs man. It would be a pleasure to go after them to collect the ship's dues. Alas, it is not a navy priority to chase a lone ship to Scotland for unpaid taxes alone." He offered Cyrus a quick smile at that juncture.

Cyrus took it as a good sign. Kidnap together with tax evasion made pursuance more tenable. The mention of Scotland, however, made him restless and eager to press on. Margaret was a clever young woman and she often asked about visiting her kin in her homeland. That would not be wise at all, for Cyrus might lose her to them. But he had assured her he would arrange a visit, one day. If that was her motivation, Cyrus rued the fact he had made even a vague promise to take her back there. He'd been concerned that she might stray if she were shown her birthplace. Now it seemed as if she might have strayed, anyway. With hindsight, he knew he should have stomped out any desire to do so by reminding her how many had been ousted by the witch hunters north of the border. Had this happened because of some wild notion about finding her kin? If it was, she had put herself in great danger because of it. A shipful of rowdy, uncivilized seafaring men… Cyrus could barely stand to think of his precious toy in such hands. She was his instrument of power, his divining rod, and he intended to get her back.

The earl pointed at Cyrus's plate. "The first rule of the sea, Master Lafayette, is to eat heartily whenever you can, for you do not know how long you will be out at sea, and rations aboard ship are far from savory."

So that was their excuse for filling their bellies while urgent matters were dallied over. The comment did, at least, seem to indicate his request to go aboard the navy ship had been approved. "I beg you to understand my dilemma, sire," he said, with false humility, gesturing humbly at his untouched plate. "I'm afraid I cannot eat. Nor can I rest, not until I know my ward is safe and unharmed."

Either his demeanor or his comment urged the earl to action. Russell rested back in his ornate headrest in his chair. "Yes, I can see why you would be so concerned, and your plan to go after them yourself is admirable, of course." He gestured magnanimously. "I will issue orders forthwith. It will serve as a good lesson to those who ignore the rules and duties of British waters. We will ensure the safe return of your ward and we'll make an example of this corrupt merchant ship. It will benefit us both."

"I am most grateful, and I am forever your humble servant," Cyrus said, and bowed his head. He was thinking of much more than making them an example, however. If even one of them had so much as touched his precious Margaret, he would take them apart with his bare hands.

Maisie awoke from a deep sleep to find the captain gone, presumably up to the deck to take charge of his ship again. Sighing, she savored the satiated state she awoke in. As she did so it occurred to her that it might have been even better if she had awoken before he did. The satiated feeling gave way to a new hunger—a hunger for more. Was that how it would be now that she'd coupled with a lover? Startled at the way her body throbbed in response to the notion, she sat up.

Nearby, on the railed shelf close to the bed, she discovered he had left a small flagon of ale. She drank thirstily. Next to the flagon stood a wooden box, inside which she found some hard biscuits, oatcakes. They were surprisingly tasty despite their rough consistency.

Rising, Maisie located the pail the captain had pointed out to relieve herself in, then tentatively examined her body before she dressed.

Her breasts were tender and her nipples peaked instantly when she touched them, quickly reminding her of the pleasures she had experienced the night before. It filled her with wonder. Whilst she knew it would be an important change in her life, both as a woman and as a young witch whose craft would be enriched by engaging in carnal acts, she'd had no idea of the newfound awareness she would enjoy. She moved her hands over her body, testing here and there. Responsive, sensitive and eager, her skin tingled. Moreover, that sense of ability that bubbled in her belly when she was sure of her magic was greatly magnified. She had indeed been enriched, and she couldn't resist exploring it.

Lifting her hands, she allowed her power to flow out from her uplifted palms, and marveled at the intensity of the heat and light that rose from her. For the first time, she truly felt that her magic came from within. The sensual fulfillment had anchored it within her. Previously, the magic knowledge that had been handed down to her was a starting point. It was something she initiated, as if she trickered the first in a chain of events. It felt very different now, as if she were the source itself, rather than the tricker.

As she stood there marveling at it, the ship encountered rougher waters and rocked this way and that in rapid succession. Tempted by that, Maisie put out her hands and channeled her vitality into the waves surrounding the ship. Whispering low under her breath, she bade the elements good day and requested calm waters. Closing her eyes, she absorbed every moment of the experience, noticing how she felt as if she were part of the ocean when it churned more gently, as if she were locked into it.

"It truly has altered me," she whispered, scarcely able to believe it.

She pushed up her hair with her hands, securing it with

several pins that she retrieved from the pocket of her gown, and even as she flexed her neck and stretched, she could feel her own power swelling within. It would be so much easier now for her to protect herself. It would be tempting to evoke change, and she knew she must keep a leash on her skills in order not to be exposed and ousted, as her mother had been.

It was little wonder Cyrus wanted to be in control of this moment, she reflected, for her power was already so much greater. She felt invigorated by the lovemaking she'd enjoyed, more confident in every way—in her magic, and as a woman.

There was great pleasure in that, too.

Moving her fingers lower, between the folds of her intimate place, she discovered that whilst she was tender there and somewhat swollen, it felt good. Pressing deeper, she found she had not been unreasonably rearranged, as she'd feared she might when she caught sight of the size of the captain's engorged manhood. Apparently her body had not only accommodated it, but already craved it again. When she moved her fingers inside, she became aroused and thought immediately of being filled by the captain's proud length.

Is this how it should be? She sat down on the bed and reclined, trailing her fingers over her sensitive folds. Standing proudly, her swollen nub reacted to the movement of her slippery fingers over it. Maisie pressed back into the mattress, her lips parting. She felt rich beyond wealth, decadent and womanly, and her powers simmered within. It was much more than she had expected, and as she massaged herself closer to release, she felt awed. Would it have been this powerful with another lover? Or was it because the captain had proved to be a skilled lover and a good match for her, once they had scrabbled through the strange arrangement and got down to the carnal act?

Shocked at herself, she pushed two fingers inside, imagining his cock probing there. Immediately a radiant sensation sprang free in her groin, and her hips rose on instinct, her fingers sliding deeper. The lingering sensitivity of her flesh was quickly eased by a surge of hot juices. It was good. It was also undeniably bound to the occurrences of the night before. When she had touched herself there before, tentatively, in her virginal state, there was yearning, and sometimes sudden flashes of pleasure, but this was different. Her mind locked on the captain's image and the way he had been so determined, so manly and virile, as he thrust inside her. Each stroke she made along her supple flesh was encouraged by imaginings and memories.

How good it had felt to have him arched over, to admire the way he pivoted as he thrust into her, bearing his weight on his strong arms as he pushed them both into ecstasy. His erection had seemed indomitable, and when he had erupted it was with barely controlled power, his pursuit of pleasure visible as he stroked his fist up and down his length.

Then her memory took her to that later encounter and the image of his head between her legs. Recalling his thick, unruly hair beneath her fingers, she felt an echo of his mouth on her, the way he had brought her to fruition with his tongue and his reverent kisses. It had been wildly passionate, shocking and undeniably pleasurable. Mimicking his actions, she remembered the way he had manipulated his hand and stroked her inside and out at the same time. While she recalled his eagerness and his smile when he brought her off, she spilled anew. Startled and delighted, she closed her eyes and her lips parted.

She could have dozed, but she was curious about him, Roderick, and what he was doing. When a creak sounded nearby, she glanced at the door expectantly. No one entered, so she arose.

Once she was dressed, she sat patiently on the edge of the bed and studied each and every item in the cabin from her perch. When she was done with that, she concentrated on the noises the ship made, those creaks and groans that sounded alarming at first, but became an almost harmonious musical performance as the hours passed.

Then her patience began to wane.

From the time they could stand on their own two feet, both she and her sister were forever running about, with a distinct lack of patience. Their mother used to comment on it often. They were easily bored, and their mother said that even Lennox, who was older and used to running about by himself, was more able to sit quietly if need be. That didn't make it any easier for Maisie to sit still now. She couldn't help it.

Besides, she had no idea what time of day it was, and longed to see the sun and the sky so that she could work it out. The captain had ordered her to stay in the cabin below deck, but Maisie could not resist the call to go above, to take the air. She might even make herself useful, which would be better than sitting here trying to gauge the time of day while the greasy candle spluttered in its lantern. Buckling on her boots, she made ready to leave the captain's quarters.

The narrow walkway outside was dank and dark, and she

put a hand on either wall to make her way along it. At its end, the wooden ladder that led up to the deck was as she remembered it, rickety and treacherous. Determined not to be put off by her strange surroundings, she carefully climbed the ladder and stepped out into the elements on deck. Closing the hatch from which she emerged, she made her way to one side. As she had the evening before, she took shelter in a corner close to the deck above, where she could hear activities going on.

Inhaling the damp, salty air, she breathed in gratefully. Out here on the ocean the elements wound their way into her, lighting her spirit. They called to her vividly as the ship drifted over the waves, freed of land and the trappings of civilized life. It made her harken back to her early life in the Highlands, where people lived in harmony with the elements and with the seasons, moving within the rhythms of time and tide.

Maisie peered across the water at the distant shoreline. It was too far away for her to make out the details, but she saw the colors of the cliffs and the changing height of the coast, the occasional bay marked by a blur of cottages. She tried to gauge how fast they were traveling. It was so hard to tell, but she knew it was faster than traveling on land by coach. That's why she had tried to find a ship to take her. Besides, the ship continued to travel through the night, aided by the tides and the wind in the sails, making progress, where a coach and horses would have to rest at an inn overnight. A break in her journey like that might mean her master would find her.

A dark shiver went through her as she considered what Cyrus's reaction to her absence might have been. She tried not to think upon it—tried to convince herself that he would not pursue her. But she knew it was futile. He had invested many years in her, nurturing her craft, using it to further his progress in government matters. Now that she was a grown woman his plans had evolved, and the hints that he had given about his ambitions—aided by her, of course—frightened her. His plans had been a long time in the making.

She knew now what he'd done. Cyrus had hunted high and low in Scotland for a suitable young girl, a magical child that he could bring up as his ward. Following rumors of witches and news of oustings, he'd traveled a trail that would also be marked by funeral pyres. Hunting down the orphans, he'd examined them for magical ability, potential and appeal. He'd wanted a child who would rely on him for her safety, a child who would be grateful enough to weave spells at his command. Maisie shuddered to think about how mercenary he had been and how he had duped Mama Beth into thinking it was her need for a child that had led him to such extreme measures. Cyrus had promised his wife that a child who had been brought up under such trying circumstances would be grateful and loving. In this twisted web of lies, hope and fear, he kept them both under his control.

Now Maisie had broken free.

Cyrus did not know where she was bound and why, but where else would she go but home to the Highlands of Scotland? He'd made promises, but he'd also tried to get her to break with her lineage and forget her young days in Fingal, making her focus instead on her mother's death in the Lowlands. The older Maisie got the more obvious his trickery was and the more wary of him she became. Her heritage was not easily forgotten, though, and neither were her siblings, Jessie and Lennóx. She had to find them. She could only hope that she would be able to disappear north, into the Highlands, before Cyrus closed in on her.

"What in God's name are you doing above deck?"

Maisie leaped with fright, startled from her thoughts by the captain's booming voice close at her side.

"I told you that you'd have to stay out of the men's way," he said, his brow deeply furrowed.

"I came up to take the air for a few moments," she retorted, rankled that he seemed so intent on keeping her locked up. She had just ridded herself of one tyrant. She did not want to replace him with another, especially when she would be with this one for only a matter of days. "I didn't think that much would be disagreeable to you," she added with sarcasm.

"It is." He grumbled and loomed over her, almost as if he intended to hide her from the rest of the men on deck with the shield of his body. To no avail. She could see them craning their necks and whispering to one another as they went about their duties.

"You cannot expect a soul to survive down there for long." She jerked her head toward the hatch.

"You'd be surprised." When he glanced back over his shoulder and saw the men hovering, many of them blatantly staring as their captain conversed with her, he grumbled some more.

His hair was swept back from his face and Maisie searched his craggy features, momentarily captured by the way he looked, and distracted from her retorts. Despite the cool autumnal air he wore no coat, and his shirt hung open to his breastbone, as if he cared little for his appearance. Why did that catch her attention? Maisie looked him over, admiring the way his body tapered from broad shoulders down to hard, narrow hips. Hips that had been against hers.

Clutching the railing at her back, she steadied herself.

"You can survive down there well enough," he added. "It's safer than being up here, especially for a lady such as yourself. Now get back below deck and be quick about it."

Maisie saw no sense in it. She looked beyond and gauged the men's reactions. Some of them frowned, while others laughed and whispered and nudged each other. "Your men have seen me now, so what is the point in sending me back down there?"

Roderick's head snapped back to meet her gaze. "If I had known what a contrary sort you are you would still be in Billingsgate begging for passage. I'm responsible for every- one on this ship, and that includes all of the shipmen and any passengers. It is for your protection and my men's sanity that I ordered you to stay in the comfortable quarters you have been given."

Maisie was about to take issue with his opinion of what might constitute comfortable quarters, then thought bet- ter of it. She hadn't seen the other cabins below deck, and if they were worse, she wasn't sure she wanted to know. But she did want to see the sky and the elements at play. Besides, she had become intrigued about life aboard ship, and how the sailors worked with the weather in order to cover great distances so quickly. "I refuse to be locked away for the du- ration of this voyage, and I am here with good intentions.

Surely there is some task I can do that will help you in the running of the ship."

The captain looked at her as if she were insane.

"Captain...Roderick." She softened her tone in an attempt to appeal to the good nature she had witnessed the night before, that which underlay this rough exterior of his. "You have been most accommodating, and I know you mean well. However, I feel sure I might be useful instead of being hidden away."

He narrowed his eyes.

She looked at him from beneath her eyelashes, and smiled.

He muttered under his breath and then glanced about again. "I suppose you might assist Adam with some of his tasks." Turning back, he ran his eyes up and down her figure. "You'll be a temptation to the men, so I must warn you not to flaunt yourself. I cannot afford to have my crew distracted and the ship land on the rocks because a fine woman has turned their heads."

A fine woman? Was that what he thought of her? Maisie couldn't help being pleased.

Closing on her, Roderick grasped the cotton of her shift where it showed at the top of her bodice, and wrenched it higher.

His action surprised her. It also aroused her to have his hands on her that way, and the tug of the cloth against her breasts was most stimulating. "Whatever are you doing?"

"Protecting your modesty."

Maisie found herself greatly amused.

When she laughed, he gave her a stern look. "If you are to be cavorting about, please attempt to cover yourself."

"Cavorting? I offered to work." The wild tingling in her breasts made her feel quite reckless. She put her hand against her bodice to quell the arousal he had set in motion, but pressing against her gown only made the situation worse. Apparently, now that she had been initiated as a woman, her state of readiness for her lover remained high. Would it always be that way for her, now that she had been awakened, or was it the prowess of her lover that made her feel that way? She wouldn't know, she supposed, until she was no longer with him. Maisie quickly found she didn't want to consider that yet. She was enjoying her time with Captain Roderick Cameron.

"And if you work," he replied, "you need to cover your bosom."

It was in such contrast to his behavior the night before that she had to quell her laughter. "You seemed more intent on uncovering my bosom last night, Captain."

He shook his head and gave a deep, heartfelt sigh. "I was aware your presence would cause me trouble. I did not realize quite how much."

He looked at her meaningfully.

Maisie saw that her arousal had affected him, too, or perhaps mention of him having her the night before. From under heavy-lidded eyes he looked at her, his lips tightly pursed as if he was holding back from kissing her.

That would be a terrible error, if his intention was to shield his men from her femininity aboard ship. "I did not mean to be a burden to you."

"What you are is a temptation, and it is bad enough that

I succumbed." The hungry look he gave her aroused her so much that she swayed toward him.

"I did not think it bad."

His eyebrows lifted. "'Tis good to see you so much less burdened, Miss Maisie. You have a beautiful smile."

"Why, thank you, Captain Roderick," she whispered.

He leaned closer. "May I perhaps take credit for bringing that smile to your lovely face?"

Laughing softly, she tipped her head back to meet his gaze. "If you mean to ask about your lovemaking, then yes, I find I am a woman fulfilled since our encounter."

His lips curled and his eyes gleamed.

How attractive his mouth was. Maisie ached to kiss it, and his stubbled chin made her want to clasp his jaw as she did so. It was far too easy to banter amorously with him and fan the flames of their mutual interest. Dangerous, too, perhaps. She should be thinking about safe passage to Dundee, about concealing her identity and planning for the onward journey, not about bedding the captain once more. However, his rugged, brazen masculinity made her want to wrap her arms around him and insist he take her back to his quarters to pleasure her again. *What am I thinking, acting this way?*

Apparently they were equally dangerous to each other, because when she glanced over his shoulder she could see the eyes of all the shipmen were riveted to the pair of them standing by the railing, barely holding back their desire for one another. Their conversation was causing great interest, which was quite the opposite of Roderick's intention. Maisie felt she must redeem the situation, or he would soon realize that himself, and become grumpy with her once more.

"Captain, set me to work and be quick about it, for you are making the situation even more of a temptation than it already was." She gave him a warning glance to indicate that she was also being affected by their exchange.

A wry smile passed over his face. "On that point we are both agreed. It seems we are well matched in carnal matters." He turned away in order to escort her across the deck, but lowered his voice as he did so, ducking down to add a final comment. "In fact, I look forward to working off this mutual temptation later, when we're alone."

His promise made Maisie breathless, and she almost stumbled as she anticipated what might pass between them later that day. Before she had a chance to respond, he gripped her upper arm with one hand, directing her across the deck.

All eyes were upon them.

As they walked, Roderick issued orders to the men nearby, sending them scurrying back to their tasks. Maisie noticed that most of them were barefoot, as if it was safer to be that way as they went about their duties on the decks or clambered up the poles and ropes.

Grappling for an appropriate comment, she gestured at a man pacing up and down the deck, dragging a broom covered in a wet cloth over the boards. "I could assist there," she said. "I'm able to clean floors."

Roderick shook his head. "It isn't cleaning. He's wetting the planks to keep the caulking tight."

As she had quickly gathered the night before, seafarers seemed to have their own language, much as those who practiced witchcraft did, using words passed down from generation to generation, understood only by their own kind.

"It keeps the ship from leaking," Roderick added, when she gave him a questioning glance. He gestured at a slender lad who stood at the far railing. "Come, if you wish to help, you can work alongside Adam. He is a young Dutchman only on his fifth month with us. It will be a blessing that he has someone to focus him. He is a mite too eager to get beyond himself and set about tasks that he is not yet ready for, but if you are by his side I warrant he will not stray."

Roderick made a gruff introduction, gave her a last lingering glance, then left them and resumed his duties on the deck above.

Maisie attached herself to the young lad, who was shy and awkward and much younger than she. His face flushed regularly while in her company. His current task was tackling a pile of filthy clothing. Maisie watched with curiosity as he tied items to a rope and then lowered the laden line over the side of the ship until it was immersed in the water.

She leaned over the railing to observe. "How clever."

Adam grinned.

Holding tight to the rope, which was obviously no easy task, he let it drag through the waves alongside the ship in an effort to rid the clothing of dirt. Maisie watched what he did, and then assisted by lifting the garments from the pail he dropped them in after their dip, and squeezing them out. The hard work felt good and she was glad to be useful, though her hands became red and sore. It was no easy life being aboard ship, but at that point in her young life the work felt honest. And the basic conditions and presence of many toiling together aboard the vessel appealed to her because of her previous isolation.

Every once in a while a bell was rung. "What is the bell for?"

"It marks the half hour, so that men know when their watches end and they can rest."

"Ah. Thank you." She smiled at the lad.

Once again, he blushed.

Maisie estimated he was no more than sixteen. Roderick had picked her a good companion to work with. The other, older men were less friendly, watching her with suspicion that aroused a sense of foreboding in her bones, the wariness that Cyrus had taught her to feel whenever attention was on her. It made her think that the shipmen might know the truth about her, but she reminded herself of the captain's warning, that the men simply did not want a woman aboard. There was no reason they would think her anything other than a normal young woman who wished to travel to her kin.

When she occasionally craned her neck she could see men moving about on the level above. Roderick was there. She noticed how he checked the wind, the sails and the waters every few moments, acting on instinct, it seemed. When he called out for a sail change, he watched as the sailors leaped into action. His crew trusted him, and he didn't want to put that at risk. He'd said he was responsible for everyone aboard, herself included. Maisie gained new, deeper respect for him as she watched him at work.

Later, she helped Adam gather rainwater from a barrel for the crew to drink as they came to the end of their watches. When she asked him a question, he often spoke in a foreign tongue before translating, the language of his own country.

"There is not much here," she commented as the lad clam-

bered almost wholly over the rim of the barrel to scoop out
another flagon's-worth from low inside.

"*Ja*. There was no time to take water on in London. Is
bad." He shook his head. "Three days out of port, there is
only rum and grog to drink, but we will call at Lowestoft
tomorrow and there will be new water then." He grinned.

"Lowestoft?" Roderick had mentioned it. She had also
heard the name before that, perhaps in her lessons, perhaps
elsewhere in conversation. It was a port on the east coast
of England. Maisie did not know how far they had traveled, so was unable to gauge how much farther it was until
they reached Scotland. The captain had said they would be
in Dundee within the week. That was pleasing enough. It
would have taken her much longer by coach.

Adam nodded his head at the captain's first mate, the man
called Brady. "He visits with his woman there every time we
pass this place, Lowestoft."

Maisie was intrigued. Brady was the one who had given
her the most suspicious looks of all the night before, and yet
he had a woman of his own, something she did not imagine
many of the other men had. Back at Billingsgate he'd shown
his disapproval of her quite openly.

She watched as Roderick ambled over to Brady, and
cocked her head to hear his voice.

"Pray for an east wind," he told his first mate, "otherwise it
will take the best part of a fortnight to reach the borderland."

Pray for an east wind. Maisie turned away quickly, lest he
see her furrowed brow.

Staring up at the skies, she observed what he had—endless
blue skies strewn with wisps of cloud that did not move. It

was her fault, because of her earlier experiment stilling the
rough waters. She had inadvertently slowed the passage of
the ship in her moment of exaltation. Her belly churned as
she realized her mistake. Now she would have to rectify that.
It was not her intention to create magic anywhere she might
be observed, but it seemed she must correct her earlier error
and be quick about it.

With her head turned to the waves, so no one might observe, she beckoned the east wind to them, quietly chanting
the ancient words that harnessed the elements. A moment
later, her hair swept up, lifted by a dramatic change in the
breeze that pulled it free of its pins. It was exciting to see
the clouds scudding across the sky once more. Her magic
had always been powerful, nurtured as it was by her guardian, but she had been able to contain her reaction. To see
her gift realized out here on the open seas caused her to be
elated. The ship swayed dramatically, but Maisie was quickly
able to adjust her stance, moving in rhythm to counter each
pitch and toss.

She didn't dare turn back and see Roderick's reaction. She
heard him nonetheless, commenting on it and referring to
their luck. When his voice faded, she glanced quickly and
saw him stride back toward the place he had called the helm.
The deck rolled and pitched, and more sails were unraveled
to catch the wind on his order.

Then she heard another voice, close by. "I recognize that
tongue. It was Pictish."

Maisie spun on her heel.

"Those words were Pictish, were they not?"

Her heart beat wildly. She'd been observed making magic.

The man before her was aged, his face deeply wrinkled, his hair and beard full and white. Maisie recalled him from the night before. He'd been one of the three men who stood waiting for the captain to return from town, and he'd scaled the nets almost as fast as his counterparts, despite the fact she could now see how bent over he was.

There was a watchful, suspicious look in his wily eyes.

The fear and caution that Cyrus had bred in her thundered back tenfold, stripping her of the pleasure that she'd had in the magical moment, unnerving her once more. "Always protect yourself," Master Cyrus had instructed. "Never let anyone know, never let anyone but me see what you can do. If you do, you risk facing what your mother faced."

It was every bit as dangerous as her master had warned. She was barely two days away from him, and someone had observed her making magic.

"Words my mother taught me," she replied. That much was true. "From an old song about the Highlands." That part was somewhat embroidered, but she was eager to deflect his attention.

"A song from the Highlands?" He cocked his head. "Now that would be most pleasing to hear."

The man was barely as high as her shoulder, crooked as he was. Yet when he peered at her, Maisie felt his scrutiny. Had he recognized the words? He knew their origins, but did he know their meaning? It was hard to gauge how much danger she was in.

She offered him a smile, hoping it might sweeten him. "I know some songs."

"All Pictish?"

She shook her head. "I know only a few lines of the old tongue, but I also speak Gaelic and Scottish. I can sing a song from the Highlands for you in English, if it pleases you."

He stared at her still, waiting on the song, beady eyes narrowed.

Maisie took a deep breath. She did not sing often, but she was well trained in protecting herself by any means necessary. Master Cyrus had taught her she should fear for her life on such occasions and do whatever necessary to avert suspicion.

She cast her mind back. Their mother would sing to them about their birthplace in the Highlands whenever they were unsettled and afraid, and her voice had made the three Taskill children calm and happy. Maisie didn't know if she could sing that way, but she thought of her mother—of the time before her life was so cruelly ended—and she heard her mother's voice in her mind. It wasn't often that Maisie went back there in her memories, but when she did they were so vivid. She saw her mother's face as she had been—hopeful in her quest to find her errant husband, the man who had left them because he didn't understand his wife's witchcraft and could not come to terms with magical bairns. Their mother's love for him still thrived, and it drew the family in his wake to the Lowlands, where they were torn apart by the death and destruction that followed.

"Hush now," her mother's voice said in her mind, *"never fear. We must be what we are, come what may, and not be ashamed."*

Maisie smarted with pain. She had been taught to live differently since her mother was put to death. She'd been taught to hide and be afraid.

But now she heard her mother's voice raised in song, proudly singing a song of the Highlands, and breath surged in Maisie's lungs.

chapter Nine

"My love, I could sing of the whispering sea,
In the calm of a winter's night,
My love, I could sing of the trembling stars,
And the flickering northern light,
And the moon, and the winds, and the barren isles,
With the clinging mists of rain,
But my soul doth flee, over the moaning sea,
To a lovely Highland glen."

Roderick stared across the deck at his unexpected passenger and found himself utterly entranced.

Her voice was the sweetest sound he had ever heard. The very air seemed to be shot through with it, making every one of the shipmen cease work and turn her way.

Roderick could not bring himself to order them back to

their tasks, for the words she sang touched him deeply, and he strained against the elements to hear every one.

"My love, the restless surges moan
In the gloom of the ocean caves,
My love, fast falls the waning moon
Beneath the glittering waves.
I could dream of isles in the tropic seas,
Where Winter's ire is vain,
But my soul doth flee, o'er the moaning sea,
To a lovely Highland glen."

Roderick glanced at the men around him and saw that they were as moved as he was, seafaring men one and all, but they kept the memory of their homeland—whether it be Scotland or Holland—close to their hearts, and the song made them think of the place they carried in their own hearts.

"Oh, give me the breath of the moorland wide,
On the breast of the azure ben,
Oh, give me the boundless sky above,
And the golden burn in the glen.
Show me the birch and the rowan tree,
And the land in sun or rain."

Across the deck she looked his way, and Roderick could see that even while she sang, she was fretful. Why? What had Clyde said to her? Moreover, why did her mood call to him, forcing him to her side, no matter what the consequences?
On she sang.

"Oh, the heath and the bracken call to me,
From that lovely Highland glen.
May I linger there with you, my love,
On a future summer day."

When she reached the final words her glance lingered on him a moment, then she looked about. Roderick could see she was startled to find the entire crew had paused to listen to her. Once again she had drawn their attention. He could not blame them. However, what he should be doing was telling her more sternly to go below deck and stay there, out of view of the men. Sight of her would only cause grievance amongst the men, for her presence broke the ship's rules. Yet when he'd set eyes on her earlier, nothing else had seemed to matter.

Gone was the deeply solemn air that she'd had about her when they first met the evening before. He was glad of that. Was it familiarity with her that made him look upon her in a different way? No, she *was* different. For a moment pride leaped in him, when it occurred to him that he had brought it out in her. Roderick could scarcely turn his gaze away. How beautiful she was, with her hair drifting on the breeze, her cheeks glowing and a smile on her face that seemed only for him—a secret smile that told him she was thinking about what had passed between them. That made him crave her again.

It was more than that, though. Moments after she had set foot above deck it was as if the day became brighter. The sun gleamed on the crests of the waves. And when she stood in the prow, chin lifted to the breeze, he could see the thrill on her face as the wind tugged at her hair. Even the wind had turned in their favor when she smiled.

He strode across the deck to her side, gesturing to the men as he went, indicating they should get back to their duties now.

She watched him close in on her and there was trepidation in her expression.

"You have the voice of an angel," he commented, eager to put her at ease.

Visibly relieved, she wilted against the railing at her back. "I'm glad you liked the song."

"The voice of an angel sounds every bit as sweet on a Jezebel." It was Clyde who had spoken.

"Jezebel?" Maisie repeated in a shocked tone.

Roderick shook his head.

Clyde gave her a toothless grin.

Roderick frowned at the old man. "You have been treated to a song. Do not cast aspersions."

"Aspersions? What aspersions? I haven't yet decided whether this particular Jezebel is a good woman or a bad."

Roderick noticed how distressed she became on hearing that, lifting her hand to her throat as if she feared for her life. He frowned. "Clyde, I forbid you to jest about our passenger."

The old sailor gave him a knowing glance, but did not respond. Nor did he move away. It was as if he truly didn't trust the woman. What grounds did he have for that? True enough, not one of them knew anything about her. Roderick had wondered about her origins several times himself that day. That was no reason to make her afraid. With a disparaging glance, he barked out an order. "You have duties to occupy you elsewhere."

"Aye, Cap'n." Clyde limped away, but with frequent glances back over his shoulder, as if he meant to keep watching.

Maisie watched him as he went, and she looked concerned.

"What did he say to upset you?"

Her head jerked up. Studying him with surprise in her eyes, she denied it. "He didn't upset me. I think he heard me humming to myself and he asked for a song, that's all."

"You were nervous to sing?"

She nodded. "I have not sung that song since I was a child."

"Now that you are Scotland bound it has come back to you."

"Yes." She lowered her voice. "I was discouraged from thinking of my homeland for many years."

"Why was that?" As soon as he'd asked, he knew he shouldn't have.

Pressing her lips together tightly for a moment, she turned her face back out to sea. "The people I lived with, they didn't want me to go back there. But it's in my blood and I must see the place again and find my kin...come what may."

Roderick knew he had intruded, but her puzzling comment made him want to know more, and he decided that he would discover her hidden story by hook or by crook. Curiosity had ahold of him. It was neither the time nor the place, though, for she was still in sight of the crew and he must remedy that quickly. "The men will accept you now, now that you sang so sweetly to them."

Her head lifted. "Thank you for your kindness. I hope that is the case."

"Don't ever repeat this, but your song was much better than what the men roll out to make the time pass more readily. A worse noise you have never heard, especially when there is rum involved."

A soft laugh passed through her open lips and her eyes twinkled at him.

Roderick was pleased he had shooed her fretful mood away.

Then something in her expression reminded him of that point the night before when her fear of their coupling had turned to pleasure, and his whole body responded, the need to hold her growing once more. It seemed that would be the case whenever she was near. Roderick groaned beneath his breath, for it was a dual-edged sword. As captain he could not afford to lose his faculties to lust every time he saw her, and yet it did feel exceedingly good when he was put in that state.

As she looked at him something in her expression changed. Had she sensed his increased need to hold her? Her lips curved, and her chin lifted as if she was ready to accept a kiss. What he saw there in her eyes reflected his desire.

"You have a canny way of capturing my interest, my lady."

"Do not let me distract you from your duties, Captain."

"It is too late for that. The moment you stepped on deck I could think of nothing else but claiming you again."

Her eyes widened and a flash of color lit her cheekbones. "Truly?"

"Could you not tell?"

"I did wonder." How beguiling she looked, now that she

was sure. Her eyes grew dark and her lower lip pouted, as if in expectation of a kiss.

Her gaze lowered to his chest. "You are a fine lover, Captain Cameron, and I remembered every moment of it this morning while I dressed. As soon as you came close to me on deck, the memory was rekindled once more."

Roderick's loins heated. Her candidness lured him. "I am close to you now."

"And I find myself ready for you again." Her eyes shone, and her bosom rose and fell rapidly as she breathed.

Roderick put his hand to the small of her back and guided her back below deck.

It took all his restraint to proceed at a leisurely pace. What he wanted to do was lift her in his arms and cart her off with the utmost haste. Once they had descended the ladder and he'd closed the hatch behind them, Roderick let loose his yearnings. Grabbing her by the hand, he pulled her toward him and covered her mouth with his.

She hummed in approval, returning his kiss.

How soft and supple she was, and how she arched against him, pressing her hips to his. Every bit as eager as he was, she plucked at his shirt with her hand, suggesting through touch that they disrobe. He had to feel her wrapped around him.

Barely breaking their embrace, he maneuvered her to the door to his quarters, and grappled for the handle. Inside, he lifted her in his arms, put his hands around her buttocks and pressed her back to the door, closing it in the process.

Sighing, she clutched at him and her legs shifted around his hips.

"Aye, this is a good fit." Thrusting his hips to hers, he

felt charged, exhilarated as never before. Was it because she wanted him so, that they shared this pleasure so joyously? Bending to her exposed neck, he rained kisses on the soft skin that led down to her collarbone.

She embraced his head with her hands, holding him close, her hips rocking against him. "Oh, Roderick, you have made me this way."

"No." He kissed the swell of her bosom. "This was in you, but I'm glad it is myself who is discovering that."

"As am I," she whispered against his ear.

That was a whole new encouragement and he had to be inside her. Holding her against him with her legs around his hips, he turned and carried her over to the map table, lowering her to its edge.

Confused, she stared down at the map on the table below her. "Whatever are you doing?"

"Having you." He unlaced his breeches and his cock pitched out. "Lie down. You will be higher here and I will be able to see you better while I bring you off."

With a whimper, she submitted and reclined, her arms twined over her head as she stretched out on the table, staring at his cock. Passion flashed in her eyes—passion so intense that for a moment it looked as if candle flames were flickering there in her eyes, and Roderick's cock jerked eagerly in response to her heated stare. Wrapping his hand around his girth, he held himself in check while he nodded at her, indicating she should lift her skirts for him.

"Here, on the map?"

Roderick gazed down as the layered skirts lifted and his

quarry was exposed. "While you are mine, I'll have you wherever and whenever I think it necessary."

"Captain, you are increasingly demanding." Her eyes glowed, and she rested her booted feet on either side of his hips.

"I do not hear you complaining."

Laughing softly, she shook her head. "I should not let you take advantage of this bargain we struck," she murmured. But she did not relinquish her hold on him, the sturdy heels of her boots embedded in his flanks as he prepared to mount her.

"Pull your skirts higher."

She obliged him, gathering the material at her waist, her eyes locked with his. She tried to hold his gaze, but he wanted to see the rest.

"Ah, yes, I am able to bear witness to your state of readiness now."

"Please, you tease me."

"No, I admire you." He smiled her way. "You will be filled soon enough."

Soft, dark hair feathered around the opening of her beautiful cunt, and he marveled at the look of her. Displayed the way she was, arranged at the edge of the table, her plump mound stood proud. Beneath it the pink folds glistened enticingly. The sight of her so slippery and inviting made him ache to be there, and he had to stem his cock, an action that drew her gaze.

It made him unaccountably proud when she looked at him that way.

He pushed the thumb of his free hand inside her, testing her, and found her slick and hot. Alluring and mysterious both, the dark channel called to him. Easing his thumb in and out, he groaned when he felt her grasp at it, her inner walls closing tightly on him. "That is quite the invitation you're offering me."

"I trust you intend to accept it."

"Rest assured I am." He withdrew his thumb and spread her silken arousal on his crown. Then he directed his cock to that hot spot, and when he did she bucked eagerly.

"Fill me, please," she cried out.

Stunned at her wild demand, Roderick wondered for a moment if he was dreaming. How lusty she was, as if it was her true nature he was witnessing now. Then she shifted her hips and her flesh gave way under his, sucking him in.

"Dear God, you are a treasure indeed." He clamped his left hand over her mound, and then thrust his cock fully into her.

Her body arched and her head rolled. She looked so eager for him. That in itself assured Roderick that he would spill in moments if he did not level his head.

He moved his hands to her thighs, stroking up and down, savoring the feel of her soft skin against his palms. That seemed to inflame her and she wriggled, her body tightening rhythmically on his cock.

"I warn you, my lady, I will fill you with my seed forthwith if you don't allow me a moment to gather my senses."

She stilled, then stared at him from under her eyelids.

"That's better. Now let me look at you, and then I will give you everything you want and more."

Her lips parted, and he thought she was about to object, but instead she watched him, waiting. It was hard not to move, hard to force himself to simply burn the sight of her into his memory—this wanton with her brazen breasts and dewy cleft, so eager for him. She made him want to hold her tight in his arms forever—a ludicrous notion for a man married to the sea.

When he glanced down to the place where their bodies were locked together, it almost undid him to see his cock buried in such a delicious place. Her swollen tickler was just visible, and he stroked it with his thumb. When he did, she tightened around his cock, her mouth opening. She whimpered loudly, then he felt her grow hotter and damper still, and she bucked against him.

Breathlessly, she begged his forgiveness. "I could not help it, I moved."

"Well, I tried to rein it in, but you have set this thing in motion now." Pulling back, he took a moment to admire the sheen of her juices over his rod, then he thrust deep once more.

In response she half sat, resting on her elbows.

Wrapping his hands under her thighs, he lifted them, encouraging her to bend her knees to her chest. She appeared to be astonished at what she felt. He rocked back and forth, making pleasure for them both, and a delighted smile lit her face.

Roderick bent right over and kissed her. Then he pumped into her hard and fast, for his sac was tight, his release impending. She jolted against the surface of the table. As she did, her breasts spilled free of her gown, and Roderick stared down at them. How bawdy she looked, with her wine-colored nipples peaked and poking over the layers of clothing attempting to contain them. The globes of her breasts were thoroughly magnificent.

She cried out as she spilled, her body arching. In a sudden and strange action, her hands fisted and went to a spot below her rib cage, while her eyes flickered closed for a moment. Then she grew limp in her release. When her eyes opened, they shone. Never had Roderick seen a woman so invigorated by a good tupping. It pleased him no end.

When he continued to thrust, she smiled, and nodded her head at the map beneath them. "Do you mean to push me all the way across the table before you finish this?"

There was a challenge in her eyes.

Glancing down at the map, he nodded. "Aye, I will not be content until I have ridden you all the way into Scotland."

With laughter on her lips she clutched at his shoulders, aiding his quest.

Roderick had all but mounted the table in order to shift her across the border before he let go, but when he did it was with total triumph.

chapter Ten

Maisie awoke in his arms. It was a chill autumn night on the North Sea, but with her cheek to his chest his body had kept hers warm.

Now he was moving and she stirred from her sleep. He'd set about extracting himself from their tangled embrace and was apparently attempting to do so without waking her, but this time she held tight to him. "You must arise?"

He paused, and when she pressed her head back into the mattress to look up at him, she thought he might change his mind and stay. His expression softened as he looked at her. He bent his head and kissed her, his mouth gently inquiring.

Maisie sighed with pleasure and wove her fingers through his thick hair.

"I must be on deck," he said as he drew back. "Alas."

Watching as he tugged on his clothing, Maisie decided she would never grow tired of looking at the male form. He was a hot-blooded stallion in comparison to the leaner, wraith-like men she had seen in drawings. He was agile nonetheless, and as he bent to pull his boots from under the bed where he had kicked them off, he pounced on her again.

Rolling her onto her back, he kissed her breasts reverently.

"I thought you were departing?"

"I am." He lifted his head, but wrapped his hand around the curve of one breast as he did so, molding the flesh in his palm, stroking the nipple. "But I couldn't leave without another kiss, not with you lying there appearing so wanton, what with your breasts bared and that brazen look in your eyes."

Was that truly how she appeared? Startled, Maisie found she wanted to know more. "What look?"

"The one that lets me know you are thinking of the pleasure you might get from this." He reached for her hand and drew it to the front of his breeches, where he rested it briefly against the bulk of his manhood beneath.

Maisie chuckled. "It is not just that I'm thinking of. I was admiring the entirety of the view. You are a fine built man."

He grinned as he straightened up.

It made her happy to see him that way.

He continued to dress while he considered her silently.

Maisie pulled the covers higher. "See, I have made it easier for you to leave, no bared breasts to distract you."

"So you did. But alas, the image is still here." He tapped his forehead with one finger.

Before he left, he paused by the door. "I suggest you stay below this morning."

Instinctively she went to object, but he hurried on.

"It won't be for long. We dock in Lowestoft later today and I'll take you on shore then. I thought you might enjoy that."

Maisie nodded. "Some time on land would be most pleasant, thank you." His thoughtfulness was an aspect of his character that contrasted to his rough-hewn looks.

"So, you will occupy yourself by preparing for that?" He waited for her to confirm her intentions.

"Yes, Roderick, I will occupy myself here until you come to take me on shore." It was a reward offered to force her to stay below, but Maisie wasn't willing to risk a proper turn on dry land for a few moments on deck.

"Good. I will purchase us a good meal in an inn there. We will talk then. You can tell me about yourself."

That was the last thing she intended to do, and it took every bit of good sense she could muster not to deny him outright. Instead, she didn't answer.

When he left, she stared at the door and fretted.

Why did he want to know about her? She couldn't tell him anything. It wasn't safe for him, or her. Unbidden thoughts of her keeper crept in on her. Why? Roderick didn't think of her the way Cyrus did—as his tool, his possession. At least she didn't think so. Her experience was limited to one guardian, but she couldn't forfeit her liberty again. This arrangement was only for their journey.

Nevertheless, doubts threatened her. Roderick was not aware of her secret craft. He was thinking of her protection, and he wanted his men to trust him. Still, she couldn't help but be reminded of what had transpired with Master Cyrus, and the way he controlled her in the name of protection. The fact that she was currently banished to this tiny room at Roderick's command unnerved her. Slumping down on the bed, she knew it was going to be some time before she could rid herself of that fear, the fear of being held hostage for her craft.

Cyrus Lafayette had nurtured her abilities, giving her time to flourish in his domain. Within a year he discovered that her talent was particularly well exploited when it involved the elements and the emotions. He was, however, a patient man, and as she later discovered, his plans were both grand and long-term.

Cyrus had a private income, and his interests lay in power, specifically in influencing government and politics. He moved in high circles. Young Margaret knew little of this until she was twelve years old, when her tutor was given specific instructions to teach her about the royalty, history and contemporary government of Britain. Mama Beth took little interest in her husband's work. She was a kindly woman and it was hearth and home that mattered to her. She didn't comment on Cyrus's affairs outside the household.

Young Margaret was curious when she discovered that he was a man of power and wide influence, because his role in her life was so very different. Or so it seemed. They spent many hours closeted together. He would debate her lineage with her in secret. These were times she both treasured, because of the subject matter, and feared, because of him.

Master Cyrus explored her world with her, but the way with which he controlled her made her wary even at a young age. She gained both knowledge and caution, but it was never easy. Maisie always feared angering him by saying the wrong thing. His attention was hers exclusively during these times. He was intense, serious, and she often found it difficult or uncomfortable to be with him. Above all, she felt in his debt. When he asked her to do something for him she did so, readily.

No more than once a week, Master Cyrus would encourage her to practice her magic in some small way, in the privacy of his study. She would move objects or extinguish candles with a few whispered words that had either been passed down to her by her mother, or learned under his tutelage. Then one day, he encouraged her to use her magic outdoors, while they were taking a walk in the park one fine Saturday afternoon.

It was a sunny autumnal day close to her thirteenth birthday. He walked alongside her and pointed out different trees, nodding his head and greeting other passersby as they went. When they were in a place where they could not be overheard, he took both her hands and encouraged her to test her magic, to stir the autumn leaves from the ground and make them dance in the air.

For Maisie it was exciting, a new beginning where she explored her craft, safely watched over by him, protected. Together they shared great enthusiasm about her talents, which made her proud, even though he warned her that others would not feel the same about her. They would be afraid of her, just as they had been afraid of her mother. Master Cyrus often reminded her of that.

"I will always protect and cherish you," he would add.

The following week, Master Cyrus took her on the same walk and once again asked her to explore her craft, but with an altogether different purpose. "I would like you to do something special for me, something like the games we play with your powers when no one is looking."

Margaret was pleased.

"We have read about love spells, and how you might influence on behalf of a lonely heart."

She nodded. It was something that fascinated her immensely.

"There is a man with whom I share many fascinating discussions about politics. His name is Gilbert Ridley. He is a widower and he is shy and doesn't seek company. However, I know a young woman who would dearly love to befriend him. I have arranged for her to pass by him when he is taking his morning walk along the river. When I pause to introduce you to Master Ridley, she will be nearby."

"And I will draw his attention to her," Margaret replied, delighted at the game.

The enchantment was woven, and of course it was a great success. Margaret thrilled at the notion that she had played matchmaker for two lonely hearts. The memory remained vivid, for it was a special moment in her life.

It was, however, the first of many times that Master Cyrus urged her to influence his acquaintances from the corridors of power. These requests were always couched in pleasantries, and the spells themselves related to seemingly inconsequential matters. She didn't begin to suspect his intentions until years later, when she discovered that Gilbert Ridley was ruined, his heart broken and his fortune stolen by a wily courtesan and her accomplice.

As the years went on Maisie discovered other such occurrences that made her doubt her magic was the powerful natural healer that her mother had taught her it was. Instead, she increasingly heard the terrible things that were spoken against witches, and her inner struggle against what she was capable of overwhelmed her at times.

Master Cyrus, however, always set her to rights. He was determined to show her it was what she was destined for.

In time, she gained confidence about her craft, whilst becoming an educated young lady. Outings were a rare treat at first, and she was never allowed to go anywhere without his supervision. Mama Beth was under strict instructions to chaperone dressmakers' visits, and Mistress Hinchcliffe never roamed from the subject matter of their lessons, lessons that the master of the house prescribed on a weekly basis.

The changes in her relationship with Cyrus Lafayette began around the time Margaret began to blossom into young womanhood. Mama Beth commented on it, and subsequently, requests given to the dressmaker for her gowns and other accoutrements became more lavish. Margaret accepted this as any young woman might, with pleasure and humble gratitude. Master Cyrus seemed to relish her transformation, and for some reason she felt painfully self-aware under his gaze.

"You are ready to discover more of the world, I warrant," he said as he watched her from his winged armchair while she was busy with her sewing,

Mama Beth encouraged her, too. "You are a proper young lady now. I'm so proud."

Margaret was not sure what discovering more of the world meant. Fear and caution were instinctive reactions. Not only because of her experiences, but because of the way Master

Cyrus kept her informed of the terrible demise often wrought on those who practiced the craft. Education was always tempered with warning.

"More of the world?" she asked cautiously.

"Master Cyrus is taking us both to the theater," Mama Beth informed her, cheeks aglow with pleasure. "It will be delightful to show you off at last."

The theater. Margaret had studied Shakespeare's plays with her teacher, but never imagined she might see them performed. These outings were a pleasure and joy to Margaret, but she also began to become suspicious, because they often encountered Master Cyrus's associates, government ministers, financiers, merchants and tradesmen of the highest order. Some were gracious to his wife and ward, others seemed lascivious and offered barbed compliments that she couldn't fail to notice. Master Cyrus, it seemed, had several enemies.

It then became apparent that when he encouraged her to use the craft, it was often in order to help him reach some personal goal. Margaret was made uncomfortable by that knowledge and began to query the full circumstances of the situation when he requested her assistance. She did not resent helping him, for he had given her opportunities in life that she would never otherwise have had. However, as time went by, the situation became more transparent, and Master Cyrus more obvious about his exploitation of her power. Alongside this, the nature of his relationship with her began to change.

At first it was small things. He told her that he wanted her to call him Cyrus, not Master. That felt odd. Mama Beth no longer accompanied them to the theater. Reasons were given, but it coincided with a change in his attitude toward Margaret. The admiration he showed her was no longer tempered, and it was no longer delivered as a guardian to a ward, but as a man with altogether different intentions.

Then one night Cyrus took her to a reception where they mingled with the actors they had seen onstage, together with personages of note, peers and lords. Margaret felt quite overwhelmed, and when she saw a young man smiling across the room at her, she returned the smile, for it seemed to bear some understanding of her predicament. Later, when the man approached, Cyrus greeted him dismissively.

"Charles Hanson," he muttered, by way of introduction.

"I was hoping to make your acquaintance," the young man had said to her.

"Thank you." Margaret dropped a curtsy.

Charles bent and drew her fingertips to his lips.

A shiver of arousal ran through her and her eyes locked with his.

The young man was about to say more, when Cyrus announced they had to leave. He called for Margaret's cloak and ushered her away, giving her no chance to say goodbye to Charles. Inside their carriage, Cyrus thumped the roof with this cane and glowered into the gloom.

"It was a remarkable performance," she commented in an attempt to alleviate the oppressive atmosphere.

"Yes, it was a perfect evening." Without looking her way, he reached out and clasped her hand where it rested on her lap.

She thought he might squeeze her hand and then return to his thoughts, but he kept hold of it, possessive and insinuating. Her skin crept with discomfort, but she knew better than to pull away. His mood was foreboding and she sensed it would be the wrong thing to do.

"Yes," he added, "a perfect evening, spoiled only by that audacious upstart, Charles Hanson. How dare he think he might court you?"

She was surprised, for she hadn't even thought that was the young man's intention. Cautiously, she measured her response. "I'm sure he was only being friendly."

Cyrus turned to face her, his hand tightening on hers. "I know what drives a man like that. He is not worthy of you."

Why did it feel so awkward? "It matters not, Cyrus, for I am sure you are mistaken about his intentions. But I am quite certain that he is far above me in this world."

"You are wrong." He shifted then and turned to cup her face in his hands. "Very wrong. You are the most precious thing in this world." His eyes glittered in the darkness, and his face was uncomfortably near to hers, his breath hot on her skin.

"Cyrus, you are embarrassing me."

"And how it becomes you," he responded, his tone low, his manner quite different to everything she had known before. He moved one hand to caress her waist. "You are not for the likes of him, my precious. Oh, no, I have much bigger plans for you."

"You have plans for me?" She blurted the question, unable to hold it back.

Immediately, she wanted to retract it, but before she could say anything else, Cyrus answered by pressing his lips to hers.

Thoroughly shocked, she froze, and then pulled away. "Cyrus!"

"There is no need to be afraid," he said swiftly, "not while you are with me. Haven't I always told you that?"

She was far too shocked to answer.

The way he sank back in his seat and eyed her made her discomfort increase. He did not ask her forgiveness for his actions, nor did he apologize. And he kept his hand over hers, as if claiming her.

In that moment she realized it had been his intention all along to keep her as his own. Not as he had done to begin with, but as something else. Something that made her blood run cold.

From that evening on, Margaret's senses were ever on high alert. Watchful and cautious, she didn't draw away from her master, her keeper. Instead she allowed him the briefest intimacy in order to learn the exact extent of his so-called plans. His true intentions toward her hadn't been honorable at all. Nor was the way he dismissed Mama Beth from their lives.

Like a butterfly from the chrysalis, Maisie's transformation into a young woman was a fragile flight into a world fraught with dangers. But deep down she was still a Taskill, and she was strong. Which was just as well, because when she discovered the true depth of her keeper's wickedness, she knew she had to break with Cyrus and forge her own path, no matter what new dangers it might bring.

chapter Eleven

"Maisie, you managed to make your way across in Billingsgate." Roderick nodded down at the plank. It had been set down as soon as they docked at Lowestoft earlier that afternoon, and had been well used between then and now.

The furrow in Maisie's brow deepened as she considered it.

Roderick found he didn't like to see her fretting. In fact, it made him quite restless and uneasy. He walked back across the plank to her side to show her how sturdy it was.

"It was dark in Billingsgate," she grumbled. "And now I can see exactly how treacherous it is."

She nodded down at the waters beneath. She was perched shipside, clinging to the railing at her back, looking down at the plank as if she wouldn't be able to manage it. He noticed how lovely she looked, poised like a figurehead for the *Libertas*. A little too nervous for that role, perhaps. Nevertheless, it made him smile.

Had she really been this afraid in Billingsgate? Things had happened so quickly that first night it hadn't occurred to him she would find it difficult. How determined she must have been to leave London. Why? It was his intention to dig to the bottom of it, but he had to get her on shore first so they might dine and talk in comfort and privacy.

"I will lead the way. Follow my steps exactly." He made a point of taking it slowly so that the board did not bounce as much as it usually would.

When he reached the dock, he gestured at her to follow. "Trust me. What can go wrong? If you fall in, I'll fetch you out."

She gave him a horrified look that made him chuckle.

That seemed to urge her on. Grumbling to herself, she edged her way along the plank. When she got close to the dockside, she gained speed, and when she stepped onto solid boards there, she visibly slumped with relief.

"You will master the plank by the time we reach Dundee, and you can step off in Scotland with grace."

"Perhaps." She didn't seem convinced. She had barely straightened up when Brady came bounding down behind her. Hearing him, she darted to Roderick's side and held tight to him.

Taking advantage of the situation, he wrapped his arm around her waist.

"Oh," she said, when she caught sight of Brady, "how foolish of me."

"Brady is away in a rush after his Yvonne."

A woman's voice called out beyond them.

They both turned to watch as the sailor and his woman greeted one another. Brady grabbed her in his arms and embraced her. Two small children stood by, watching. When

encouraged by their mother, they stepped forward with of-
ferings for their father.

Roderick glanced down at his companion. She appeared
to be intrigued. "How did she know he was coming?"

"He sent word from Billingsgate. He pays highly to have
someone ride ahead to deliver a note. As soon as we dock in
England he sends word. Then she has the port master inform
her when he catches sight of our masts."

"Like two spinning stars closing on one another," Maisie
whispered. "It's quite lovely to witness their reunion."

Roderick had never thought so, for this reunion meant
he might lose one of his best men. But he could see that a
woman might be smitten with such a touching scene. "It is
not without problems. Brady is a man of the sea. No sailor
should be tethered to the shore by a woman, for it tears him
apart inside."

Maisie frowned. "You cannot believe that. He clearly loves
her."

"He does love her. That is exactly the problem."

Maisie frowned at him, then watched as the couple hurried off, each with a child by the hand.

Offering his temporary companion his arm, Roderick
adjusted the neckerchief he had put on for the occasion. He
was not used to such finery, and he'd had to hunt high and
low amongst the men and their belongings to find something
suitable to borrow for the event.

They stepped out together, promenading through the small
town. Roderick was proud to be seen with her. He had gone
ashore before she was even aware they'd set down anchor, and
sought out the best inn he could find to make arrangements.

"I have organized a room where we can dine in comfort," he said, as they mounted the cobbled lane that meandered from the harbor into the heart of the town.

"Why, Captain Cameron, you are being most charming. That wasn't part of our bargain, surely."

"Oh, I shall hold you to the bargain, never fear."

She smiled and glanced at him most seductively.

"However, I want us to talk, to know each other a little better. I am most curious about my lovely passenger."

Her smile vanished. Roderick felt her withdraw. Even her grip on his arm loosened. That was not good. Perplexed, he gestured at the inn ahead.

Maisie nodded. She didn't say anything, but looked rather pensive.

Once inside, he caught the innkeeper's eye, and the man took them to a private room. It was small but well presented, with a dining table, two chairs and a stoked fire. Candles stood in a row on the mantel, as well as in wall sconces, and there was a thick woven mat before the fire that gave it an air of comfort.

"It's lovely," Maisie commented, and smiled.

He was relieved to see the pensive look had gone.

She went to remove her cloak, but Roderick stopped her, stepping behind her and placing his hands over hers on the silver clasp at her collarbone.

She glanced back over her shoulder. "Thank you."

The look in her eyes heated him to the marrow.

Aboard ship she appeared ladylike, moving elegantly all the while. Even when the ship tossed, or she was half-stripped, or was undertaking menial tasks alongside Adam. Here in the relative comfort of the private room in the inn, where candles abounded and the log fire crackled and hummed, she seemed even more elegant, sparkling like a rare jewel before his eyes.

He held out a chair for her.

She had pinned up her hair, and the pale skin of her nape was revealed to him as she took her seat. Roderick stared down at her, and before he moved away, rested his hand on her shoulder a moment, needing to touch her.

Taking the seat opposite her, he was glad the room was so well lit. It meant he could admire her. The way her throat curved into her collarbone made him want to kiss her there. The swell of her breast at the edge of her bodice had the same effect.

The innkeeper brought mugs of ale and assured them they would enjoy a good meal. When he departed, he left the door to the room ajar. The cheer of the crowd in the inn beyond— whilst amiable and infectious—made Roderick want to have her completely to himself again, much as he did in his quarters aboard the *Libertas*. Later, though, he would have that and more, and the thought kept his lust well stoked.

"Tell me," she said, "how did Brady come to have a woman here?"

Roderick thought back on when it was. "We set down anchor here around five years back, in order to careen the hull."

When her eyebrows drew together, he explained. "The outside of the ship gathers unwelcome baggage, barnacles and weeds and all manner of strange creatures. When they make their home on the boards they slow us down. They can also make the ship more vulnerable to taking on water.

We dropped anchor in Lowestoft in order to take dry dock, to hove down, do repairs and tar the boards."

"I didn't know there was so much involved in your way of life."

"It never ends, that is the truth of it, but it's a wild old life and we welcome it. Careening is just one of many tasks that have to be undertaken to keep the ship seaworthy. On this occasion we'd been in warmer seas off the coast of North Africa, and the task took longer than expected, and while we were here Brady met his Yvonne. After we left he was so miserable that we started to call on the port whenever we were nearby. After a year he married her and secured her a cottage. Now there are two bairns to feed, but he is happiest when we sail closer to this part of the world."

Maisie considered Roderick with a half smile. "You are a generous captain."

"It was not just me that made the decision. I sail with a partner. He has been on land these past six months on family business. Together we talked Brady around to this arrangement. He loves the woman, but he also loves the sea. He is a good first mate. We did not want to lose him entirely."

"A woman can do that, draw a seafaring man back to land?"

"Oh, yes," Roderick replied, with irony. "Losing crew to women is a hazard we have often encountered. Many a seafaring man will suddenly find his land legs if lust is involved. Worse still, if his mind is addled by romantic notions."

Roderick had never understood it, but when he stared across at his companion he began to see how it could happen. Maisie Taskill could easily lure a man to land if she set her mind to it. Which was exactly why he should be keeping his distance, not spending every possible moment with her, and endeavoring to find out her history. Yet he couldn't help himself. Natural curiosity, he told himself. That's all it was.

"You thought he would stay with the *Libertas* if you did this to help him?"

"Gregor thought it would be the case, but I think we may lose Brady yet. He gets melancholy when we are away too long. It is better for a seafaring man not to grow attached to one woman."

Maisie sat back in her chair, a curious expression on her face. "Gregor?"

Roderick thought he'd offended her with his plain speaking, but it was Gregor's name that had caught her attention. "Gregor Ramsay is the man I share joint ownership of the vessel with. He is in Fife at the moment, settling a score."

She shifted in her chair and tapped her chin with one finger. "The name. Something about it seems familiar. I am fairly sure I don't know it, but I have the oddest feeling I should."

How would she know Gregor Ramsay? Roderick wondered. "Did you hail from the East Neuk of Fife? Perhaps you heard of him there?"

She shook her head. "I was born in the Highlands. I have never spent time in Fife." She lifted her shoulders. "No matter."

"The Highlands, aye. That accounts for the wildness I witness when you lose control of your senses."

"I have no idea what you are referring to, Captain." Her smile and the flash of her eyes assured him she did.

"What took you to England?"

For several moments she didn't speak at all, and she looked wronged. It was as if he'd asked her a terrible thing. When she did reply there was tension in her voice. "Something that turned out to be a very big mistake."

"We all make errors."

"That is true enough." There was wariness in her tone.

"This life is not easy, nor is our path laid out straight and fair."

She nodded, then lifted her mug of ale and sipped from it. "No, but I did not make the error."

Roderick pressed on, his curiosity rife. "Who did?"

Again, she thought about her response at length, then gave a forced smile. "The man who thought he could bend me to his will and keep me."

Roderick lifted his brows. Apparently she'd had a suitor, one she hadn't given her virginity to. Yet she'd given it readily enough to him. A puzzle lay therein. It was the sort of puzzle that he and some of the men would enjoy debating at length while they shared a flagon of rum on a night and made entertainment for themselves. More intriguingly, she showed a deep determination against being kept by a man. Any man, or just this suitor?

"You have an unusual strength of spirit," Roderick commented.

"For a woman?" she retorted.

"Aye. And more than many men, too."

She looked away and into the flames in the hearth. "I had to be strong."

"Why so?"

She flashed him a warning stare. "It is better that you know nothing about me. I have said too much already."

Irritation built in Roderick. "I do not agree."

It was more than idle curiosity now. He had a bad feeling about the things she said, and their physical union—whilst only a temporary arrangement in lieu of a fee—made him believe he had a right to know.

"I have given you my body, nothing more."

Unaccountably, her glib comment made him feel even more irritated. "As your captain, I have your life in my hands. You should trust in me."

"I trust no man." Her stare was bright and determined, and Roderick felt her strength of will. She wanted him to feel it, he knew, for it was a warning.

He frowned. One moment they were at ease with one another, then this disagreement had arisen. "I don't claim to understand the fair sex," he stated. "I never have. But you, madam, only serve to show me that I never will."

Affronted, she responded by rising to her feet. "You cannot hold all women to account on the actions of one. That is unfair and unreasonable."

"Why not? It is the way you treat men. You said so yourself, moments ago."

Color rose to the skin on her cheekbones. In her anger, she was even more beautiful. Despite the tension between them, Roderick found himself roused by her, and if they had been in his cabin he would have had her on her back in a flash.

Mercifully, the door opened and a serving wench bustled in with a cauldron of stew set upon a wooden board. Steam rose from it.

Roderick nodded across at Maisie. "Sit yourself down."

She pursed her lips and stood her ground, as if unwilling to obey.

He held up his hands. "I will pry no more." Once she took her seat again, he could not resist adding, "Although you are willful and you are wrong to mistrust me."

She folded her arms over her chest and glared across the table at him.

The stew was set down between them, and a second serving woman brought bread, bowls and spoons. Even after the wenches had gone, Maisie held her position most deliberately.

Roderick's belly grumbled. He reached over and dished up the hearty stew into each of their bowls. "Come now, eat. You won't get a meal this good aboard the ship."

"You didn't have to point that out. I have already gleaned that much knowledge myself," she retorted.

Roderick gave a dry laugh.

When she looked his way, she snatched up her spoon.

The food was good and they were both hungry. They ate in silence, but still Roderick studied her, wondering.

"You will not force me to tell you my story," she commented, when she caught his eye.

"No, I won't force you…."

When he smiled at her, she echoed it, albeit slightly.

"And you," she asked. "Why were you leaving Billingsgate docks so hastily?"

So, she can ask me and expect a response, despite her own stand. Roderick had to fight back a sarcastic retort. "The excise men do not take kindly to merchant shipmen such as us, because we don't abide by their rules."

That seemed to amuse her. "You don't pay excise on goods you carry?"

"We are a crew made up of Scots and Dutch. There is little love amongst any of us for the English soldiers, despite the supposed union with Scotland. We find ways to avoid the excise men."

Maisie nodded thoughtfully. "You remind me of Scotland."

"Because I hate the English?"

She gave a low laugh. "Not only that." Eyeing him curiously, she explained. "You are barely tamed, and you answer to no one. Scotland runs in your veins. You carry it everywhere with you."

Roderick had been about to deny her comment, but when he thought about it he realized she'd seen something deep in his character that he hadn't even been aware of himself. It was uncanny. Yet he could not fathom her, except when she was on her back. He seemed to have a knack for handling her then.

A small mercy, he thought, with irony.

"Would you avoid the law if you were on land, in Scotland, or is it because you are at sea?"

Her comment amused him. It was a topic they often debated aboard ship. "There are ways, even on land. In the border country the smugglers have trained ponies to follow a path along a low ledge on the cliffs. They carry smuggled goods inland for them, so that they won't be spotted by the excise men." Roderick grinned. "I've seen the clever beasts myself, from the sea. Quite a sight it was, too. They needed

no man to guide them. They follow the path to their destination quite happily."

Her mouth quirked and he could tell she was picturing it.

Roderick felt the urge to share more of his thoughts on
the matter. "The truth of it is that men will sometimes do
anything to feed their kin, and sharing what little coin they
earn with the taxman is hard to do when their mothers are
ailing or the bairns are crying for food."

Maisie nodded.

"Does my lawlessness shock you?" He swiped up his ale
mug, knowing already that it did not shock her at all. He
wanted to hear her opinion on the matter.

"No. I have seen men even in high and respected places
twist and control a situation purely for their own gain. Your
tale seems almost noble in its cause in comparison to some
of the things I have witnessed and heard tell of."

There it was again. A curtain had been pulled back, briefly.
What a strange comment it was, too. Did the things she had
seen account for the wisdom beyond her years? Roderick
thought about asking her what she meant, but quizzing her
directly had brought nothing. Her comment had, nevertheless, revealed something about her. What it was he couldn't
immediately fathom, but he stored her words away in case
they made sense in different circumstances.

"How do you avoid the excise men when sailing into the
harbor?" she asked, turning the conversation back on him.

Roderick would rather have spoken more about the matters she had hinted at, but he acquiesced. "It isn't easy, for
they watch every move and are often in their rowboats and

boarding before you have time to set down anchor. But there are ways."

"There are?"

She was so much happier learning about him. Roderick felt torn. He liked to see her happy. "One is to create a diversion."

"How do you do that?"

He loved to see the spark in her eyes. She liked to learn, he could tell. "Send men ahead in a rowboat or by foot along the coast. Spread a rumor that there are goods aboard another ship, and then dock and unload while the excise men are otherwise occupied."

"How clever."

Roderick found he enjoyed her interest in their seafaring ways. "It may seem unlikely, but there are even ways to hide an entire ship from view."

"Hide a ship? Surely that isn't possible."

"It is. It's about knowing the coastline as well as you know the back of your own hand. Canny seafaring men make note of every convenient bay or island outside the established harbors. There is one along the coast from here, for example, and if we had set down anchor there we would be within an hour's walk of Lowestoft, but no ship here would be able to see the *Libertas* because of the shape of the intervening coastline."

She sat back in her chair, obviously impressed. "That is most canny."

It was common practice amongst free traders and merchant shipmen, but Roderick was glad they'd found a subject that did not irritate either of them.

"Yes," he added, "if a seaman knows the coast well enough he can make a ship disappear from view—" he flickered his fingers in the air "—as if by witchcraft."

He thought she might chuckle, but instead she looked at him aghast, her eyes widening. What in God's name had he said now?

He was about to ask what was wrong with her when she rose from her seat and turned away to stand by the fire, warming her hands. A moment later, she turned back and offered him an apologetic smile.

Roderick frowned. He would give anything to understand this woman, but her thoughts and actions baffled him. All that he could glean from this latest oddity was that she wanted to be closer to the fire.

He took action. "Come, if you are cold we will draw the chairs to the fireside and I will request a glass of port for us to enjoy there."

"You are most thoughtful."

"I attempt to put you at ease."

"I know you do." She smiled, as if to herself.

Was there some underlying comment there? He didn't want to consider it, for it irritated him again. Instead, he reorganized the chairs. A moment later he called for service and requested a bottle of port. When it arrived they sat either side of the fireplace, each nursing a crystal glass filled with the potent liquid.

It took him back to a childhood memory he had long forgotten, of his parents sitting this way. Of course, they didn't have fine crystal or port, but it was the notion of a man and wife either side of a warm hearth at the end of a hard working day that struck him and made him feel rather odd, as if he had been cast into a different life to the one he was currently used to.

I should be thinking of the tides and who is on duty on deck, not what passes between a man and his wife at the end of the day. Such landlocked notions were irrelevant to Roderick Cameron, or should have been.

"Thank you for this evening," Maisie said, pulling him back from his thoughts.

When he looked at her, he found she had her head cocked on one side, as if she had been watching him.

"You really are a considerate man, aren't you?"

Was she teasing him now? "I try to be, even though I am not used to a woman's company or the finer things in life."

"That much is obvious." Mischief flickered in her eyes.

Roderick raised his eyebrows.

She blinked at him in a languid, sensual manner.

How could such a simple thing affect him so? He had the wild urge to fling her over his shoulder and cart her off to the bedroom. Something about her made him lose rational thought from time to time. That was dangerous. No man, let alone a man of the sea, could afford to be so thoroughly distracted by a woman that he reacted irrationally. Roderick needed to be more sensible about this arrangement. It was imperative that he forgo his curiosity about her background and focus on his ship and the voyage.

He brooded on that fact awhile and stared into the flames.

When he looked back at her he realized she'd kept studying him from under lowered eyelids, and she had that certain glow about her that she got when they came together to couple.

"When do we have to be back at the ship?"

"Not until after the turn of the tide, at dawn."

"Oh." Her eyelids fluttered beguilingly as she thought about it. "Will we stay here at the inn?"

Her question was quite innocently delivered, but he saw that she was thinking on it, and her demeanor was considerably more agreeable than it had been during their meal. Was this a ploy to keep him from asking her more questions? It mattered not, for he knew he shouldn't care about the woman's origins.

She arched her neck and leaned toward him.

It quickly stirred his desires, desires that had been simmering steadily all the while. "I have secured a room for the night, one with a decent, roomy bed and a roaring fire."

"I see." Her mouth lifted at the corners.

Roderick decided she was a temptress. That part of her, at least, was no mystery. "Does that arrangement suit you, my lady?"

"Most definitely."

The irony struck him. Now that they were talking of intimacy she was so much more agreeable and forthright. Moreover, she did not attempt to hide her interest, like most maidens might. A Jezebel she was indeed, just as Clyde had proclaimed, for she had cast aside her shame along with her virginity.

Nevertheless, it still rankled that she wouldn't confide in him. "Yes," he deliberately drawled, "we do seem to get on so much better in matters of a carnal nature."

She gave him a quizzical glance. "Beware your sarcasm, sire, or I shall develop a headache."

Roderick rose to his feet. "I do not intend to give you time to have one."

Reaching over, he took her by the hand.

"It is a good thing I find your prowess as a lover makes up for your lack of good manners, Captain," she said as she stood up. Humor shone in her eyes.

Roderick shook his head, not allowing himself to say any more, not with the serving girls hovering by the door, waiting to clear the table. But once he got her alone he would say and do plenty, and none of it would involve good manners.

chapter Twelve

"Does milady need a maid to assist?" The innkeeper looked at the pair of them with barely concealed amusement.

"That will not be necessary," Roderick replied before Maisie had a chance to speak for herself. "I am quite willing to assist the lady with her disrobing."

Much as it was tempting to chastise him immediately, Maisie restrained herself until they were alone.

"I'm sure you are, sire," the innkeeper replied, somewhat sarcastically, and then retreated.

As soon as the door was closed Maisie folded her arms across her chest. "You care nothing for any pride I might yet have maintained."

"Ah, so you have abandoned your shame but not your pride?"

Maisie's mouth opened. Then she thought better of saying anything, because he was right. It was the way of her kind. Those who were closer to nature did not see any shame in the act of lovemaking. It was a powerful, magical thing. Even more so when affection was involved.

"That innkeeper knows even less about you than I do," Roderick continued, apparently relishing the taunt. "What is your honor to him or anyone we might encounter?"

There was truth in that, but she wasn't about to agree, because it was obvious it stemmed from his annoyance that she wouldn't confide in him. "You are a scoundrel."

"I don't deny it." With that pronouncement he pounced, scooped her into his arms, carried her across the room and threw her on the bed.

Winded by his sudden action, she attempted to rise up and support her weight on her hands to glare at him. "No, instead you seem set on proving it."

His gaze, heavy with lust, raked over her.

Maisie knew she should have been offended by his actions, but there was something deeply arousing about the way he handled her, as if he'd been harboring the need to strip her and make her his all evening. As much as she wanted to keep her private affairs private—and it was safer for him that way—she found it thrilled her immensely to have him so wild-eyed and possessive.

"You are a disagreeable wench when you want to be."

"Why so," she retorted, "because I know my own mind and don't buckle under your questioning?"

He laughed and began stripping off his coat, neckerchief and waistcoat.

Maisie stared, unable to do anything else as he tore off each garment with speed, emphasizing his imminent intentions to bed her. When he lifted his shirt over his head and tossed it aside, she almost forgot to breathe while she took in the sight of his bared chest in the candlelight. The way he stretched and moved made his muscles gleam, showing them to good advantage. No wonder he could lift her so easily, she thought. He was completely undressed before she had a chance to shift from the place he'd deposited her on the bed.

When he lifted his head and looked her way, his expression was both determined and roguish. His eyes glinted, and she knew he was about to pounce. When she tried to get up she was too slow, and hampered as she was by her rigid bodice and corset, he was on her in a flash.

"My intention is to pleasure you until you beg for mercy, but even then I don't think I will be able to find it in me to give you a reprieve. You have driven me to distraction this evening and I intend to work off my lust most thoroughly, even if it takes all night long to do so." He crouched over her on his hands and knees, like a wild hound that had pinned down its prey, his smile victorious.

Instinctively, she turned her face away, but her thighs squeezed together, her anticipation building all the while. How was it that it thrilled her to have him threaten her with a lack of mercy? She wanted to deny that, simply because he was so arrogant, so sure in his power over her.

"The idea appeals to you, my lady. I can see it in the flush on your cheeks." With the back of his knuckles, he stroked the outline of her jaw.

The touch, gentle and subtly persuasive, inflamed her.

"You are so sure of yourself," she taunted, then wriggled and rolled from beneath him, her aim to scamper away from the bed and make him wait a while longer, just to show him she could.

Roderick was up and after her before she'd left the bedside. One large arm locked around her waist and he hauled her back to him. She reached for something to hold on to, but he had her.

"I'm sure of what you need, Maisie." He dragged her back to him, sat down on the bed and captured her in his lap. "I can tell you enjoy this tussle as much as I do."

Before she could even try to resist, he'd reached around and was lifting her skirts.

The urge to spar with him did not decrease. "You flatter yourself, Captain."

No matter how she tried to wriggle from his grasp, he was easily able to cage her in his arms, even while he hoisted her skirts up and bunched them at her waist.

His hands around the top of her thighs made her squirm again, but when she glanced down, she was mortified to see that her ungainly position on his lap exposed her private places. "Unhand me."

"Oh, no," he whispered close against her ear, "you are mine for the week. It is my fee, and if you kindly recall, those were the terms you yourself offered."

The comment only served to arouse her even more, and the hard rod of his erection pressed against her bottom played its own part in making her want fulfillment. Maisie battled him, incensed that he had such a hold on her, in every way.

Then he planted one large hand over her exposed mound, cupping it tightly in his palm. For a moment she fell completely still, distracted by the rush of sensation there at the seat of her pleasure, where he squeezed and manipulated her without mercy. His other hand closed over her bodice at her breastbone, holding her steady against him while she wriggled in his lap.

"Yes, rub yourself against my hand, enjoy it," he whispered, his tone heavy with humor and lust.

"No!" But Maisie was already rubbing herself against him, her hips rocking to and fro, her body responding of its own accord.

"What is it that you need?"

Shuddering, she moaned uncontrollably when he held her nether lips apart with his fingers and rubbed her.

"This?"

Awash with humiliation at her predicament, but desperate for relief, she nodded.

"Good girl."

Between his words and actions, her body ached to be filled, to be taken roughly and ridden until they were both overcome with a hearty release. But she wouldn't admit that.

"Oh, yes, I'll have you after I feel you spill into my hand." His voice was husky, indicating how aroused he was, how ready for her.

Anticipation coiled deep within her.

He stroked her more rapidly, until she was breathless and panting, almost to the point of pain in her tender, swollen nub, but still she met each touch, moving on instinct, seeking release.

He lifted his hand and licked his thumb, and when he returned it to her and thrummed her flesh once again, her body swayed in his grip. Feverish and restless, she moaned aloud.

On he went, until her back arched and she cried aloud, her sudden spending making her hot and restless from the top of her head to her toes.

"You're a lusty wench."

A more powerful one, too, she thought to herself, feeling her magic building inside her, a reserve that was being constantly stoked by his attentions. Everything she had been given to read on the subject was true. Her craft was invigorated by this. Just as two sticks rubbed together could create fire, the passion of lovers brought potency to her magic.

Before she could even catch her breath he rolled her onto her side, then placed his hand beneath her left knee and drew it up toward her chest, holding it there. Within the confines of her corset and bodice, her chest swelled. Her position meant that the base of her corset massaged her lower belly, and her sensitive inner flesh throbbed wildly.

She wouldn't have thought it possible for him to take her while he had her that way, but he knelt over her, one knee on either side of her prone leg. Shocked that he had her so thoroughly pinioned in that position, she could only brace herself for what was to come.

Then she felt the head of his cock at her entrance.

When he entered, it was at an angle that made the experience even more intense than on previous occasions, for his erection moved up along a particularly sensitive area as he fed her his length.

"Oh, Roderick, I might faint."

"I will see to it that you won't, by holding your attention." Gruff and mocking, his tone assured her he meant to push her to her limits.

Glancing back over her shoulder, she watched his face as he eased his way in, his jaw tight, his eyes focused, his chest rising and falling. Copious juices dampened her thighs, and it was a mercy, for the girth of his manhood alone made her feel weak, as if with a fever. She panted for air, her skin misting with damp heat. As the walls of her channel were stretched apart, her head dropped to the bed.

He pushed inexorably on.

She mewed aloud when the head of his cock pressed against her deepest point, the sheer pressure of his erection there making her dizzy. Then he began to pump back and forth, and she could not withhold her vocal appreciation.

"You see, you are too busy enjoying yourself to faint," he taunted, in between thrusts. "Admit it," he urged, "you enjoy the tussle."

"I will admit you're a clever lover," she managed to respond, her voice wavering as she received his rapid thrusts.

"That is good enough for me." His grip on her was unforgiving, as if he had his own war to win, and she couldn't have moved even if she wanted to.

Maisie was helpless beneath him, her entire nether region aflame as he rode her relentlessly, churning into her over and over until she spilled again, crying out as she did so.

"Ah, your grip on me is too good." He paused and stroked her hair back from her face with one hand before he changed his pace, moving in more shallow thrusts.

Maisie clutched him again, and found her own pleasure was lengthened in the process. She reached around to touch him.

He meshed his fingers with hers.

The tender gestures, offered while he was so bound up in his quest for release, affected her strangely, and when he pulled free to spill his seed elsewhere, she found herself wishing he had not left her at that point.

Be careful, she warned herself.

If her affection for him grew, it would be more difficult to deny his questions and keep her secret nature safe. Yet when he rolled her into his arms a moment later, so that she faced him and he could cover her in kisses, she melted anew, unable to pull away.

chapter Thirteen

The autumn sky on the following morning was glorious, and as the *Libertas* sailed out of Lowestoft Harbor, Maisie breathed the air in, reveling in the moment. Her body felt sated, womanly, and rich in carnal magic, and the elements seemed to reflect her vitality.

Gulls wheeled overhead, circling above them as they made their way out to sea. They were on their way once again to Dundee, and as the distance between her and London grew and she spent more time with her Scottish captain, she anticipated the onward journey and the reunion that she hoped waited at its end. She watched in awe as the land appeared to slide away from them as the morning breeze caught the sails. She would have fond memories of Lowestoft.

Turning, she looked up at the deck above, where Roderick directed the ship's path through the waves with his strong hands on the wheel, issuing instructions to the men and watching over their actions. He'd attempted to get her to go below deck when they came aboard that morning, but she had insisted on aiding Adam in his chores. Roderick didn't fight against her too hard, most likely because the men had already given her a good scrutinizing as she mounted the rail and landed on their deck again.

No sooner had she turned Roderick's way than he noticed and smiled across at her, acknowledging her stare. His attention kindled her passions afresh. Now that she'd begun to understand his ways and she had gained the measure of him, she'd even begun to enjoy bantering with him. Being wary and cautious was still foremost in her mind. She couldn't risk him learning about her secret nature, nor the true reason why she had left London. So long as she kept that in mind, she was able to enjoy his company. Even when he was arrogant and demanding. Perhaps even more so then.

The notion made her blood heat. Why was that so? She had vowed never to be cowed and controlled by a man again. It was different with Roderick, though. His demands were borne solely from his passion for her.

That was no small thing.

When her stare lingered on him, his smile became brooding, as if he was thinking of the bed they had shared the night before, as she was. It had been a long night of passion. Yet when they had risen that morning he had been most debonair and gracious. Their long night of lovemaking had apparently mellowed his gruff humor, as if being with a woman directed his life force onto a steadier course.

Before they left the privacy of the room at the inn, he'd kissed her—her mouth, her forehead, her cheeks and eyelids—then he'd sighed deeply. When she had started to ask him why he'd done that, he'd put his finger on her lips, then told her they had best get back to the ship.

Moving into action now, she set about her tasks aiding Adam. Whenever she could, she stole a glance in Roderick's direction, watching him and his easy manner as he strode about the place, checking on the men individually as well as issuing orders from above. He had gained their trust. That was no small thing, she knew. Perhaps these men had never had reason to mistrust others. She certainly had, yet she recognized in Roderick a quality that she hadn't found in the only other man she knew well. A forthrightness that was not only admirable, it appealed to her immensely.

Over the course of that morning Maisie learned how to milk the goats. As Adam demonstrated, she recalled watching her mother do the very same task in the Highlands, when she was but an infant and stood in the croft with her twin at her side, waiting for the warm milk. The memory, unbidden but welcome, touched her, and made her grateful once again that she'd been brave enough to break from her sheltered life in London to undertake this journey.

Under Adam's guidance she managed to coax forth one eighth of a pail of milk. It took a great deal of time to master the ability, but she was determined to do so and not resort to magic or assistance. Adam chuckled at her failed attempts, but encouraged her on, and eventually the wondrous sound of the milk hitting the side of the pail gave her cause to cry out in delight.

"You have done well. It took me much longer to learn. The milk will be used to enrich the porridge for the morning."

"I had a good teacher." She smiled up at him as she continued with the task.

"If you were to stay with us beyond Dundee, I could help out with the sails." He shielded his eyes from the bright morning sunlight and looked upward, and she could see that he longed to be climbing the masts.

Maisie had overheard the other men teasing him about his woman's work. It hadn't occurred to her that someone must do it until a new ship's hand enlisted. Adam would never move on if there wasn't a new lad to take his place. It made her think about what it would be like for a woman to live a life at sea. A strange life indeed. When Maisie looked back at Adam, she could see that he was following his own thoughts, too, looking longingly at the young lad who was currently keeping watch from the nest high above.

That afternoon she and Adam sat on short stools either side of a large pot, peeling and dicing root vegetables.

"We'll add salt beef, then I'll take it below," he informed her.

"Is there a scullery with a fire, below deck?" Maisie had not even wondered about the actual cooking.

"An open grate. We can only use it if the conditions are right." He shook his head, his eyebrows drawing together. "If the sea is rough it is too dangerous to risk lighting the fire."

Maisie nodded. Now that she thought on it, she saw that the ship would be vulnerable to fire.

"With luck it will be calm enough to prepare a hot meal for tonight."

"If it isn't?"

"Salt meat and oatcakes again. If the captain thinks the

voyage will be smooth enough the men's bellies start to rumble. I must sit with the pot the whole time, watching in case the fire catches the boards." He looked rueful, and she knew it was because he preferred observing the activities above deck.

"In that case," she said, "I will finish the vegetables and you can do something else, until you have to go below deck with the pot."

He stood up, smiling gratefully. A moment later he joined a group of men who were discussing which of them would wet down the boards that day. Adam volunteered.

Once he was gone, Maisie returned to her work and sharpened her hearing in order to listen to Roderick instructing the men. Even though she didn't understand many of the terms he used, his voice made her feel warm. It also made her remember how the timbre changed when he was making love to her. At those times his voice seemed to vibrate right through her, an intimate call that she alone could hear. Once again she thought how lucky she'd been with her random lover. Roderick had stirred her affections as well as her passions. That she could no longer deny. She cared for him, for his safety and happiness. Could she halt that? Probably not, but she would leave his side quickly at Dundee, unwilling as she was to put him in danger by association.

During the course of that day the men seemed friendlier toward her. Clyde, who had been suspicious of her at first, and had asked her to sing, stopped to talk to her.

"Not many women would brave this deck. You are a strange one."

Was that a note of admiration she heard in his voice? "I

am trying to make myself useful. Tell me, have you decided whether I am a good woman or a bad one?"

"I'm still thinking on it." He ran his fingers over his beard as if suddenly concerned for his appearance.

"The captain told me you carried a woman passenger once before."

"Aye. She was nothing like you, though. She would never have sullied her hands preparing food or milking the goats. She did try to order the captain about, both him and Master Ramsay who was aboard ship then. Treated them as if they were her servants, or tried to."

"It's little wonder the captain was reticent when I requested passage."

Clyde's eyebrows flickered. It clearly interested him that the captain had not immediately agreed to her plea.

"It took some persuading," she added, "and I was most eager to travel north, to my family."

Clyde nodded thoughtfully. "The captain is a generous soul and you appealed to his good nature. It is his first term as captain of the ship without Master Ramsay at his side to discuss matters. It is important that the men do not doubt him."

Was that a warning? When Roderick told her to keep out of the crew's way, she hadn't realized it would reflect badly on him if she didn't. It was too late now, but because she was particularly wary of Clyde she took his words to heart. "Do the crewmen think I have brought disrepute on the captain?"

She hoped that was not the case.

"Some of the men believe it is bad luck to have a Jezebel flaunting herself about. Others merely think it is no place for a woman."

"And you? What do you think?"

"Sometimes I see the captain watching you, when he ought to be watching his men."

Maisie swallowed. That definitely sounded like a warning. This man doubted her, recognized her Pictish tongue and thought her a Jezebel.

Before she had a chance to respond, he broke into a grin. "I cannot blame him, for you are much prettier than the men."

With that, he limped off, leaving Maisie to think through what he had said. The man clearly had his misgivings about her presence. He was a riddle, though, because she knew he was trying to get the measure of her, but he was giving nothing away. Had he known the words that he overheard that first morning? She still wasn't sure. What she did know was that he was watching her closely. It reminded her all too readily of Cyrus's threats and warnings. Icy fingers flitted over her spine. She braced herself and pushed the thoughts away, fixing her attention on the work at hand.

Maisie was nearly at the end of her task, with only two turnips left to peel, when a commotion broke out overhead. One of the ropes that harnessed the sails had become entangled with the material, and a young man was climbing the mast, his intention apparently to free it. There were mutterings and shouts, and a moment later she realized the young man in question was Adam. He had taken it upon himself, even though the older men called him back.

One man in particular, a fellow Dutchman, shouted up in his own language.

Adam called back, and as he did he lost his grip and swung in an ungainly manner from the rope he had been working on, his legs coming free from the mast. The rope rapidly unraveled and the lad descended, his body twisting on the descent.

Maisie's heart thundered in her chest, fearing as she did for his safety. Instinctively, she mustered an enchantment, but there was no time to prevent the accident. Adam hung precariously in a tangle of rope like a great fish caught in a net.

Maisie covered her mouth with her hand and rose to her feet. Men swarmed to his aid, two climbing the rigging to assist from above, while others eased him down to the deck. Adam cried out in pain on occasion, and Maisie could see the hand that held him tight to the rope was twisted and bloodied.

"Take the wheel," Roderick shouted to Brady, then darted over to the scene to examine the lad. "Take him below and tend him," he instructed two of the men.

The sailors moved quickly, lifting the lad. One of them shifted his injured arm, laying it across his chest so it would not dangle as they carried him, and Maisie saw the extent of his injury. Blood ran down his forearm from scraped knuckles, but that was not all. Two of his fingers were badly misshapen, in all likelihood dislocated.

Turning on her heel, Maisie made her way quickly below deck to the captain's quarters, where she retrieved her bundle from under the bed. Checking through it quickly, she reassured herself that she had dried agrimony leaves, a vulnerary herb that she could bind around his fingers in a dressing to aid healing.

When she returned to the deck, the men who had been tending Adam had disappeared, taking him with them. The hatch at the far end of the deck, where the men emerged when they came up for their watches, stood open. Without a second thought, she hurried over and clambered down the ladder, clutching her bundle as she went.

The ladder was longer than the one that led to the captain's quarters, taking her deeper into the ship. She found herself in a dark and crowded place, where the air was stifling and wooden bunks were stacked one upon the other on the walls. It took her a moment to become accustomed to the gloom, and when she did she saw that the slots acted as beds for the men.

Beyond them, she saw hammocks lined up at the far end of the space, as well. There were only a couple of lanterns here and there to light the way, and she stepped carefully around piles of clothing, goods and boots littering the floor.

As she passed, a man stuck out his head from one of the slots and she jumped.

He gave her a grin and settled to watch her, apparently amused by her appearance in their quarters. She was just about to ask the man where to find Adam when she heard a frightful scream from beyond. Whatever they were doing to him, it was not good. She hurried on.

Half a dozen men surrounded the spot where they had Adam stretched out on the floorboards. His head was propped up on one man's knee while another poured rum down his throat. The liquid spilled everywhere, staining Adam's shirt and making him cough.

Maisie grumbled to herself when she saw that his hand appeared to be in worse condition than the last time she'd seen it. Marching over, she quickly instructed the men to leave him alone. "I will see to him. Leave the task to me."

A couple seemed dubious, but one of them was agreeable and he took charge. "His hand needs to be strapped tight." He gestured at a pile of tattered fabric beside Adam's body. "His fingers must be made straight now, or they never will be again."

Maisie nodded. "Have you a small splint I can use?"

The men mumbled amongst themselves and one walked off and returned a few moments later with some spliced pieces of wood to offer her.

"Thank you." She stared at them, waiting for them to leave.

"If he gives you any trouble," the man in charge added, "call out for us and we will feed him more rum."

Rum was their answer to everything, or so it seemed. Maisie Taskill had more than that to help his recovery, though, but it was important they did not observe her. She jerked her head, indicating they could go.

When the men left Adam's side, she peered around the gloomy corners of the place and saw that there were other men about. Some were resting, some were watching her. Sighing inwardly, she realized she'd gone down there without even thinking about her own safety, but there was nothing else to do now but proceed. And even if she'd thought about it beforehand she would still have come to his aid. Cautiously.

Kneeling at Adam's side, she took a moment to calm him, stroking his forehead. He blinked and looked at her with unseeing eyes a moment, then offered a weak smile when he recognized her. "It is Maisie from Scotland," he whispered.

"It is me, yes, and I will tend you." She cupped the elbow of his injured arm in her palm, allowing him to get used to her touch before she began her task. "That is the first time you have called me by my name."

"It's what the captain called you, when he asked me if I would look after you."

Maisie from Scotland. It touched her deeply to think that Roderick called her that to the men, when he had been so doubtful of her origins on first hearing her voice.

"You looked after me well, Adam. And now I must look after you."

She saw a troubled, pleading expression in his young eyes. "It is going to hurt a lot, isn't it?"

"I will be as gentle as I can, I promise." He was sure to hear her enchantment, and she knew many pairs of eyes were observing from the dark shadows all around, so she had to find a reason for it. "I will sing you an old Scottish song to soothe you while I see to it. Rest back now."

She began to hum a tune about the lochs and the mountains in springtime as she examined his hand, and after a few moments she whispered a soothing enchantment amidst the song. It worked instantly, and with a much greater effect than she was expecting. The lad visibly slumped on the floor, and looked as if he was asleep.

Startled, Maisie realized it must be due to her enhanced ability. It pleased her, but she also knew she would have to be more cautious than ever, and especially so if she made magic in fear or anger, for the results would be far more than she had previously been able to achieve. It was difficult for her to gauge how forceful it was without some time alone to explore her newfound levels of ability.

"That rum surely is potent stuff," she commented as if to herself, but loud enough for the benefit of the onlookers, and shook her head.

There was a bunched garment beneath Adam's head, so she made a show of plumping it up to make him comfortable. Then she continued with her song.

The flesh around the dislocated joints was already swollen, and the fingers badly distorted. In the state the lad was in, barely conscious as he was, he would not feel much pain. Realigning bones in a person was not something she had experience of, but she wasn't afraid. Under Cyrus's guidance and encouragement she'd healed sick and injured birds and animals in order to test her magic. Moreover, there were many healers in her family line, and it was a particular skill of her mother's. Maisie had always wanted to heal, and working on small animals had given her the deepest satisfaction.

Inhaling slowly, she tentatively felt her way around the first dislocation. When she had the measure of it, she quickly shifted the bones back into place, and used one of the straightest bits of wood they had given her to support the finger, then aligned the second finger against the splint. When the second joint cracked into place, Adam rolled his head and murmured, roused from his sleep, and she was glad of that much for her audience. Hurriedly, she crouched over her patient to obscure the view any of the men might have of her, and pulled the dried agrimony from her bundle. She laid several precious leaves within the bandages that had been left for her to use, covering the grazed knuckles and swollen joints with them. The plant had healing properties and would also protect the torn skin from infection.

Resting back a moment, she studied her patient. "Poor lad, I think he has passed out with the pain."

She stroked his head and shuffled the makeshift pillow beneath his head again. Then she arranged his arm across his chest, so that the hand was supported there.

It was when she was rising to her feet that she heard whispers that unsettled her. Sharpening her hearing, she distinguished their hushed words from the creaks and groans of the ship and the other distant voices and sounds. Two of the men had seen her retrieving something from her bundle, and were speculating about the contents therein. One of them called it the devil's work, and questioned the fact Adam had fallen silent, despite his earlier bellowing.

A leaden weight settled in her belly. Some of Roderick's men suspected her actions and her motives.

Maisie's first reaction was to counter it by magic. That would be even more dangerous, for she was not sure which of them or how many had seen her.

Tying her bundle tightly, she gripped it in one hand, and lifted her skirts in the other as she made her way through the crowded quarters. She lowered her head so that she did not draw attention or meet anyone's gaze.

The risks were there, but she had done her best to cleverly conceal her magic. If they ousted her now she might never complete her journey to the Highlands. Still, she did not regret it. It was unfortunate, but she couldn't have left Adam that way.

Whatever they did to her, she would endure it. It was better than being Cyrus Lafayette's instrument of power. Once she'd learned his true nature, and what he was really capable of, she knew there could be no worse fate.

chapter Fourteen

The day that Maisie Taskill traded her virginity for passage aboard the *Libertas* would forever be etched in her memory. It had begun badly, and grew more frightening and regret-filled as every moment passed.

Cyrus had entered her bedchamber that morning while the maid was still dressing her hair. He had done so several times since Mama Beth's illness kept her confined to her bed, and he did not even knock or have his visit announced. "Good morning, Margaret, my precious beauty."

Suspicion and fear roared in on her, filling her senses. He was circling ever closer, like a bird of prey getting ready to swoop.

"Cyrus." She inclined her head. She had already begun to think of herself as Maisie Taskill again and not Margaret Lafayette, and that helped her, giving her something to cling to that was nothing of his.

He stood behind her, admiring her refection in the look-ing glass. "Put on your best gown tonight. The one with the

gemmed bodice that becomes you so well. We'll be attend-
ing the opera. I wish to show you off."

He wove his fingers into her hair and drew some of it to
his face, breathing it in.

Maisie glanced over in order to see the maid's reaction.
The girl looked startled. Even she saw it. Master Cyrus was
no longer treating Miss Margaret as a daughter, but as a potential consort. Even while his wife lay ill in her bed and
close to death he was ready to begin a new life with Margaret as his companion.

Maisie forced herself to keep still, when what she really
wanted to do was turn on him and push him away. It was
important, however, that his suspicions were not aroused
while she decided what to do. "Shouldn't I stay at home tonight, with Mama Beth so unwell? The physician informed
me she is very ill indeed."

His mouth twitched. "She would not want you to miss
this opportunity. Lord Armitage himself has invited us to
join him in his private theater box."

Maisie inclined her head, but all she felt was a sense of
foreboding, one that was so strong she knew she would have
to act upon it and do her utmost to discover the truth.

"Cyrus," she said, and met his gaze. "What will become
of me if Mama Beth passes on?"

It was a weighted question, for she had begged him to
allow her to use healing magic on his wife, and he'd refused.
His mouth lifted at one corner. He beckoned for the maid
to leave, and then leaned over her, whispering, "You will be
everything that we have dreamed of, and more. Your mighti-

est powers will unfold and we will wield them together, for pleasure and benefit."

Her heartbeat faltered. It was all true. The suspicions that had grown over the past months were warranted. He'd stated his intentions quite clearly, and there was no denying it now.

"I will make you my own," he continued. "Forever. My queen and my wife."

Maisie's heart turned to stone. Wife? She'd already gleaned his nefarious aims and his lust for her, but had never once thought he meant to marry her. What of Beth?

He bent and kissed her bare neck, as if he couldn't resist doing so now that the subject had been so thoroughly broached. His mouth on her skin repelled her. It seemed like such a betrayal.

Dare she use her magic against him? Would it even work, given his role in her life? Maisie couldn't be sure. She didn't feel powerful enough to thwart him that way, because he knew so much about witchcraft. What she did feel was his lust, pent up and dark, both fiercely carnal and greedy for power, and her need to run from him grew desperate. Soon. If she made him suspicious he would have her more closely guarded. She was already aware that he had her every move watched and noted. Averting suspicion was paramount. Instead of flinching, she clung to the edge of the dresser with her fingertips and forced a smile.

"I will be with Lord Armitage until the opera begins. I'll have a carriage readied to bring you directly to The King's Theatre, where you will be escorted to our box when you give your name."

"Thank you, Cyrus."

He seemed content with that and left.

Maisie didn't move from that spot until she heard the sound of movement outside the building. The familiar shout the coachman used to urge the horses on indicated Cyrus had left in his carriage. Then she rose and went directly to Mama Beth's chambers.

Requesting some private time with Mistress Beth, she assured the two servants and the nurse who currently cared for the mistress of the house that she would call for them if they were needed. Once they departed, Maisie entered the bedchamber and walked quickly to the bedside. She'd spent many hours there in recent weeks, but she'd kept a bright mood and hopeful spirit, relating the household events and other such chatter in order to help Mama Beth feel content, and enable her to fight the illness. This time she had to be bold and ask questions, questions that might otherwise never be answered. It felt selfish and harsh, but at the same time Maisie knew she must. If Mama Beth was distressed by the discussion, Maisie would wipe the memory away with magic.

She was so pale, drawn and frail in her bed that it was hard to bear witness. Maisie loved this woman who had been so generous and kind to her. Guilt weighed heavily on her, too, guilt for Cyrus's shift in affections over the years.

"Margaret, is it you?" she said, her eyelids fluttering.

"It is." Mustering a smile, Maisie bent to kiss her forehead. "Do you feel any better, Mama Beth?"

She roused a weak smile, but did not answer directly. "How fares the household today?"

"All is well there."

She squinted at Margaret. "You appear thoughtful. You have something else on your mind, child?"

Could she even broach the subject? *I have to.*

Maisie nodded. "I'm afraid I must burden you with my personal concerns, and I must ask you some questions that might be difficult for us both."

Beth studied her face for some time, then looked at her with sympathy and with love. "I knew you would come to me when you were ready to ask."

Her response, so simply stated, so knowing, buckled Maisie's legs. Tears quickly dampened her cheeks. "I'm so sorry for what I must say. I feel that I've been foolish and blind."

"Hush, child. You are no fool, and Cyrus is clever at concealing his true plans."

Maisie wiped away the tears. How much did Beth know? "How long have you guessed his plans for me?"

"I don't think he intended to become quite so obsessed with you, not when you first came to us. That came later."

Maisie nodded, relieved. "You must believe me, I never thought of him...in that way."

"I know that." Beth lifted her hand from the bedcovers, seeking Maisie's.

"Oh, Mama Beth, I'm so grateful for your understanding." Maisie grasped her hand and bent to kiss it. These past few weeks witnessing her declining health had been difficult enough, without the need to broach this painful subject.

"I always knew that he honored your intelligence, your... special abilities."

Maisie lifted her head. Cyrus had always told her not to

reveal her craft in front of anyone but him, stating that not even his wife knew.

Beth smiled weakly. "You thought I didn't know?"

"Cyrus told me you didn't."

"Cyrus tells us all what suits him. I knew. When I wanted a child he told me of the poor orphans, the ones left behind after their parents were put to death. He said it would be easier to find a child I might keep under such circum stances." Beth had a faraway look in her eyes. "I was later told we could have adopted a child here in London, and soon enough I realized that he was nurturing that magical side of you. Perhaps I should have intervened, but I could see how you flourished under his guidance."

"I have, and I am grateful for that, but I cannot be what he wants."

"No, I see that now."

Maisie was startled, for the comment revealed Beth hadn't been sure, that she perhaps wouldn't have said anything if Maisie hadn't broached the subject. That twisted the knife a little bit more.

"I hesitate to say it," Beth continued, "but I think perhaps Cyrus is afraid he will lose you, and by making you his bride he might keep hold of you."

Maisie's thoughts raced. She recalled that when she had turned fifteen he'd talked about how her magic would transcend all that had gone before when she was made a woman, by a man. She shut her eyes, because she saw it now—saw his face again as he'd said those words to her. She also saw how he'd protected her until this time, how he'd turned away potential suitors and discouraged her from spending time with people her own age. It was because he was the one who intended to introduce her to her full potential. Cyrus wanted to be her only lover.

Beth's eyes had misted, and Maisie knew that in her heart this woman was every bit as betrayed as she, if not more so. "Tell me, Mama Beth. I sense your troubled thoughts."

"It is not how I thought things would end," she whispered. "But you must know something else. It would not be fair of me to conceal from you the wickedness in his soul."

Darkness seemed to crowd in around them.

Maisie swallowed down her trepidation. Beth was trembling, and it was so uncharacteristic that Maisie knew not if it was from her illness or from fear.

"I haven't been well for some time," she began, "and then it became apparent to me that Cyrus was eager to be your husband, instead of your guardian. At first I couldn't comprehend it. But it began to make sense. I grow weaker now and I lie here hour after hour, and I seem to see things from afar." Beth squeezed her hand. It was a feeble grip, but Maisie felt her effort. "I think he has hastened my path to the grave. That is how much he wants you."

Maisie reeled, horror-struck.

Then she understood. The physician had told them Beth was growing weaker, but would be with them for many months, perhaps even years, if properly cared for. But within a matter of days her health declined rapidly. Listless and unable to rise from her bed, Beth faded away from them. The physician gave little hope. It was around that time Cyrus had made his intentions known to Maisie. He'd started to be seen out about the town with her more regularly, ordering lavish gowns to be made and bringing her expensive trinkets on a daily basis. That very morning, when he had told her he would make her his wife, it all fell into place.

She gripped Beth's hand, looking deep into her eyes. "Beth, mother of mine, I trust you implicitly, but I must ask...are you sure?"

"I doubted it myself at first, and then I watched him. He asked to sit with me during my suppers. One night I saw him add something to my broth once the servants had gone. I asked him what it was, and he assured me it was a tonic. He wasn't offended when I said it might be making me ill. He had a black look in his eyes and his answer was too easily given. I turned the food away, hoping I would improve, but I fear it is too late. The damage has already been done."

Maisie wiped away the flood of tears that gathered. "You should have told me this before now."

Beth moved her head against the pillow. "I made my own mistake with Cyrus, long before you came along. I agreed to stay with him no matter what, for he supports my family, and they have no other income."

"Your sister and her children?"

Beth nodded. On the last Sunday of every month Beth had visited her widowed sister.

"I often wondered why you never allowed me to accompany you on your visits. I thought you might be ashamed of me."

"Good Lord, no. Cyrus said it wouldn't be appropriate for a young lady such as you. Perhaps he feared you would discover my debt to him."

The hidden secrets rolled out, each hideous treachery dependent on the other. Maisie rested her head on the bed-covers a moment, for she ached with grief. Could it be true that Cyrus had poisoned his wife, in order to be with her instead? She felt as if her heart was breaking.

"I've always wanted you to be happy, child. When you walked in here with such fear and regret in your eyes, I knew I had to tell you everything."

Everything Beth said only added to Maisie's turmoil. Beth would have slipped away silently if Maisie had been happy with Cyrus's advances—that's what she was inferring.

"I'm so confused. This morning I felt as if I must flee from him, but I don't want to leave you, especially not now."

Beth's lip trembled, but she squeezed Maisie's fingers in her own. Her life force was fading all the while.

"I can scarce believe he has done this to you." Maisie shook her head. "I will attempt to make you well again. I believe it is possible."

"No, you must go. Escape this trap he has set for you."

Escape this trap. The words echoed in her mind.

"Go home to your birthplace, Margaret. Cover your trail well and live a safe and happy life in Scotland."

"I have thought on it often. I do not know if I am strong enough to undertake the journey alone."

Beth breathed a laugh. "You are. You will find your true kin."

Maisie lifted her head. A new dread filled her. "Cyrus told me they were safe, Lennox and Jessie."

Beth shook her head. "We know nothing of them. Cyrus lied to you about that, too."

It was the final confirmation, the thing that mattered the

most to her. She had been duped and betrayed for all these years, while she thought her siblings had been offered salvation like her. All those times she'd felt concern for their well-being, Cyrus had reassured her. It was all lies. The reality of her situation struck her anew.

"That day, he selected you when he looked across at you from the coach. He paid highly to have you brought to us unharmed. I saw your sister that day, too, and it broke my heart to split you from her. I begged Cyrus to take you both, but he refused."

Jessie. Maisie covered her face with her hands and wept.

Mama Beth touched her forearm, encouraging her. "Go, go now. There is some coin in my special jewel box. You'll find it in a red satin purse. Take it and anything else you think might help you."

"I cannot leave you." The frustration that she'd felt about Beth's illness still haunted her. She was sure she could cure her by magic. Maisie had never undertaken such a thing, but she could try. "I will bring healing herbs and you will get better. Now that I know about Cyrus, I will guard your food."

Beth shook her head. "No. We cannot go on this way. Neither of us will be safe. I'm ready, and I am weary of this life. All I wanted was to watch you grow. You're a fine young woman now, so I am at peace to say goodbye to this life of mine."

The ache in Maisie's chest grew. Tears spilled from her eyes.

"You must go now. Please. I will pass on peacefully, knowing you are safe."

Maisie couldn't force herself to rise to her feet.

"Please, child. Go quickly."

"I cannot."

"You know you must. Hush now, be strong. Go to your kin, find them. They will keep you safe."

My kin. Are they even alive? Beth had said the right thing, for Maisie had to know. She forced herself to her feet, then bent to kiss her adoptive mother on the forehead. "I love you, Mama Beth."

"And I love you. Make haste, my girl. And forgive me. I loved you very much, and I am guilty, too, for I didn't want to lose you, either."

It was hard to walk away from Beth's bedside, but with her words echoing in her mind, Maisie managed those difficult first steps.

I did not want to lose you, either. Cyrus didn't want to lose her. He would stop at nothing to get what he wanted. That was his way. He had groomed her, and now it appeared he might even have assisted his wife's untimely passage to the grave in order to have her.

Instead of going to the opera, she had to leave that very day. She couldn't meet Cyrus and be seen on his arm like a jewel he had secretly been polishing until he could bring it out and show it off to London, while his wife died alone in her bed.

Maisie dressed in her plainest gown and covered it with a somber cloak. She'd already decided it would be too risky to hire a carriage to take her north, for it would be a long, slow journey and Cyrus would be fast on her trail. She might never reach Scotland and her kin if she went that way. Instead, she determined that the best way, the quickest way, was to go by sea.

That afternoon she set off on foot and then hired a carriage to take her to the docks. There she sought word of vessels that were bound for Scotland.

She heard mention of the *Libertas* at the dockyards. She made note of the captain's name. The vessel was due to sail on the late tide, but she could find no one who would tell her if it would take a passenger. She couldn't afford to wait and secure passage, and she couldn't return to Cyrus. He would not be happy, for he had invested much in her, years of his time, including his future. But she couldn't be part of it.

Forced to act quickly, she returned to the house to avert suspicion. The closer to the turn of the tide she waited, the safer it would be.

After her maid dressed her for the opera, Maisie gathered together a few cherished possessions, what little jewels and coin she had, thanks to Beth, and the sacred objects that would keep her magic safe and rich. Then she pulled on her cloak and made her way out of the house, leaving by the servants' entrance before the coach could be called to take her to Cyrus.

If the *Libertas* had already sailed, or the captain refused to take her, she would have to go back, attend the opera and find another way to leave, another day.

Maisie could scarcely bear to consider that option, and fixed her hopes and her will on escape. Not since the day of her mother's death—the day she'd been taken from Scotland—had Maisie Taskill known such intense fear and dread.

For the first time she would be without her protector, alone with her forbidden craft and vulnerable to discovery. The unknown path ahead loomed dark and foreboding, with danger lurking at every hidden turn. And yet it was eminently preferable to staying at Cyrus Lafayette's side.

chapter Fifteen

"It's true enough, that Jezebel did something ungodly down there." Brady shook his head and looked at Roderick with a warning in his eyes.

The fact that Brady had adopted Clyde's name for Maisie annoyed Roderick almost as much as the fact that they were accusing her of witchcraft. "Caring for an injured man is ungodly?"

"She did more than care for him. She sang awhile, but there were words in there that none of the men understood. And Adam…why, he scarcely breathed at all, let alone cried out when she straightened his hand."

The captain sighed. The men were troubled, and a large group of them had gathered on deck to confront him, for the word had passed quickly amongst them about what Maisie had done. As if they hadn't troubles enough. The lad could have been killed, the rigging had been damaged, and Roderick had only just set the sails to rights. Now this nonsense.

While he was busy overseeing repairs he'd caught sight of

Maisie emerging from the hatch that led to the men's quarters. He'd assumed—correctly, it seemed—that she'd gone to Adam's aid. Yet now the men were doubting what she'd done, and her intentions. As he thought back on it he recalled that she'd scurried off to his cabin immediately after the accident, without seeking him out, which had struck him as odd.

Not odd enough to cause this mood amongst the men.

"Adam gave himself a fright, and he probably fell dumb when he thought about what he'd done and what might have happened," Roderick clarified. "He was too eager, and realized what a fool he made of himself. You should be grateful he isn't as badly hurt as we thought."

Roderick didn't like the way they were talking about Maisie, and he'd heard one of them whisper something about getting rid of her. It troubled him greatly, because when something stirred them up this much it was difficult to keep them in check.

"Witchcraft is what it is." Brady shook his head. "It's not right, I tell you. Gilhooly said he saw her wrap Adam's hand in some strange dark thing, and there were whispered chants, words that had no known meaning to good God-fearing folk. What does that tell you?"

"We woke the lad from his slumber after she'd gone," one of the other men added, "and an unnatural sleep it was, too. He remembered her being there and thought it a dream. When we asked him about it, he remembered nothing of his hand being fixed, but said he dreamed he was in a beautiful place. He'd felt the sun on his face and warm grass at his back, and he wanted to stay and sleep there."

"Dream?" another man stated. "A nightmare is more likely, if she is what you say she is."

Roderick sighed again. How quickly the whispered suspicions grew into so much more than what they first appeared.

Brady's frown grew. "We had to reassure Adam that it was not a dream. It took some amount of rum for him to be able to rest."

Roderick's patience was wearing thin. "If he hadn't had so much rum the previous night the lad wouldn't have been so reckless in the first place."

He glared at his crew. As he looked over the crowd, he noticed that Clyde was there, but said nothing. He was the one who'd started this speculation about Maisie, and yet he was observing the other men while remaining silent. Roderick wondered what thoughts were in his mind.

That could wait. His first responsibility was for the safety of the ship, and for that he needed the men content.

He took his responsibilities seriously, and he was concerned on many fronts. The young Dutchman should likely have been given a bit more responsibility earlier, for he'd grown bored and hotheaded doing laundry and peeling potatoes. Moreover, Roderick now felt he should have supervised the tending of Adam's injury himself, then all this nonsense would have been put to rest. Most worrying of all, he felt the wild urge to put up his fists when anyone made suggestions about Maisie's good intentions. That was no way for a ship's captain to act, and yet he could not help himself. It was because she was his responsibility, as well. As captain, that was the way of it. Reasoning with himself, he paced up and down.

"I order you back to your duties. I will quiz our passenger on this matter. Meanwhile, we will have no more of this nonsense. The injury was minor, and he is young and healthy and will heal. Now rest your heads and I'm sure by sunrise you'll see there is no cause to worry. If not, we will convene again then and I will hear you out. Those of you not on duty go below deck and be ready for your watches."

With a few grumbles here and there the men dispersed.

Clyde remained.

"Clyde?"

"Captain."

"You have something to say now. I noticed you said nothing before."

Clyde considered him at length. "You care for the lassie."

Roderick couldn't tell if it was a criticism. The man's tone gave nothing away. The comment did, however, make him think on it, which was perhaps the old sailor's intention. In that moment he couldn't answer with conviction, so he answered by logic. "She is a passenger. Therefore she is my responsibility, every bit as much as you men are."

"If she is practicing witchcraft on this ship, we are carrying more than a passenger."

Roderick's gut knotted. "You clearly think the accusations are true."

Again Clyde thought on his words. "If she is, it does not mean her intentions are wicked. If I thought they were, I'd be the first one to have her walk the plank."

"No one will be walking the plank while I'm running this ship." He spoke between gritted teeth and his chest grew tight.

Clyde lifted his shoulders and for the briefest moment a smile passed over his mouth, as if something had been confirmed in his mind. "Many healers hail from the Highlands, is all I am saying."

Roderick calmed somewhat. "A healer, is that what you think?"

Clyde nodded. "And many of our men have begged for healers when we have been in foreign lands, regardless of what magic and strange potions might be used on them."

"True enough. You've made a good point. Thank you."

"Whatever happens, be careful not to let your affections cloud your reasoning, Captain."

Roderick was about to respond when Clyde turned and limped away.

With a few well-chosen comments, the old sailor had sent him into a pit of confusion. The argument about healers was a good one, though. Healing was a gift. Clyde meant well and was a canny observer.

For some time, Roderick remained rooted to the spot, wondering if he'd developed affections for Maisie, and if that was indeed clouding his judgment.

He wasn't able to deny it.

She did call to him, but that was because he'd never known a woman like her in his life, and she made him feel vital, as if his course in life was clearer. Was that the nature of a woman's lure? It troubled him greatly. Why, he'd even warned Gregor Ramsay to be wary of a woman's lure when Gregor had left the ship six months earlier. And yet he'd now forsaken his own advice.

I am the captain of this ship. I will not fail. No woman was going to make him lose his good sense and his command of the men. His brain was addled because of the pleasurable tousles they shared, that was all, and Roderick knew he must keep his head. Yes, that was what Clyde was telling him.

Roderick stayed above deck overseeing the night watch for a full hour before he retired, filling his thoughts with matters of ship routine. But as soon as he prepared to make his way down to the cabin, caution ran alongside the rife curiosity that was always in his blood. What would he say to her? Would it be necessary to quiz her about what she had done?

He paused to collect some provisions from the locked store, realizing that she mustn't have eaten since they left Lowestoft. Even that caused him to worry over her. It was nothing he had experienced before, this concern for a woman's welfare. The sooner he delivered her to her destination the better.

Maisie rose from the bed, where she'd obviously been sitting, awaiting his arrival. When he held out the apple and the hunk of cheese he'd brought for her, she nodded and thanked him, but did not reach for the food.

He could see the tension in her expression, and he longed to hold her in his arms. There it was, unbidden and instant. His inability to step away from her remained, despite the unrest going on all around them. "I'm sorry I didn't come down earlier. There was much to see to above deck."

"I'm afraid it was all my fault, what happened with Adam."

Roderick frowned. It was the last thing he expected her to say, and it unsettled him greatly. He set the food down nearby, hoping she would eat later. "Why so?"

"I encouraged him to leave me with the cooking pot until

it had to go below, and that meant he was tempted to try other tasks that appealed to him."

Relieved she meant nothing more sinister than that, he stepped over to her and wrapped his hands around her shoulders so that he might study her while they talked. "It wasn't your fault, don't think that. Adam is often ahead of himself. I should have taken charge of his supervision myself weeks ago. It was time to give him some mannish work to engage him."

Studying her, he could see that particular worry was not the only thing on her mind. She seemed fretful and the glance she gave him was beseeching. It took him back to their first encounter. She'd been so much stronger since then, and he hated to see her look this way again. Was it because she sensed the crew mistrusted her?

A chill went up his spine, a feeling of fear for her. Even if it were true what they said about her, he could not believe she would harm them. "Why so fretful, my lady?"

"What did they say about me?" She blurted out the question and wrung her hands together as she spoke.

"Fear not. It's only the men growing restless about your presence. I did warn you."

Her expression did not change.

He smiled, attempting to put her at ease. "You're a woman, and you made them feel inadequate with your good and kind care, tending Adam's injury the way you did. Having a woman aboard is no easy thing. It is a betrayal to some of the men. Many of them will mistrust you. Most of them will desire you."

His gaze drifted over her body, and he imagined how he might feel if he was watching and wanting, while only one man amongst them was able to take her to his bed. It was little wonder the mood was tense.

"Roderick, please do not think badly of me. I care very much for your good opinion."

"Hush now, I don't think badly of you." It was important to her that he hadn't been turned against her. Roderick knew why: he was her protector aboard this vessel. He didn't flatter himself it was more than that. This woman had been desperate to travel to Scotland when she offered herself to him. He couldn't believe that she might ever harbor any affection for him or care for him. It was a lucky encounter, for him. He had enjoyed her immensely. For her it was only a necessity, a bargain struck. The mystery surrounding her actions and her reason to leave London in such haste was something he might never fathom. Almost everything about her had remained a mystery. Unless her secret was indeed witchcraft… He wasn't afraid of her, even though some of the crew thought he should be.

"What did the men say?" she repeated.

She would not rest until she knew.

He kissed her forehead. "You should sing more."

"Roderick…"

"I'm serious. When you sing to them above deck you have their hearts."

"And when I do not sing to them all?" Stubbornly, she pursued the subject.

"It's something and nothing. Some of the men have it in their heads that you used Pictish words, and that's not a good sign."

Her eyelids dropped and she pulled free of his embrace,

stepping aside. "It's only because they are words my mother said to me."

Roderick wondered how old she was. It was the first time the question had occurred to him. He had the suspicion she was younger than he'd at first assumed. Her solemn eyes and her serious approach—and that wily bargain coming from her lips—had made her seem older. "Are you going back to your mother in Scotland?"

She shook her head. "My mother died when I was a child. It was a cruel death, too, one that my siblings and I were forced to witness." Maisie took a deep breath and met his gaze again. "The old words make me feel closer to her, and to my beginnings. That is all."

Her eyes flickered and for a moment Roderick had the odd feeling that she was not telling him the whole truth. He wanted the truth. He also wanted her. The two combined to make his lust ruthless, and he felt as if he truly could fuck the truth out of her, given long enough.

Ashamed of himself for such a base reaction, he turned aside and reached for the bottle of rum that was wedged between the maritime books on one of the lower shelves. Swigging heavily from it, he offered it to her. When she declined, he had her portion, as well.

She pushed her hair back from her face. "Do they think it means I am bad in some way? Because I know some of the old Pictish songs and sayings?"

Would she confide if he was more honest? "It raises their mistrust."

His own level of trust was far from stable when it came to this woman, and yet Roderick still wanted her. Wanted her with a passion. The movement of her fingers through her hair as she eased it back made him want to do that, to have her sitting in his lap while he studied and explored her.

"And you? Do you mistrust me?" Her expression was challenging in its intensity, almost as if she wanted him to confess he did.

"I know nothing of you, Maisie, not even your family name. And when I try to understand you, you battle me every step of the way. That's what makes this situation difficult for me."

Her lower lip trembled. "Forgive me. My family name is Taskill. Maisie Taskill. I didn't tell you before because I thought it would be safer for you that way. A powerful man wanted me for his own, and if he discovers who it was that aided my escape from London, he will show no mercy. I said nothing about myself because I didn't want to endanger you or your men."

Their gazes locked, and it seemed as if nothing else existed to him, only her and the way she looked at him, as if his good opinion of her was the most important thing in the world. He felt that way, too. While the circumstances that brought them together had been uneasy, he had managed them well enough. Now it felt as if everything around them was in danger of fracturing. He didn't know what the morning would bring, but even if he kept the crew in check until he could get her ashore in Scotland, the men did not trust her and wanted rid of her, and that tore him apart.

"I couldn't bear it if you came to any harm because you aided me." Her eyes shone with tears. "I find I have fast grown to care for you."

Roderick had to hold her in his arms, had to claim every part of her. Inside a moment he was against her, his arms enclosing her while he devoured her mouth. She clung to him, just as frantic and eager for him as he was for her. He didn't care what had been said about her, didn't care if it was true. That problem could wait. This could not.

"Make me yours," she whispered.

"I will." Taking a deep breath, he set her at arm's length. This time it would be no hurried coupling, and he wanted her completely naked so that he might know every part of her. It seemed imperative.

In the gloom of his cabin he undressed her, carefully dealing with each fiddly hook and eye, each complicated lace and tie, until all that was left was her woolen stockings, fastened with ribbons above her knees, and her boots. Roderick could scarcely bring himself to take them off because she looked so pretty. Her hair had fallen loose down her back, and she gazed at him intently. The whole time he'd undressed her, her eyes had followed his every move, and when he smiled at her, her head lifted and she looked deep into his eyes, as if she could read his thoughts. Could she? If it were possible, she would see only how much he wanted her.

Lifting her onto the bed, he slipped off her boots, then undid the ribbons above her knees and rolled the stockings down, discarding them. He undressed hastily, because he knew that when the time came, he might not be able to pause long enough to do so, and he wanted to feel her naked skin against his.

When he was stripped she held out her arms to him. Roderick took her hands in his and kissed each palm in turn.

Every moment seemed precious. Folding her arms across her chest, he noticed the fretful look in her eyes. "You will have me soon enough, eager one. I mean to kiss every part of you first."

Her eyes widened. "That sounds as if it might test me somewhat."

He nodded.

Sitting on the edge of the bed, he explored her, tracing every inch of her body. He followed his fingertips with his lips, kissing her everywhere, from the soft skin behind her ear down across the curves and planes of her figure until he reached the top of her feet, and back up. When he nudged his jaw around the curve of her breast, she moaned.

"My beard is too rough on you?"

"No. It feels…good. It arouses me immensely."

How very much that pleased him, and he decided to kiss the soft warm crease beneath her breast, scuffing her with his beard there, too.

"Oh, oh, Roderick, you master me so easily."

Could he be happier? When he ran his tongue over the taut surface of her erect nipples, each in turn, she reached for him and clutched him to her. While she was distracted, he slipped his fingers between her nether lips, where he found her slick and hot.

It was so inviting that he rearranged his position. Opening her legs, he looped one over his shoulder so that he could access her there. The soft pink folds of her pretty cunt gleamed with her juices and he bent to devour it, his tongue scooping her up. Her essence was like nectar to him, the aroma and taste of it making him harder still, mindless in his desire for her.

Her body arched and she pushed her fingers into his hair. Glancing up at her, Roderick saw that she was close to coming, and he centered his attentions on her tickler. Lapping the swollen ridge from beneath, he was fast rewarded by the sound of her strangled cry of submission, her body shuddering in release.

He lifted his head to watch her, adoring the way her head rolled from side to side and a flush bloomed on her cheekbones and chest, as if the heat of her release flowed through her entire body from the place where he'd stimulated her.

Moments later, she opened her eyes and looked at him.

Those eyes of hers seemed to reflect the candlelight for a moment, as if the flame was right there inside them. He drew back in wonder. Then she blinked and it was gone.

She sat and looped her arms around his neck, squeezing him tightly.

"Roderick, is it always this way?" she asked as she drew back. Her expression was candid and serious.

"It has never been this way for me. For me, it is you that makes this…what it is."

She searched his face for a long moment, then nodded. Cupping his cheek, she rested her other hand against his chest. "I want to explore you the way you have been exploring me, with my fingertips and my mouth."

Roderick inhaled deeply, for the very thought of her doing such things made his cock throb. It was already rock-hard and had been for some time, inflamed with the need to be inside her.

She glanced down at his erection as she meshed her fingers in his. "And I want you to show me everything."

"How so?" he queried gruffly. The way she looked at him, with such passion in her eyes, made him sweat.

"All the different ways that we might…"

"Ah." His cock lengthened, growing painfully distended. "Be careful when issuing such a broad invitation to a man who is already inflamed by his desire for you."

She laughed softly. The sound of it was heavenly to his ears. Stroking his jaw with one hand, she sighed. "I want to know everything, and I want you to show me."

As she considered him for a moment longer, Roderick saw the deep desire in her eyes, as well as the invitation. "Ah, sweet Maisie, you should be learning such things from a fine gentleman, someone worthy of you."

"There is no such path for one such as me. My life has been tainted by tragedy and pain. The best I can do is return to Scotland to find my kin, my twin sister, Jessie, and my brother, Lennox. I must try to find my way again, with their help. Being with you…this has brought me happiness I have never known before."

It pained him to hear that she'd had times that were so unhappy. "Maisie…"

Then she kissed him, her tongue beckoning his into the warm cave of her mouth, silencing him. Roderick savored her sweetness, his mind and body surging for her, his cock ready to answer her request.

He'd been about to encourage her to say more on the matter. More than that, he wanted to reply, to promise that he would help her find her kin. He wanted to protect her while she sought them out. Then she wrapped her hand around his shaft, and for a while he didn't think anymore— couldn't do anything but feel. And when he drew back from the kiss, startled, she ducked her head to kiss the crown of his cock instead.

Roderick silenced the curse of disbelief that rose inside him when her lovely mouth closed over it. Her lips moved while her tongue swept the underside. When she took it deep, riding it in and out, her moves threatened to make him spill far too quickly, and he wanted it to last and last.

Staring down in wonder, Roderick noticed how much she enjoyed the act, how sensual and appreciative she was. This woman had been born for passion, and her newfound confidence revealed itself in the way she handled him, taking control. Before his very eyes she was transforming into a woman who knew, a woman who wanted and did.

As if she became aware of him looking at her, she lifted her head and caught his eye, quickly smiling his way. Then she gripped his cock around the base and kissed it from tip to root before taking it between her lips once again.

"My lady, please." Roderick gave a ragged moan and stroked her hair, unable to resist touching her. He had to show her how much it meant, how good it was.

"It is my turn to enjoy you now." Maisie laughed softly, her hot breath tantalizing his erection, and then set about him even more eagerly. Stroking the underside of his cock head with her tongue, she cupped his sac with her free hand.

"Maisie." It took immense control to spin this out, but Roderick wanted the night, and he planned to fill it with memories that would burn in them forever.

She drew back, wiping her mouth with the back of her hand as she did so. It made her look even more wanton. She rose to her feet, but before he had time to act, she moved. Holding his shoulders, she mounted him, so that they were face-to-face and her legs wrapped around his hips. Stunned at her forthrightness, he groaned with pleasure to have her so eagerly in his lap that way.

"We are made to fit this way, too," she whispered, eyes bright. She licked her lower lip and gazed down at his erect cock. There was a wild look in her eyes, hungry and powerful, and he knew he was lost to her.

"That we are," he responded gruffly, his chest unaccountably tight.

The intoxicating aroma of her arousal made him feel drunk. Her breasts crested perfectly, crowned with peaked nipples and close to his face, and he molded them in his hands, lowering his head to kiss and suck each nipple.

"Oh, Roderick."

Her back arched, her breasts rising to meet his mouth. He tongued her liberally, his cock jerking with the need to be inside her. Oh, but she was a siren, luring him. Was it witchcraft? Was that her secret? In that moment Roderick didn't care. With one finger, he stroked her slit. She was sticky and wet, her juices trickling like thick honey, and he pressed his upright cock against her hot niche. He nodded down at the place where his member stood upright before her mound, like an acolyte worshipping at her temple.

Maisie moaned and writhed, her body moving rhythmically while she stared down at the place where his erection rose proudly against her splayed flesh. Rocking back and forth, she rubbed herself against the hard surface of his cock, catching the sensitive skin on the underside. "I must have you," she whispered, her fingers tightening on his shoulders.

He breathed out loudly. Each sensation was pleasure incarnate. He held his shaft around the base, directing it to her. With her bottom lip captured between her teeth, she sank down onto him and settled herself on his hips. The pull of her body sucking his cock inside was exquisite. He closed his eyes, relishing the intense pressure when it was fully installed inside her tight sheath. "Maisie. Oh, Maisie."

Whispering words of encouragement, he praised her when she began to rock back and forth on him, her face flushing as she gripped his shoulders and rode him with determination.

"My beauty," he said, adoring the way she looked—like a sea goddess, a siren, her hair trailing down over her naked body as she rode him with abandon. So what if she was no normal maiden? He would have this night with her.

He cupped her buttocks and leaned his face into her chest, every moment sending him nearer to the edge. It was the closest to ecstasy he had ever been, and as she milked him to fruition there was nothing else in his world but her.

She moaned softly, and he saw damp tears on her cheeks.

His cock was rigid, his sac high and tight, his balls aching to flood home with his seed. Their movements became fevered. The candle spluttered out. She did not let him pause to find another.

In the darkness, in the heat, they melded as one.

Her eyes flashed in the gloom, luminous as twin candle flames. Strange it was, but he accounted for it by thinking the candle still spluttered on.

He stemmed his release, shifted her to the bed where he lay her facedown, because the urge to lock her in his quarters forever—to hold her in his arms and never let her go—built inside him alongside the imminence of his release.

Within one beat of his heart, his eager cock found its way home again and he plundered her depths from behind. Her body arched, a cry of pleasure issuing from her open mouth, his name on her lips once again. Roderick thrived on it, showing her how roughly he wanted to claim her. He slammed into her, the change of position making him endure.

"Oh, yes," she cried, her hands pushing out against the wooden plinth at the top of the bed. "Fill me. Satisfy me!"

Roderick cursed aloud.

"I want to feel everything," she said. "Make me feel everything, Roderick. I know you can."

Those words, and the feel of her supple body, prone but rising up against him, swamped his mind with every dark image of fornication he had ever seen or imagined. "You do not know what you are saying."

"Show me what it is. I want it all."

Manipulating her bottom with his hands, he shifted his thumbs to her crease, moving them up and down there, brushing over the tight ring of her anus.

Her skin was misted with sweat, but she undulated beneath him, showing him that she enjoyed his touch. "Oh, oh, that. Your touch there, why does it thrill me so?"

He pulled his cock free, but only so that he could dip down and kiss her there in her crease. When he did, and his tongue roved over her bottom, she moaned. It was a pleasured sound and her body flexed. She liked it.

Roderick's cock throbbed. "You are a wanton indeed."

"For you. You have liberated me in every way."

Her words seemed to burn in his chest. He wanted to know all of her. When he continued to stroke her along the groove of her bottom, she moaned and did not chastise him, so he moistened one of his fingers in his mouth and pressed it against her opening, sliding it in a little way. Even in the darkened room he was aware of her clutching at the bed, her torso lifting.

"Does it trouble you?"

"It does, but," she panted, "I find that it feels oddly just and right. I want more. Is it wrong, to feel this way about something so lewd?"

It made him smile, that she was asking his guidance even while she ordered him to satisfy her. His candid novice was an experience like no other. "Nothing is wrong, if it is between two bodies in the night who come together willingly, as one."

He eased his finger deeper, holding his free hand around the base of his cock to stem it. Stroking his finger in and out, gently, holding back, he allowed her to get used to it. Moments later, her body began to rise and fall, welcoming him in the way it did when he was inside her sweet cunt.

"Can you take more there?"

"Oh, Roderick."

"Can you take this?" He removed his finger and pressed the head of his cock to her anus. That act alone threatened to undo him, the tight ring exerting pressure on his swollen crown. He held the position, scarcely trusting himself to breathe.

She moaned and writhed. "Is it possible?"

"It is, but if you don't want it, you must say."

"I want to know," she cried out, "I want to know it all, and I want you to show me." With those words, she pressed back to him, and Roderick arched over her, shifting position so that when he lay against her, his cock was there. Scooping up her copious juices, he lathered them on his cock so that it would slide home easier. Maisie spread herself wider still and pushed up her bottom. He eased the swollen head of his cock into her tight opening.

"Oh, yes," she cried, "make me yours, Roderick, there, too."

Grappling for her, he pushed his hand beneath her in order to clutch her mound in his hand, to bring her off.

"You are mine," he managed to respond, before he drove deeper and sent them both into a spiral of intense and visceral ecstasy.

Later, as he held her body in the crook of his arm and she slumbered against his chest, Roderick found himself dreaming of keeping her, of setting up a home somewhere as Brady had done with his woman, so that he might keep and visit her. It even crossed his mind to set down roots on land, in order to be with her all the time. But when he looked at her, he saw an educated lady, one whose hardships might always remain a mystery, too. Could he ever hope to win a woman like that?

"I'm glad you were my first lover, Captain Roderick Cameron," she'd said while he washed them both down, readying them for sleep.

Roderick couldn't reply, because what he wanted to say was that he should be her one and only lover, forever. Instead, he'd dried her off and taken her back to bed and held her tight to him.

As the night deepened, however, his thoughts grew more troubled. His crew's earlier comments about her haunted him. Most of all he wondered if it was true, if he was blinded from the truth by her. He had been distracted, there was no denying that. He should never have brought a woman aboard in the first place. The men had made their feelings known as soon as they saw her, but since then they had quieted, some even seeming to enjoy her presence. Especially when she sang for them. If Brady and others amongst the crew were unhappy, so be it. To blacken her name with the suspicion of witchcraft, however, was intolerable.

Roderick frowned, tried to force the thoughts back, while clutching her warm body to his. The troubled images wouldn't leave. They had a rule aboard the *Libertas*. No women. So why had he been swayed that night on Billingsgate docks, when she'd stepped out of the darkness and begged for safe passage? Was it witchcraft? Or was it just that he wanted her? God knows he wanted her now. Passion arose between them even though the doubts were there, even though it had come to this—arguments and surly behavior amongst the men.

Still, he could not keep away from her. Tonight had showed that clearly enough. He wanted her more than any other woman. That, above all, served as a warning to him. He was a seafaring man, and had no right to be thinking the way he was. He had obligations, to his crew and to Gregor

Ramsay. He couldn't let a woman beguile him, lead him off course.

Then she shifted in her sleep, waking slightly, holding tight to him still, before drifting off again, and Roderick could only be glad of this moment.

chapter Sixteen

Cyrus's frustration had reached its boiling point. The excruciatingly slow journey was made worse by the tedium of being at sea. Whilst the navy shipmen seemed happy and busy at their tasks, he was left to fester in his narrow quarters, where the roll of the ship made him reach for the piss pot to vomit in. The only alternative was to pace the deck, gripping the rail and staring ahead at the blustery clouds and the horizon, as if he could bring it closer faster, could wish it by magic. If only he could! But alas, his precious source of magic had been whisked away from him.

Tormented with questions and possibilities about Margaret's whereabouts and her safety, and sickened by the sea travel, he could not sleep or eat. Most of all it was her intentions that plagued him. Surely she could not mean to leave him? Bile gathered in his gut when he considered it. No, she'd been swayed, or she'd been mistaken in going aboard the vessel. There had to be a reason. Seething silently over her departure, he found his anger growing with each passing moment. Even if she'd been influenced she should have known better. Margaret was an intelligent young woman. He'd spent enough on her education. Maybe too much. Perhaps he should have kept her ignorant and grateful, the way she had been at first. There were no acceptable grounds for this scheme of hers. He was wasting his time and energy fetching her back. Once he had her under his command again she would have to learn to accept her servitude to him more gratefully.

Cyrus was also exceedingly frustrated by Captain Giles Plimpton. The man's attitude gave him no confidence. Cyrus had the feeling it was merely an urge to impress that motivated the captain, and not a true dedication to the mission. This was especially noticeable once the captain discovered that Cyrus was a notable orator. Captain Plimpton subsequently detailed his own personal history and expertise at length, and stated that he hoped Cyrus would report favorably on His Majesty's navy, now that he was experiencing it firsthand.

Cyrus had to force a suitable acknowledgment. He would be much more likely to speak well of him if the captain showed any sense of urgency. Captain Plimpton commanded many men aboard three ships, for two smaller vessels followed their own, and yet it seemed as if they would never catch up with this ship called the *Libertas*. Now, for a second time in their two days at sea, they had dropped anchor and were waiting on a rowboat that had gone ashore for some reason unknown to Cyrus.

Cyrus watched the boat disappear off toward the harbor and then eventually make its return. The day before, when he'd asked the purpose of this diversion, he was told they collected navy papers from Harwich, where there was a large naval establishment. This time, however, the two men that had been dispatched brought back no extra goods or supplies, which irritated Cyrus immensely. Another waste of time.

He was just about to turn and head below deck to the pitiful quarters he had been allocated, when he heard the captain call his name.

"Master Lafayette. It seems the *Libertas* stopped at Lowestoft overnight. It was noted by several of our informers." Captain Plimpton smiled broadly.

Cyrus's attention sharpened. "How long ago?"

"A day since they set sail. We are gaining on them." Captain Plimpton looked rather smug. "They are bound for Dundee. We'll have them before they reach the Tay estuary, maybe even by Berwick."

"I'm most impressed, Captain."

"You will be. We'll find your ward even if we have to take the *Libertas* apart board by board."

"Margaret must not be harmed," Cyrus retorted.

"Leave that to me. We will secure your ward before any subsequent action is taken."

"Excellent. I will speak highly of your talents in my record of this endeavor."

Plimpton beamed. "Rest assured there are no ships faster than the British navy vessels."

No ships faster, Cyrus thought to himself, *except perhaps the ship with a powerful young witch aboard.*

They were gaining, however. Soon enough he would have his prize back. Cyrus thought on their reunion. She would be grateful and subdued once again, ready to take on her role as his wife. It was her place, because there he could best control and exploit her. It would be soon, and then he would bed her. Maybe he wouldn't even wait until they were married. Too long it was already that he'd savored the anticipation of the event. He'd watched her grow into womanhood, her pale skin enticing him, the swell of her breasts a constant torment while he imagined her virginal body beneath his as he claimed her for his own. Yes, that would be a pleasure indeed.

Then he could reap the rewards of her empowered magic, and she would acknowledge that he was the only man in the world who knew how to protect her, how to make her feel safe and flourish.

Roderick sighed, inwardly fuming at the turn of events.

After his restless night he awoke to rough seas, and he'd come above deck to find a grim day overhead, with no break in the clouds and the ship pitching and tossing as if it were trapped on a knife edge between winds from the east and the west.

As soon as he appeared on deck, one of the men went below and shortly afterward a crowd of them emerged. Even as they came toward him they were mumbling amongst themselves about what they'd seen of Adam and his injury. Roderick found that the men's thoughts and opinions about their passenger had grown only more dark and determined overnight. He knew what had brought it about—too much discussion fueled by too much rum. When they had a good subject to argue about, his men could spend the whole night doing so. But he would not have any of it. Maisie was not the black-hearted Jezebel they were currently describing.

"Rest assured that I, as captain of this ship, have quizzed our passenger," he told them. "The young lady has a way with nursing the afflicted. I discovered no proof of male-faction." If that did not quell them, he had a secondary plan that would.

They were not content to let it lie. Brady led them once again, detailing the latest discovery, while others added their own commentary.

"It was not nursing. Healed he was, Captain, his fingers perfectly straightened again!"

"It was as if there had been no injury at all," someone else added.

"The injury cannot have been as bad as it first seemed," Roderick stated firmly.

"It was," Brady argued, "you saw it yourself. His hand was all twisted up and the skin broken and his knuckles raw."

"I saw it, too, and the lad was crying out in pain," another man added.

"Not damaged at all now. Wrong is what it is." Brady shook his head. "She wrapped his hand in some strange potions, and there were whispered chants, words that have no known meaning to good God-fearing folk. What does that tell you?"

"It tells me nothing, because no one has been harmed. No one has been thwarted in their duties and our ship is safe." Roderick kept his voice level, maintaining command and reassuring his men, even though his loyalties were divided.

Brady was the ringleader, and that was not good. "I took

it upon myself to unbind his hand, to reveal what she had done," he said.

He should be Roderick's closest man, and yet he stood with the rest of the crew instead. The atmosphere was mutinous. Roderick saw the irony of the situation, for Brady was a man who kept a woman himself. Surely he knew the female sex was different to men, and that was not necessarily a bad thing? Apparently not.

"There were strange potions indeed," Brady continued, "ancient leaves with a putrid aroma. But that was nothing compared to the evil doings she created with this potion. There was nary a mark on him. No grazing, no swelling. It was as if it had never happened. The devil has her enslaved, and she spins magic to bring him more souls."

Roderick scowled at them. "I have seen several of you men here beg for a healer when you were sick or injured, and yet you accuse this woman of evil when she has done nowt to deserve it."

"We have never had one aboard our ship, one who could turn on us and destroy our vessel, our livelihood."

"She has blinded you to her true nature, Captain Cameron, blinded you with her magic and her feminine wiles." It was Brady who made that assertion, and it sent Roderick dangerously close to reaching for his cutlass. Amidst the stream of objections the men had raised, Brady insinuated that she had ensorcelled him into bringing her aboard.

"Do you think the same of your Yvonne?"

Brady smiled, slow and sure, and Roderick saw the trap he had fallen into.

"No," the man responded, "but then my Yvonne is no witch."

"Witch!" someone repeated.

"I wouldn't be surprised if she'd been found out, and that is why she was so eager to leave London," Brady added.

Could it be true?

"See her off the *Libertas* and spare us from the devil's woman, please, Captain," another added.

Several of them had a murderous look in their eyes, and Roderick knew that was not easily going to be changed. He'd tried to straighten their thoughts the night before. That hadn't worked. If he didn't take charge of the situation soon, they would turn on him, as well. Several of them were looking at him suspiciously, as if he'd lost his mind, as if he'd lost his soul because the Jezebel pleasured him in bed.

What angered him most of all was that they put questions in his own mind. Some of what they claimed fitted. He struggled to recall what it was that she'd said when she'd begged for safe passage. *Her liberty was at stake,* that was it. Why so? Were there witch hunters after her? Roderick scrubbed his jaw in his hand while he shooed those treacherous thoughts away.

Now there was only one thing he could do, and that was to take charge of the situation and lock her up for her own safety. It would be damnably hard, but he would also have to be canny and put on a good show for the men in order for them to rest easy.

For the first time, Maisie didn't want to go above deck that morning. Instead, she sat on the bunk and tried to focus on the path ahead, how she would travel from Dundee to the Highlands once they made land. But she couldn't think upon it, because trouble was afoot. Above deck the mood had turned dark amongst the men, she sensed. That darkness sank down through the aged beams and boards, permeating the captain's cabin and reaching out to drag her spirit down.

They were saying things about her and making Roderick doubt her. How much had they said? She'd made a mistake helping Adam, had been incautious and aroused their suspicions. Uncertainty twisted in her gut, and that familiar feeling taunted her—fear for her life, for her kin, for those she cared for. Even though she'd been protected for so long, Cyrus had kept that fear alive in her mind and heart, reminding her how well he watched over her. And when she felt the crew gathering against her, whispering their doubts and concerns to each other, it took her right back to the moment her mother had been tugged away, leaving her and her siblings to watch as she was tortured and persecuted.

Maisie sensed the men approaching the captain's quarters before she heard them, and she knew they were coming for her. Rebellion and anger built in response. She sat on the edge of the bed she'd shared with Roderick, clutching her arms around herself while she attempted to push the dark emotions away. They would only make her hotheaded and careless, and she couldn't afford to say or do the wrong thing.

There was a loud banging on the door.

It sprang open before she had a chance to answer.

She rose to her feet.

Brady, the first officer, and two other men stepped into

the captain's quarters, crowding the space with their bodies and their obvious animosity toward her.

"You will come with us." It was not a request.

They all lowered their eyelids in her presence, avoiding her gaze.

Maisie's blood quickened. "What is it? Why have you come for me?"

"Mistress, if you please, the captain and the crew are gathered and we need you to come above deck."

Being led out this way was not good, but she rose to her feet, and when they stepped back to clear the path to the door, she went through it.

Up on the deck, the entire crew had gathered. A tense conversation was ongoing. Roderick was at the center of the group. When he caught sight of her, he fell silent.

The look in his eyes affected her more than she imagined it could. He had listened to the men, yet what she saw in his expression was reassurance. He cared most of all what she thought. *Roderick.* How she ached for him. How she ached to undo the trouble she'd brought to his ship.

"Seize her, Captain." The man's voice jolted through her.

Another shouted, "Aye." The look in their eyes was horribly familiar, taking her back to the moment her mother had been accused.

Maisie clutched at the railing by her side and fought for breath. The pitch and toss of the ship barely reached her, and though her senses registered the whip of the wind and the salt in the air, signaling rough seas, she could not address it or counter it as she had done on the previous day. It was as if her feet had been nailed to the boards. Unwilling to move, she stared across at Roderick.

His gaze flitted from her to the men and back again. "I'm informed that you may have been performing some form of—" he paused, his scowl deepening "—witchcraft, while you have been aboard the *Libertas*."

"There is no might about it," a man shouted above the whistle of the wind. "I saw her with my own eyes. She cured the lad by some strange power, using words that the witches use. When Clyde questioned her about it, she tried to sweeten us, but we know what we saw. She has powers. You cannot trust her, Captain. She will bring bad fortune, mark my words."

Roderick did not take his eyes from her while he listened to his men, each adding their own comments. It sent turmoil through her, yet he looked calm and in control. "Is it true? Did you save the lad by means of magic?"

Why did he ask her that? Desperate for his understanding, and frustrated by the scowls and jeers surrounding her, she fisted her hands and struggled against the hold the men had on her.

"Stand your ground, my lady," Roderick stated, "and answer me." He strode closer, until he was between her and the crowd.

"I have hidden nothing from you." It was the best she could muster, for fear and anger roiled in her. Panic set in. He claimed to care for her, and yet he was as bad as the rest of them—eager to turn her away now that the truth was out. How could she have let herself trust him? Worse still, care for him?

Roderick shook his head.

Maisie tore her gaze away, her heart sinking.

Yes, she had hidden things from him; they both knew that. It was only for his own protection. The less he knew of her troubled history the safer he was. He and his men. Although now it looked as if they didn't share the same concerns for her. How foolish she had been, assisting them in their work aboard ship and healing the lad.

"Cast her out, tie her up and throw her overboard!" one of the men cried, and hurled a rope toward her.

Maisie froze. The line landed close to her feet.

Roderick's face turned thunderous. For a moment she thought he would do as the man had suggested, but instead he turned on him. "We are not witch hunters, nor do I wish to be one."

Roderick's eyes blazed, his rugged face made even fiercer in its masculinity by his mood. Her heart leaped in her chest at the sight of his torment.

Just then a shout attracted their attention. A man emerged from the hatch that led to the captain's quarters. In his hand he brandished her velvet bundle. Maisie watched in horror as he opened it and spilled the contents across the deck. "I found this hidden beneath the captain's bed," the man declared.

Maisie stared down at her precious lodestones as they rolled hither and yon. Her carefully preserved healing herbs and powders spilled free and were fast lifted by the autumn wind and swept away into the sky. There were other items there that were close to her heart, trinkets that Beth had given her. Most of all it was the lodestones that tugged on her heart-strings, for they had been with her for many years, and as she had enriched them, so their powers had enriched her and harnessed her magic to her when she coupled with Roderick.

The man who'd brought the bundle out kicked the stones about the deck. "Tools of her evil trade," he said.

Roderick stood between her and the unruly crowd of men who hovered, readying for action. "I am captain of this ship. I will deal with this."

Cursing loudly, he snatched up the rope that had been thrown at her feet.

"It was foolish of me to bring a woman on board," he said, shouting over his shoulder to the men, "let alone one that is driven to dark ways." He grabbed her arms, but did not look her in the eye. "I will not let you put my men at risk."

Enraged, Maisie struggled against him.

Mercilessly, he carried on, binding her wrists together despite her efforts to fight him off, and tying the rope tightly.

"You have not put your men at risk," she hissed at him angrily. "I have only brought the wind into your sails and healed Adam."

Roderick hushed her. "Trust me," he whispered.

Trust me? Confused, she tugged away.

He jerked her arms up and over her head, holding her that way while he stared into her eyes. "So you admit it? You have influenced this voyage?"

Maisie squirmed, dangling like a fish on a hook. It was imperative that she convince him she was not out to harm him, and yet everything she said only seemed to pull her deeper into the tangled mess. Fury bit deep into her bones, fury she had never experienced the likes of. It was because of what had passed between them the night before, when they'd seemed so close they were almost as one. Now he turned on her, and that made her mood black. Her power roiled within her, troublesome and uneasy and close to the surface.

"I paid you and I paid you well," she stated beneath her breath, holding his gaze. "Don't you forget that, Roderick Cameron." She wanted him to feel her outrage.

"You'd be wise to hold your tongue," he said, low enough for her ears only. His eyes flickered. His men had influence over him, though. Their opinion on the matter was crucial. He could not afford to risk mutiny.

For a moment she thought he was warning her out of good faith, but then he held her at arm's length, as if he wanted nothing to do with her.

Anger and frustration twisted inside her, and it was she who now felt betrayed. The eternal struggle not to show her power was in danger of being cast aside. Instead, she wanted to make these men afraid of her. But doing so would only prove them right. If she demonstrated her power, it would give them an excuse to do away with her.

Roderick nudged the back of her shoulder, pointing to a hatchway on the opposite side of the deck. She'd seen supplies being carried out of there, and it was where the pot was taken below, for cooking on the grate. A bad feeling turned over in her belly. "No, I will not be locked up like a petty criminal. I have done nothing wrong."

"I forbid you to say another word." Determination shone in his eyes.

Was this man who she had seen as loyal and passionate and jovial growing distant? Was he an enemy to her because of what she was? Behind him, the crew urged their captain on.

She had been too foolish in trying to aid them in their work. Now they were turning on her, turning as people so often did. Cyrus had told her this would happen if she left his side. His purposes were much more nefarious, but that part of his litany was true.

When she refused to walk ahead of him, Roderick dragged her by the rope, muttering angrily as he did so.

The men stepped back as she passed, clearing the path and giving her a wide berth. She caught Clyde's eye, and she could see he was not sure. A heavy frown scored his forehead. She had thought him about to sway, to accept her. Now he stood with the others, unwilling, it seemed, to speak out. It made her think of all the books Cyrus had made her study. The accounts of witch trials and hangings. He'd done it to instill fear in her, to make her cautious and wary. But now it was becoming as real for her as it had been for her mother.

Roderick showed little mercy as he forced her down the ladder behind him, tugging on the rope and ordering two men to follow. Brady was there, his boots on the step above her head like a threat he would willingly deliver if she did not hasten down after the captain. The ladder was long, and rickety from overuse, and with her wrists tied she was ungainly and almost slipped several times. Once she reached the bottom, she realized that what little light there was came from above. Glancing up, she saw that one of the men who followed carried a covered lantern. Once he stepped down, Brady took the lantern from him and passed it to Roderick, who then led the way.

Maisie scarcely noticed her surroundings as she followed Roderick's broad back down the gloomy corridor. But she could smell the fetid air, the dampness in the wood and something else that made a shiver run down her spine.

The sound of keys rattling made her lift her head. Roderick was unlocking a heavy door made of wood and iron. When it swung open on its hinges, he put his hand at the back of her neck and forced her on.

Maisie stumbled over the threshold.

When Roderick secured the lantern in a wall sconce, she saw the place was a dank storeroom. The sound of water sloshing came from nearby, and the groaning of the ship seemed much louder and more frightening down there. She clung to a wooden brace that ran the length of the space, a massive beam that had supplies tied to it here and there.

"I'll deal with her," he shouted over his shoulder to Brady and the others. "Attend to matters above deck."

"Be sure to secure her tightly, Captain," said the man who had carried the light.

Secure her? Maisie trembled. If she denied them this power—if she used her magic to put a halt to it—it would only confirm her guilt in their eyes. They would descend as one, a fearful and crazed crowd. She had seen it before and never wanted to see it again. She had been educated to avoid it. Maisie willed herself to remember that.

"Aye, I will," Roderick replied in a growl.

Maisie fought back the urge to cry. He intended to do as they said.

"Are you sure you can manage her?" It was Brady who asked, as if he was uncertain whether he should leave or not.

"I've handled her this far, haven't I? See to the wheel. No doubt we are off course by now, and I want to reach land

and hand her over to a magistrate as soon as possible. I will secure her and watch her, lest she spin magic and wreak havoc for us."

Maisie cursed aloud.

That seemed to convince Brady, though, and he left them alone, albeit reluctantly.

After he'd gone, the door swung on its hinges, creaking violently. Roderick stomped over and slammed it shut. He stood there with his hand on the latch, as if not wanting to turn back and look at her.

She sensed he was not comfortable with this. Hope flared within her. "Roderick?"

He strode back to her side. "Don't test me, Maisie." His expression was determined. "I didn't want any of this. I'm doing it for your own protection."

His gaze, frantic and angered, swept over her. He shook his head, as if denying what had passed.

"Protection?" She glanced about, drawing his attention to their surroundings.

His jaw set hard; his lips pressed together. "I asked for your trust. If I hadn't locked you up they might have cast you overboard."

Her anger was only fueled by that remark, shot through with fear as she was. "Trust you? You had me hauled out there to be judged by your men! Why should I trust you? You won't even hear my tale." She couldn't help herself. Her magic boiled up inside her, heated by the injustice she felt. Blurting a call for chaos, she showed him her fire.

He recoiled, and she knew he could see her power in her eyes.

"Maisie, no." He swallowed, but did not turn away.

"I would not harm you. Why do you believe that I am a danger to you? I have done no harm to you or any of your men, and I do not intend to."

She could not let him leave her, not without saying more on the matter. But it was too late, for the words spoken in the midst of her fury had let loose chaos around them. The ship tossed and pitched more violently, and Roderick, who was always steady on his feet, was thrown to one side. Goods shunted and something fell from a shelf. A sack of potatoes pitched and the vegetables spilled across the boards. Somewhere above, a beam creaked. The sound of wood splintering reached them. Roderick stared at her, aghast.

Twisting her wrists within their restraint, she tossed the loose rope out, cursing as the heavy weight of it snaked across the floor. But still it hampered her. She would need a knife to cut it loose. "By nature's oath I swear I will not be left here to die. My heritage is a curse and always will be, but I will not be lowered to this by a man I gave myself to."

"You need to calm down and think on this arrangement with a clearer head." Roderick grasped her by the shoulders, shifting her back to where the room narrowed. He flung the loose end of the rope up and over a beam overhead and hoisted her so that her arms were stretched high and she dangled there, her feet just touching the boards beneath them.

"Don't do this," she begged, frightened to her marrow. The way he'd strung her up made her wild, because she was all but standing in her mother's boots.

"This is for your protection. Stay quiet, and I will find a way to set you free."

Struggling against him, she battled the urge to fling herself into his arms instead. To bury her face against the comforting warmth of his chest, so solid and real.

"Your eyes," he said, and backed away from her. He shook his head. "I cannot witness you like this, for it proves them right, and I didn't want to believe that was your secret. I fought for you up there. They are my men and this ship my responsibility. I vowed no woman would ever alter my path. Yet I kept them from ending you, and it makes me sick to the gut that I am such a fool, for I would still rather die myself than see one hair on your head damaged by another man."

Staring into his face, she saw he spoke the truth.

His eyes gleamed with withheld emotion.

She went to respond, to query him, but he turned away and headed to the door.

"Roderick?" Struggling against the bands at her wrists, she called after him. Even though she was frantic, her heart swelled in her chest. She hated him for turning away from her, but she loved him, too.

How could he leave her down here?

Before he got to the door, he lifted the lantern as if to take it with him.

Panic flooded her.

Death tainted the air and she sensed the rats lurking in the dark corners. She couldn't protect herself with a ring of fire as she might on open land, for it would endanger the ship. "Please, Roderick," she cried out, "do not leave me here alone in the dark, I beg of you."

chapter Seventeen

Roderick knew he shouldn't turn back. Lord knew he tried not to. His men were correct in their assertions. She was a witch and a Jezebel, and she had played him far too well. That didn't stop him from wanting to save her, to free her and let her loose on dry land, with the instruction to run for her life and not look back.

"Roderick, please…"

Her voice reached out to him like ethereal fingers swooping across the space to touch him, just as it had that first night in Billingsgate.

"Please, at least…at least leave the lantern."

He put his fist against the door frame, urging himself to climb the ladder away from this place, away from her. Frustration held him to the spot. He shouldn't trust her. She'd all but threatened him moments before, showing him what she could do to his ship with just a toss of her head and a few magical words. "What, so that you can control the flame and threaten to burn us all?"

"No! I would never do such a thing. It's because I'm afraid. There are rats. I hear them. And this place…it reeks of death."

Roderick's gut turned over. It was the fact she knew— that she could sense someone had died down here… It had been one of his men, afflicted with a fatal fever and sadly untreatable. The sailor had insisted on taking himself down here to die alone, before his burial at sea. None of them had been happy about it, but it was the man's last request, and represented his dignity.

More than that, Roderick didn't want to leave her. Everything in him balked at the idea of her alone and afraid. Yet the fact that she could sense death only proved what she was—a witch.

"You are afraid of nothing. Why would you be, with your powers?" He shot the words back over his shoulder, and as he did the image of her hanging there—so thoroughly vulnerable and compromised—made his lust flare. He quashed it down. "I cannot even look at you for fear of your magic. The way your eyes glow…I should never have brought you onto the ship."

"I have never influenced you by magic."

Roderick squeezed his eyes tightly shut. How he wished it were true. How he wished he could believe her. All he wanted to do was take her in his arms.

Her voice softened. "Roderick, listen to me. I promise I will not create magic, but there are things I need to say to you."

How beguiling she was, and he couldn't even see her. Even her voice touched him, turned him. "I will give you a few moments more, if you promise you will not look at me with those eyes."

There was silence at his back.

Eventually, she responded. "In that case you must cover them, for my gaze is always drawn to you. Please, for what we have shared, spare me a moment to hear me state my case."

That troubled him, as he knew it was meant to. She hadn't been given a chance to speak. Once his men had become riled, he'd had to act and fast.

He strode back, bringing the lantern nearer to her. The flame flickered wildly, sending light and shadow skittering across the dark hold in the bowels of the ship.

Her beauty and her vulnerability seemed exaggerated by the circumstances, and he quickly lowered the lantern to the floor. "Turn your face away."

"My eyes are closed." Nevertheless, she did as instructed and turned her face to one side.

Hurriedly, he looked about for something to blindfold her with, lest she turn on him. Pulling his shirt free of his breeches, he went to tear it.

"You may use my petticoats," she whispered.

Roderick pressed his lips together, ducked down and lifted her skirts.

As soon as he did he regretted it. The light from the lantern he'd set on the floor lit up her slender ankles as he lifted her skirts, and he was flooded with memories of how it felt to have those legs wrapped around him while he thrust deep between her thighs. The way she'd mounted and clung to him the night before, so bravely accepting him and claiming he was her master, all of it conspired to make him crave more of her. Doubts crowded into his head. He'd never been so thoroughly beguiled by a woman before. Was it as Brady had suggested? Was he under her spell?

"I hope I do not live to regret this," he muttered, as he tore a length of linen from her petticoat. Dropping her skirt back into place regretfully, he rose to his feet and quickly blind-folded her with the wrap he'd torn from her underclothing.

Maisie hung her head down between her bound arms to aid him, keeping her eyes shut all the while. Roderick was struck by the sight of her like that. Her submission, after all the fire he'd witnessed in her, made his lust surge.

How could that be? *Because I yearn for her constantly. To see her this way only shows me how much I want her submission for my own benefit.*

"Roderick?" Her whisper, so tentative, revealed how afraid she was.

"What is it you need to say?"

"I have not tricked or swayed you, I promise you that. I healed Adam and I called upon the weather to hasten our journey, but that is all. What happened between you and me was purely borne of our passion for one another."

Roderick gritted his teeth, casting his mind back. Then he shook his head. "What of those strange things you did when we were alone, and the way you were at the moment of your release? You lit up the cabin when there was no candle."

Her head rolled against her arm, her soft, lush mouth turned down at the corners. "It is so hard to explain briefly, but in offering myself to you and sharing our passion, my magic grew stronger. That is what you saw."

He jerked back. "So you were—"

"No!" Her very posture forbade him to think further on that path. "It happened, it empowered me, but it was not used as a tool against you, never."

Oh, how he wanted to believe her. Had she really been as cold and calculating as Brady had suggested? Was their lovemaking part of a plan to bend him to her will? It trickled through his mind again, every strange thing she had done, every brazen suggestion and whispered word. "Why are you this way? Where did this magic come from if not from the devil himself?"

"It is in my lineage. We hail from the Highlands, where my kind live a life closer to nature than to any prescribed by a god. We cherish the lessons of the seasons and the elements, and we live by those lessons, not by laws passed by church or magistrate. The old magic that thrived in the hidden glens is passed down the line from mother to child. Like my kin, I have the ability to call on nature and to wield its powers...for good."

Roderick frowned. It seemed fanciful. As a seafaring man he had a healthy respect for the elements. The rest was beyond him. She explained with such conviction, though, it was difficult not to believe in it. "You use these powers only for good?"

"Unless we are threatened, or...or if we are tricked into it." She paused, and he saw how upset she was by that admission. Who tricked her? "I can defend myself by magic," she continued, "but I choose not to. I want you to trust me because of the rest of me—what I say and how we are when we are together."

That much was true, he was sure of it. If she could heal

Adam's hand and direct the wind, she could easily have averted this situation with her strange talents.

"You have never used your magic for gain, or to hurt anyone?"

She sighed and hung her head. It made him fear what she was about to say.

"Not knowingly. I was kept, in London, sheltered by a man who understood my craft, but I didn't know he meant to use me as a tool. When I discovered his true intent, I fled." She lifted her head. "And you aided my flight."

That was why. It was not because she was being sought out by witch hunters. She had fled to escape a man who would use her. All this talk of laws of the natural world and the power of the elements as a life force, it dazzled his mind. He did not claim to be anything but a simple man, and yet he felt as if she believed it all. He knew he couldn't trust her, for she had hidden so much of herself from him and he couldn't identify the overriding emotion he felt in response to that. Was it anger, frustration or grief? All those things flitted through him. It left him torn between the need to cast her out, and to punish her for not revealing this secret nature to him earlier, so that he might have been prepared for it.

In that moment none of it mattered. Still he had to listen.

"This man, he had me create magic, but I didn't know he would gain from it. I was innocent of his true nature. There may have been wrongdoings. It breaks my heart to think of it."

He had to see her eyes in order to be sure of her honesty. He untied the blindfold, knowing even while he did that it might be a trap. "This man you speak of, is he the one who made you mistrust all men?"

She nodded. That solemn look was back in her eyes.

This bastard from London, whoever he was, had put it there. "Is he the one who wanted you for his own?"

"The same man, yes. But I didn't want him, and because of that I found you, and you've been the best part of my life."

"And you mine." He trailed the back of his fingers down the soft curve of her cheek.

"You have spoiled me for other men. I know I'll never find another lover like you."

There were so many ways he wanted to reply to that, but he knew it would be wrong to make false promises. Reaching out, he allowed himself to touch her. With one hand around the back of her neck, he embraced her softness. If it was a mistake, he didn't care anymore.

She moaned softly and turned her face to his arm and kissed it.

That simple touch made his reason trip and stumble, good sense flying from his mind. "You have me, my lady. God help me. You are like a siren calling to me, luring me to my end—"

"Never."

It mattered not. He was hers. Embracing her, he lifted her from the floor as he kissed her, taking the weight from her arms.

The way she trembled against him, her body flexing in his arms, made him wonder if he would ever tire of this. Her kiss was every bit as hearty and passionate as his. Roderick reminded himself that her motives had been self-protection, nothing more. Learning that fact heaped scorn on the vague notion he had of making her his for much longer than this troubled journey. Roderick knew that whatever her thoughts on the matter, and her reasons for offering herself to him, he adored her. Her virginity had come in exchange for her passage to Scotland; she had not lied about that. But he also knew that she wouldn't do such a thing without great deliberation. He'd learned that much about her.

Was there evil magic and twisted games at play? Did she have a black heart?

Even if it were all true, he still adored her.

He would aid her escape. She would be gone from him soon, gone to follow her mysterious path, and he would never regret this, despite the danger and the black looks in the eyes of his men. He could not regret it, because in his heart this was the woman he wanted to call his own. "I see it," he whispered. "I see it all now. I understand your plight."

"And you still want me?"

"Yes, fool that I am."

Her head dropped back, and she gave a soft, wry laugh. "You're not a fool. And I want you, too, Roderick Cameron. Even though you have me tied up down here like a criminal and you are willing to leave me alone in the dark with the rats. I cannot help myself. I want your embrace. Please hold me again."

Was it a trick? She wanted to be held, and he knew he shouldn't take the risk, but he moved his hands beneath the curve of her buttocks and hitched her higher against him, until she wrapped her legs around his hips. The swell of her breasts jiggled against his chest and he lowered his head to place a kiss upon the place where they bulged from her bodice.

He struggled to think, to breathe more evenly, but he could only act upon his desires.

Mine. Covering her open mouth with his, he kissed her again.

She moved her hips, beckoning to him, as willful in her lust as she had been the night before. He felt her heat and he was hard as a rock.

Urgently, he pushed her skirts up. She moved, tightening her grip on the rope above her head, her body opening toward him. He shifted his feet to a wider stance, ready to savor that moment when he thrust inside her, losing himself to her.

Her cheeks were flushed, her hair tousled and hanging over her face.

His cock ached for her. *No denying this.*

Holding her safely to him with one hand, he freed his cock.

Maisie pivoted, staring down.

His cock twitched in response.

Nudging the swollen head into her opening, he eased inside her, his blood pounding inside hers. Her hips were angled to take him in, her flesh melting onto his length.

"Your cunt is hotter than hell and sweeter than heaven," he whispered, and thrust deeper still. His fingers locked around her bottom while he thrust home.

Maisie cried out, her head falling back. He held her locked in place, then moved his face into the curve of her neck, breathing her in. She felt so good, smelled so good.

She was wild with it, too, her hands twisting around the

rope that bound her wrists while she pivoted her hips to his. Leaning back, her head lolling, her lips parted, she looked wanton—every bit the Jezebel the men had called her. A woman eager to be taken, eager to be pleasured. Roderick dug his fingers deeper into the gathered skirts, holding her hips while he rode in and out. The slick, tight grip she had on him was unbearably good, her channel slippery with her juices, her body embracing his shaft with each and every stride he made.

Having her so thoroughly bound and submissive and eager to be his prize led him to a new destiny, one where he knew beyond doubt that he would never forget this, and forever crave it. As the thought took hold at the back of his mind, he imagined having her like this again and again, and it made his cock reach even farther.

Maisie moaned loudly when the head of his cock was buried deep in her most tender spot. Roderick could scarcely bring himself to pause, but he did. "I'm not hurting you, am I?"

"Yes, no, but it is the sweetest pain I've ever felt and it makes me glad you have me this way."

He could not bear it. "Hush, I cannot bear your words."

He was close to losing his mind. Then her cunt tightened. She had him so deep. He felt the heat of her climax sucking at him. He tightened his hands on her hips and began to slam home. She cried out in ecstasy. And again. He was there. He thrust again.

Her head rolled back, her body clutching at him, over and over. She bit her lip between her teeth, but being quiet was beyond her, for she whimpered and moaned. Roderick felt his spine turn rigid, his sac riding high, the urge to let loose inside her building, pounding right there at the base of his spine.

"Let me feel you," she pleaded. "Don't pull free."

Those words made it impossible for him to do anything else but loosen his seed within her, his release barreling through him. He could scarcely stay upright, but when he saw the rich, magical glow in her eyes, and her body undulating as she accepted his seed, it held him to the spot, for he was in awe. A witch she was.

He had loved a witch, and lived.

He stayed inside her as long as he could, his cock painfully sensitive to each flex and ripple her body made. When he kissed her, her lips parted under his, defying her captivity to share the pleasure a moment longer. In the aftermath, he clutched her close to him, unwilling to break with the moment, to address the problems that surrounded them.

Roderick craved her as he had craved nothing before, and it broke him apart inside to have to keep her this way. Kissing her face, he held her gently against him, cosseting her the only way he could.

He lowered her to the floor. "You are safer here."

When she started to deny him he covered her lips with his fingers. "The men are unhappy, and when they get like this they are a law unto themselves. I would lay down my life to protect you, Maisie." He paused when she shook her head, but it was true. "I would. Please don't disbelieve me."

"I don't. I've always been able to tell you were honest with me. It is your men you have been vague with since I came aboard."

Clarity shot through his mind, and he felt a queer pain when he realized how wily she was. Every bit as wily as the men said, in fact. And yet he still loved her. Yes, it was love, he did not deny that. He had fallen for a troublesome woman indeed.

"Then you will believe me when I say that I'll ensure your safe delivery into Scotland, as I promised at the outset." Forcing himself to draw back, he continued with caution. "I will come down to check on you often, and when we near the Tay estuary I will row you to land myself."

"You said you would hand me over to the magistrate."

He shook his head, then pulled his breeches into place, securing them. "No. That is for the men's peace of mind. I will free you before that time."

For a moment he cradled her cheek in his palm, and she turned her face, kissing his callused hand. Roderick braced himself. "I'll ask this question once more, because it plagues me most. Tell me the truth now, were you weaving spells when we bedded together?"

"No. But I cannot deny our match made me stronger. It is the way of my kind. We ally ourselves to the natural world and the powers incarnate there. These are particularly powerful in the act of lovemaking."

Roderick remembered the first time, how hot the cabin had become. It was not just a virgin becoming a woman, it was a witch riding high on the magic she felt.

"It was strong because we are a...a good match." She bent her head, growing silent.

At first he thought she had become suddenly ashamed

of her lusty ways, but then he realized she was thinking of something.

"I told you that I'd been split from my kin when my mother suffered a cruel and horrible death."

"Yes."

"She was called out as a witch." Maisie's voice broke on the words, her lower lip trembling. "Much as I was, up there." She jerked her head toward the decks above.

Roderick could not stand it when tears spilled from her eyes. He felt her pain. Why he felt it so intensely baffled him, but he wanted to ease it. He held her jaw in his hands, lifting her face, and kissed each salty tear away. "Hush, you are safe. I will not let my men hurt you."

"I know." She nodded. "And I understand you must keep me here."

When she looked at him, Roderick drew away. He did not trust his own promises, when she might yet try to escape him by magic.

Dragging a sack of root vegetables closer, he stationed it behind her so that she might sit upon it and make herself more comfortable. Then he went to retie the blindfold.

He paused when she whispered his name.

"Roderick..." She shook her head then, as if she'd thought better of what she'd been about to say.

"I must cover your eyes again and keep you bound. It isn't because I want it that way, you know that. But if I don't the men will suspect, and they will turn on us both. Bide your time and I will come to you and take you ashore by rowboat. I will set your feet on Scottish soil, just as I promised the night we met. That has not changed."

"Oh, Roderick." She hung her head. "Forgive me for being angry."

"You were afraid."

She nodded.

Roderick took one last look at her beautiful eyes, then covered them. He left the lantern where it was docked and headed for the door.

Before he stepped out he stared across at her, a tortured young woman, so slight, so feminine. Yet he had seen her power, and even though he believed she would not harm him, there was still so much he didn't know about her. In the space of just a few days she had filled his mind, body and heart. That didn't seem right, and he couldn't shake the feeling it was just as the men had said, that he'd been blinded by her. That's what women did, anchoring men to them, instead of to their own destiny.

As he looked over at her he had the strangest feeling he might never see her again, and it crossed his mind that she could vanish by magic. Would that be for the best? Maybe, but he couldn't accept it.

As if she sensed his thoughts, she lifted her head. "I'll never forget you, Roderick Cameron."

"And I will never forget you, Maisie from Scotland."

chapter Eighteen

Cyrus lay on his back, staring at the damp wooden beams above his bunk, resisting the urge to vent his frustration on his meager surroundings. He could happily smash the lone wooden chair into a thousand pieces, the wait was so intolerable. All night he'd lain there, arranging his thoughts in order of retribution and justice, imagining how he would punish Margaret, and then bind her to him forever.

A knock sounded at the door.

"Enter."

A uniformed soldier stood in the doorway. "Begging your pardon, sire, the captain has asked me to alert you. The ship we seek is within our sights."

Cyrus was up and pulling his boots on before the man had even finished delivering his message. He followed the young soldier up on deck, thoroughly delighted that this moment had finally come. Out in the chilly morning air, he searched the skies. It was blustery and gray, scarcely dawn, and mist clung around the ship. He stepped quickly to the rail and looked beyond to where the various naval officers were focusing their attention. At first he saw nothing, and craned his neck. Then he saw it, a much smaller ship moving along the coastline in the distance.

At last. She was almost within his grasp. Not long now, and he would have her, and he would make her feel his wrath. The need to do so heightened his senses, invigorating him, making his pulse race.

A voice at his side drew him from his thoughts. It was Captain Plimpton. "I have issued orders to our sister ship. We idle here awhile, until everything is in place." Plimpton smiled. "We will have some sport with these vermin."

"Excellent," Cyrus replied.

He trained his eyes on the distant boat, thinking of her, and his appetite for power sharpened.

Roderick didn't sleep that night, nor could he rest in his cabin. Instead he remained at the helm, watching the night sky, waiting for dawn. His ability to ensure Maisie's safety wasn't worrying him, for he would simply tell the men he wanted rid of her, and take her to land. It was as if he was already mourning her departure, though.

How could it be? He was a man of the sea, and no woman had ever called to him this way. It wasn't even as if she were a normal woman, a woman he could wed and set up in a harbor somewhere, a woman he could visit like Brady's Yvonne in Lowestoft.

No, Maisie was something strange; he admitted that to himself, now that he'd had time to think on it. He'd known that first night that she wasn't a lowly sort, but he'd never imagined she would be so thoroughly shrouded in secrets, nor that she practiced the forbidden craft. Now he saw the immensity of the risk he'd taken bringing her aboard. A woman was bad enough, a forbidden passenger, but her secret nature made her sex seem as nothing in the scale of danger he had courted.

The image of her lowering her hood, with that beseeching look in her eyes, flashed through his mind. Her lips had trembled when she thought he wasn't going to take the offer of her virginity. It had intrigued him, and now he knew why. There was a wisdom about her. She was young, but with eyes that knew too much, had seen too much. And yet there was an acceptance about her, too, for her pride was tinged with desperation. All of those things and her strange beauty had left him unable to turn away. If he had, he knew he would never have stopped wondering about her.

As dawn split the horizon, he peered toward land. They had kept the coastline in their scopes. He could take her to shore at any time, but he waited as long as he could, unwilling to say goodbye. They'd passed Saint Andrews, and now he was looking toward Fife. He'd been born in the Lowlands of Scotland, across the Tay from Saint Andrews, in a back room of a tenement in Dundee. Lurid tales of witches and their burnings had been part of his childhood. He'd never pictured one looking anything like the woman he had been consorting with these past few days, though. Despite his dark mood, Roderick gave a wry smile at that thought.

During his years at sea, visiting many strange lands, he'd heard stories of people with magical powers, and oftentimes those people were revered and respected, not put to death as they were in his homeland. Maisie's mother had been one of those victims. That was a harsh realization for him. No matter how humble his beginnings—and they had been humble, hampered by poverty and misfortune—he hadn't had such a dark history as Maisie. No wonder she'd looked so afraid when she was brought above deck and the men had threatened to end her days because of her forbidden craft. Roderick couldn't blame them, for he couldn't claim to understand her, either.

Witchcraft. He never would have guessed it. There was something strange about her, but not that. He'd never been a believer, but there was no denying what he'd witnessed, and in matters of their joining, yes, there had been much that was not easily explained. He'd been so taken with her, it had been easy to ignore. At first.

Once again he looked at the distant shoreline and at the sky. They were almost within sight of the Tay estuary. It was time to set her feet on dry land. She could go where she was destined.

Roderick decided it was the right thing, no matter how wrong it felt. While the majority of the men still rested, he would instruct Clyde to lower a rowboat. He could trust the sailor to do it without question, he knew, because Clyde had been wary of her, but had not called for her to walk the plank. The old man had been wise about her from the outset, and had made good points about her. Clyde knew she meant them no harm. He watched Roderick even now, a glint in his eye as if he was running a wager with himself on how this matter would play out.

If any of the men argued with Roderick, he had a perfectly

good reason for escorting her away from the ship. Depositing her on dry land would rid them of the burden of carrying a witch, well before they reached their destination.

He called to Clyde, and was about to instruct him to lower the rowboat and prepare Maisie to leave the ship when a whistle sounded above their heads.

The watchman pointed at the horizon. "Ship ahoy, Captain."

Roderick reached for Clyde's eyeglass and focused it in that direction.

A large vessel was headed their way. At the top of the main mast a familiar flag was flapping. "It's a navy ship. If they're patrolling the waters, they wouldn't be headed straight toward the coastline."

He approached the starboard railing, looking back over their wake at the tossing waves. "They have come in from a distance. If we were closer to Saint Andrews, I'd think them headed there, but we're almost at the Tay now."

Brady ran up the steps from the main deck. "The ship appears to be making ready to engage. They are coming for us, Captain," he added in an alarmed tone.

For me, no doubt. Roderick frowned. But would they go to such trouble for the taxes owed on a small merchant ship? Perhaps they would pass by.

Brady called out for all hands on deck. The order was passed quickly, men relaying it along the chain of command.

Roderick strode to a wooden trunk that was built in close to the wheel. Unlocking it, he pulled out his cutlass and sword belt and wrapped it around his hips. When he returned to the wheel, men were pouring out on deck, hiving off in all directions. Several clambered onto the rigging, shifting into positions on the spar above, ready for his instructions.

"Full sail, veer hard to port. They are coming up fast and if we cling to the coastline they might pass us by." The instruction was passed and the crew set about adjusting the angles of the spars, rolling up sails to change direction at speed through the turn.

Roderick clenched his jaw while he watched through the spyglass. The navy ship was fast. It had the advantage, and wouldn't take long to come up on their stern.

It was a command ship, and in the distance he saw another ship behind it. Scanning the horizon, he caught sight of a third vessel, approaching from the north. Roderick lowered his eyeglass and looked Brady's way. "There are three vessels. They have us surrounded. Even if we gain speed, that third ship will block our passage north."

"A carefully planned entrapment," Brady commented.

"Indeed." Roderick frowned. "And yet when we docked at Lowestoft we were not approached by navy officers."

"It is a puzzle."

Roderick and Brady studied each other a moment.

"Guns at the ready, Captain?" Clyde asked.

Roderick pressed his lips together. It would be a token gesture for his men, nothing more. There was little they could hope to do against three naval ships that had dominance in these waters. "Aye, but not visible."

Safeguarding the ship and the crew was his priority. The navy vessel was coming up on them, but before he had a chance to issue any more instructions, a loud boom sounded.

It was a warning shot, for it was not followed by another.

"They wish to board," Brady said.

The command ship approached with its cannon at the ready. Uniformed naval soldiers lined up on the nearside, guns trained on the *Libertas*. A brazier flamed on the deck, men standing by with bows and arrows held aloft.

"They are ready to take out our sails, Captain," Clyde called out.

"Drop anchor," Roderick instructed. When no one moved, Roderick repeated the instruction, louder.

He looked at Brady, who rolled his eyes. "No other option," the first mate agreed.

"Not a good time to have a store crammed with illicit French wine," Roderick commented.

"Nor an angry witch tied up in the hold."

Up until that point Roderick had not made a connection between their passenger and the trio of ships that had ambushed them. Neither had Brady.

They frowned at one another.

"You don't think it's her they are coming for?" Brady asked.

Roderick swayed, his concerns growing rapidly. *Witch hunters?*

"She was eager to leave London. Perhaps this is why."

Roderick nodded, but he looked away, focusing on the command ship, and prayed that was not the case. If it was, he wouldn't let them take her. They would find her, though, even if they only came to search the ship for contraband goods.

Brady, however, brightened at the prospect. "If they truly

are after the Jezebel, we will be rid of her sooner than expected."

Roderick didn't acknowledge his comment.

Clyde caught his eye and the old man shook his head.

The command ship set down anchor nearby and two rowboats were lowered. Six men bearing arms accompanied a commanding officer in the first. Two more men followed in the second.

Roderick watched as the rowboats closed the distance. As he did, he tried to plan for every possible outcome, but until he knew what had led them here, he could not even begin to decide how to act.

The naval officer stood up. "Captain Cameron of the *Libertas*," the officer bellowed.

"We're behind you, Captain," one of his men called out to him. "Just say the word if you want us to take action."

Roderick approached the railing with a deep sense of misgiving. Something was badly amiss. The number of men and vessels was unprecedented for a simple case of excise evasion. As he pondered it, his thoughts went to Maisie. Had they come to try her? Was she known in London, and was that why she had to leave so hastily?

"I am Captain Cameron," he shouted down.

The officer stared up at him, sour-faced and disapproving. "We believe you have a passenger aboard, a young lady by the name of Margaret."

Roderick's heart sank. He would rather they'd come for him.

"They have come for the witch," one of the men close by said to another. Whispered conversations began and Roderick's tension grew as he realized his men were pleased. He was not. "We do not carry passengers," he announced.

"You were observed taking a young woman aboard this ship in Billingsgate," announced the officer. "Her guardian seeks her safe return, and if you deliver her to us unharmed, we will be lenient when addressing the extensive list of excise charges against your name."

Roderick was relieved that no mention of arresting her on a charge of witchcraft had been made. However, if this guardian of hers was well-meaning, why had she run away? Was it the same man who wanted to keep her? He tried to recall if she had referred to him as her guardian. If only she had confided more in him, he would be able to judge and know how best to respond.

Meanwhile, at his back, the men were already taking action. "Fetch her up. Let them take her and we'll be rid of her and her twisted ways."

"Stand your ground," he instructed, shooting the order back over his shoulder.

"If you do not hand the young lady over," the naval officer continued, "a charge of kidnap will also be listed against your name, and no mercy will be shown to you or your men as we come aboard."

"Look at the trouble she has brought upon us," a shipman spat.

"She is a crime against God, that woman," another one agreed. "Let them deal with her."

Roderick's heart thundered against the wall of his chest. He was trapped. There was no way they could escape the navy. Neither could he decide whether Maisie would be safer with them than she would be with his own men, who had turned against her.

If only he'd managed to get her to dry land before this occurred.

He addressed the officer below. "The woman you seek is safe and well."

"So, you do have the young lady. If you do not take passengers, we must assume that you have indeed kidnapped her." His sour expression altered into a sly grin.

Roderick's mind raced. From what little Maisie had revealed, he had been able to glean that the man who wanted to keep her had wealth and influence. Influence enough to set the Royal Navy on them? If that was the case, then they intended to take her back to London. Torn, he considered the dilemma. She would be safer with the navy—who apparently were unaware of her forbidden craft—than with his own crew. But could she escape the master from whom she had run before if the navy took her back to him? Roderick could only hope.

He had to be sure they were not acting on behalf of witch hunters. "I have a duty to ensure the young lady is safely delivered onto land. Are you charged with the same duty?"

The naval officer turned to pass comment to a man behind him, before he answered. "Given that *we* are rescuing the lady from *you,* that is somewhat of a strange question, Captain Cameron." Sarcasm dripped from his voice.

Behind him, Roderick heard his crew whispering, and there was laughter, too. At least the mood had lightened amongst them, he thought wryly.

Brady came closer to his side. "Don't be a fool, Roderick.

Let her go. She will be their problem and they've assured you our men won't be harmed."

"And you believe that?" Roderick lifted his eyebrows.

Brady scowled at him. "I have a family to feed. I *have* to believe it."

As I have to believe Maisie will be safe once she is dispatched to the navy.

"Bring her up from the hold," Roderick commanded.

chapter Nineteen

Maisie rose to her feet, her hands clutching at her tethers. She hadn't been able to rest easy, even with the stuffed sack Roderick had left her to sit upon, but the distress she felt up until that moment was nothing compared to the sense of doom that encroached on her now.

It closed in all around her, ominous and far-reaching, and building all the while.

The ship lurched, as if changing direction.

Something bad was going to happen. Panic hit her. She sought an enchantment to free her from her bonds. Then the ship seemed to still.

Sails had been drawn in and she heard them drop anchor. Was it because Roderick was taking her to shore? If that was the case, the men would be uneasy, which might explain the sense of impending doom she felt. It would be dangerous if the men found her freed by magic, so she stayed as she was.

Then she heard a loud boom, followed by silence. Distant voices reached her through the bowels of the ship. Someone shouted, but she could not understand what was being said. Time passed. Then the sound of footsteps close by took her attention to the door. Moving her head in that direction, she listened closely, trying to work out if it was Roderick. If it was, she would truly have to say goodbye to him. It would be hard, for she felt great affection for him, but she knew he could do no more than take her to land and set her free.

Why didn't that make her happy, as it should?

A key rattled in the lock and the door creaked open.

Several men entered the room. She sensed three, maybe four.

"See?" one of them said. "Even the captain was afraid to look at those eyes of hers."

"I am surprised, for I thought him smitten with her."

The second man sounded familiar. Brady, perhaps? They circled her, three of them.

None of them was Roderick.

When they began to untie the rope that bound her hands, Maisie reacted. "Where are you taking me?"

"Fear not, Jezebel, it is not the plank that awaits you."

That was definitely the old man, Clyde, for not only did she recognize his voice, she knew he'd been the one to saddle her with that name. She turned her face in the direction of his voice.

"What's happening?"

"You've been rescued by the British navy, who seem to be under the assumption that you were kidnapped by our captain."

"A fine story indeed," one of the other men said. "Any

fool could see she came aboard of her own volition. Duped our captain with one of her spells, no doubt."

"Didn't need no spell to dupe him, if you ask me," Clyde responded. "I wager that one look at her was all he needed, and he was sold on the idea of bedding her."

"I wager, I wager," the other man parroted. "Do you do anything but wager with yourself?"

"It keeps me sharp in the head."

Maisie barely registered their words, stricken as she was by fresh concerns. Whatever did they mean, the navy was here for her? "I do not understand. Who has come?"

As soon as the words were out, dread swamped her. Who else would come but Cyrus?

No, not that.

Hands reached behind her head.

"What are you doing? Are you a fool?"

"She cannot climb the ladder blinded. Look away if you are scared. I am not afeared. I've been given no reason to be." Swiftly, the blindfold was removed.

Maisie blinked and squinted. It was Clyde who stood before her. A quick glance showed her the two men with him had averted their eyes. She had the wild urge to tell them it wouldn't help, if she chose to make magic, but she resisted.

"Be quick about it, Clyde." It was Brady and he was annoyed.

"The British navy have come for you." Clyde peered into her eyes, observing her closely. "Your guardian?"

"My tormentor." It was a whispered comment that she couldn't withhold, but Clyde heard her.

He put his hand on her shoulder and squeezed gently.

Compassion, from this man who had recognized something different in her that first morning they set sail? It touched her deeply. Her lower lip trembled as tears gathered in her eyes. They were so close to landing in Scotland. She'd begun to believe Roderick would be able to see her onto land, after all. Now this. Cyrus had taken action. He'd sent people to hunt her down.

"They wanted to charge our captain with kidnap," Clyde said, and she felt the hand on her shoulder tighten.

This was important. Maisie listened even more closely.

"Said they wouldn't press charges or harm any of the ship's crew, though, if you are safely delivered to them."

A deal had been done, and Maisie felt as if it had been made directly with her. If she went willingly, Roderick would be safe. Given such a good cause, she would do so.

Brady had set about tugging down the rope from the beam.

Pain shot through her shoulders as her arms were lowered, pulling her back from her thoughts. She was prodded, encouraged to move. Clearly, the men did not want to touch her.

Clyde, however, guided her with one hand still on her shoulder.

"I knew there was something not right about you," Brady commented from behind them. "But as long as you're gone from this ship with your witchcraft and your wicked ways, I'll be happy."

"Good luck to them, I say," the third man said. "Once they realize, they will hand her over to a magistrate."

They were glad to be rid of her. Did Roderick know what this meant? she wondered. How could he? He wouldn't guess that Cyrus was capable of swaying people in power to pursue her.

Staggering up the rungs, she rubbed her sore wrists and then felt her way with her hands. Fresh air reached her. Blinking in the bright light as she emerged, she found all hands were on deck, and yet an eerie silence encompassed them. Scanning the small crowd, she quickly sought out Roderick's familiar face amongst the gathered men, and saw immense concern creasing his brow.

Then she looked beyond him, and what she saw made her gasp aloud.

Even though she'd been told about the navy ships, she hadn't been prepared for the sight of them. A great array of masts on one side of the *Libertas*. Glancing around her, she saw that the three much larger navy vessels caged them in, with the coastline on their free side. As she scanned the closest ship she caught sight of uniformed men with raised weapons. Stepping closer to the railing, she saw that many cannons were pointed in their direction, too.

Roderick came to her side.

"I'm so sorry," she said.

"They haven't mentioned your magic," he said quietly. "They have come to escort you back to your guardian." He put his hand on her upper arm, gently embracing it. "If you go with them you'll be safer than with my men. But if you don't think you can outwit them and escape your persecutor in London, say the word and I will put up a fight to keep you."

He knew. He'd unraveled the puzzle. Maisie looked into his eyes, saw his determination, and her heart nearly broke.

"Roderick, I am no expert in such matters, but even I can see you would stand little chance against three much larger ships with their cannons trained on you. Your offer is kindly appreciated, but do not concern yourself. I will go with them. I will find my way to the Highlands, somehow. As you know, I am set on doing so."

Tension was building around them, and an impatient voice called out, requesting information.

Roderick's grip on her arm tightened. "Promise you will do that...and that you will protect yourself with your magic."

She nodded.

"If you need me, I believe I would know."

"I believe you would." She smiled at him. "Let me go and all will be well on the *Libertas* once more."

Roderick stared at her with blazing eyes, the breeze lifting his hair. Studying him for a moment, Maisie absorbed the precious memory, then turned away quickly.

Clyde gestured to her. A rope ladder had been rolled over the side in preparation for her departure. She nodded and accepted his hand in guidance.

Two rowboats waited below. The one beneath the ladder carried two men, one at each oar. The other held seven men, four of them with their weapons trained on the spot where she stood. Another man was standing, presumably the officer.

Maisie lifted her hand, acknowledging them.

"Thank you," she said to Clyde.

"Hold tight to the ropes...and to the song in your heart," he replied.

Maisie nodded. Tears welled in her eyes, but she forced them back.

She grasped the rope, took a deep breath and clambered over the railing. Holding tight to the ladder, she waited until it stopped swinging about, then found her footing. The climb down was treacherous, but Maisie scarcely thought about how dangerous it was, and acted on instinct, for her mind was elsewhere.

The men who waited assisted her on the final rungs and encouraged her to take a seat at the head of the boat.

"Escort the lady back to the ship." It was the officer in the other boat who issued the command.

The two men began to row determinedly.

The boat laden with armed men remained.

Maisie stared wretchedly at the water for most of the journey across, and then it occurred to her. *Cyrus.*

Lifting her head, she looked up at the ship they approached. There he was, at the railing, staring down at her.

He'd come. He'd come himself, to recapture her.

Dread filled her and the urge to fling herself into the water and swim to land was great. But how far would she get with these men in pursuit?

Must reach my kin. Must keep my wits about me.

What could she do? There was only one option—to handle Cyrus by means of magic. She would have to convince him she was glad to be reunited with him. She had never dared—never believed she could—for his knowledge was so great she was afraid he would recognize it in her. But these past few days away from him had changed her immensely, and she was no longer young Margaret, indebted to him. She was a woman, and a witch empowered, because of the time she'd spent with Roderick. Her captain had given her the strength, she was sure of it. She would manage Cyrus until they were well away from this place and Roderick and his men were safe and free. Only then would she find a means to escape once again.

They were closing on the navy ship, where another ladder awaited her.

Then she heard a voice from behind her, and realized that the naval officer who'd stayed behind on the other rowboat was issuing instructions to the crew of the *Libertas* once again.

"As you have handed over the young lady, a charge of kidnap will not be raised. However, you will forfeit your ship as recompense for previous misdemeanors and avoidance of taxes and excise duties. The *Libertas* will be commandeered by the Royal Navy of Great Britain for the service of His Majesty King George."

Maisie jerked her head around and looked back.

Her hand went to her chest. How could they take his ship?

"Any man who wishes to stay aboard will be offered gainful employment as a member of the king's navy. Those who wish to stand by your captain are urged to lower your rowboats and depart the vessel forthwith."

"And if we do not agree?" It was Roderick's voice, and it tugged on her heartstrings.

"There are currently eighteen cannons manned, loaded and pointed in your direction, Captain Cameron. They will be discharged if you do not abandon your ship immediately."

Maisie listened, horrified.

"Your ship and all its crew will perish."

chapter Twenty

Cyrus craned his neck, trying to catch sight of Margaret's face.

All around him, orders were being issued and instructions shouted, but Cyrus Lafayette could do nothing but watch as the rowboat carrying his precious cargo came closer. His mood had been black for the past several days, and frantic. Now a deadly seriousness had come upon him. He would not settle until he knew the reasons for this. Could it be that she had truly been kidnapped? If it was true, he found it hard to believe that she could not outwit and escape her captors by magic. No, she must have instigated this. He would much prefer to think she had been led astray, or followed someone's advice on a whim.

Just then she lifted her head and looked up at him.

Cyrus stared down at her. She did not wave, and he could not read her expression. His fingers dug tightly into the wooden rail beneath his hands. She looked away. The rowboat had pulled alongside the ship and the two oarsmen held the boat steady while Margaret stood up and mounted the rope ladder.

The captain appeared at his side. "Master Lafayette, if you would step back, I will assist the young lady to climb aboard. I need to ascertain her state of well-being before I decide whether further action needs to be taken on Captain Cameron." The captain patted the pistol that hung from his belt. He smiled, as if he anticipated the prospect.

That suited Cyrus. He nodded and stepped back, allowing the captain to stand by as Margaret climbed up to the railing. Two of the lower ranking men all but pulled her over it, setting her on her feet. She thanked them, but then looked back at the *Libertas*.

"Miss Lafayette, I am Captain Plimpton of the British navy. Welcome aboard. May I ask if you have come to any harm during your time on the ship known as the *Libertas?*"

"Harm?" She looked at the captain and seemed bewildered.

Cyrus's suspicion grew. She was avoiding his eyes.

"Forgive me for being indelicate, but I must ask. Did they hurt you or...defile you in any way?" Plimpton pulled the pistol from his belt.

Margaret stared at the captain as if distressed.

"Point out the man who defiled you and I will finish him." He pointed his pistol at the crew of the *Libertas* climbing down to the rowboats beyond.

"No, Captain. None of those men hurt me."

Plimpton nodded. "Well, it seems we'll have no further sport from this one." He sighed. "What a pity."

Cyrus wanted him to blow the lot of them out of the water

and have done with it, but before he had a chance to offer his opinion, Margaret spoke.

"Captain, is it your intention to carry out the threat to... make them all perish?"

The captain chortled. "If they haven't harmed you there is no absolute need to do so. Unless you would prefer I did?"

She shook her head vigorously.

Cyrus's mood turned sour. She wished to protect those brigands. "Margaret?"

What struck him most when she finally turned his way was her beauty, which seemed strangely enhanced out here in the wild ocean breeze with her hair flying free and her eyes wide and bright. She looked pale and tired, though, and her gown was damaged and torn in several places. She had no belongings with her. The foolish woman. Cyrus wanted to drag her below deck and berate her.

She closed her eyes a moment, and when she opened them she broke into a weak smile. "Cyrus, you are here."

"Of course I am here," he said with barely concealed anger. "You are mine and I will not suffer you or your precious... *talents* being squandered."

Her eyes flickered with fear. She was still terrified of being exposed as what she was. Cyrus smiled. That pleased him greatly. He could work with that to keep her more strongly in check. As he approached, she held out her hands, beckoning him to her.

Cyrus cocked his head, trying to understand her actions. He'd expected her to reject him if she had run away, or fling herself at him if she had been kidnapped. However, she took his hands in her own, staring into his eyes as he joined her.

"You must tell the captain if there is any cause for concern."

She held his hands tighter still. "Cyrus, no, I was not harmed, as I have already told him."

She gave the captain a sidelong glance. There was a fretful look in her eyes and she kept peering back over her shoulder. She seemed restless or confused, and she whispered some words in Gaelic or Pictish, he was sure of it, but for some reason they were swept away on the wind. He was about to quiz her when his mood softened. It didn't matter, because she was there and he was holding her. The very sight of her... it was pure and simple delirium to have her back after these days of rage and hardship.

Again she spoke, but he could not catch what she said.

Why did she keep looking at the *Libertas?* Cyrus followed her gaze and saw that the men from the ship were now clambering down nets into rowboats. There were some thirty of them, and they were watched over by one of the navy officers. Why did she seem so fretful? The question echoed in Cyrus's mind, but he found it hard to voice it. Had some rogue frightened her, or worse still, stolen her virginity from him?

Captain Plimpton looked at Cyrus and frowned. "Are you quite well, Master Lafayette?"

In the distance, the sound of men jeering at the navy reached them.

Margaret pulled her hands free of his and ran to the railing.

What horror was this? Cyrus stared at her back and the joy he'd felt a moment before fast dissipated. Instead, he grew angry. Had one of those men befriended her? Worse still, become aware of her powers? A seething jealousy bit into him. Stepping over to the captain, he reached out and took the lowered pistol from his hand. Striding to the railing, he trained it on the man who stood up in one rowboat, watching Margaret through a spyglass.

"Master Lafayette, you surprise me," the navy captain stated in an amused drawl. "I take it you still seek recompense?"

"I would be much happier if you had rid the seas of all such vermin as soon as we had my ward safely aboard," Cyrus muttered. "However, I will take the task upon myself." He cocked the pistol.

Margaret was at his side instantly, attempting to halt him. "Cyrus, no!"

Cyrus did not look away from his target. "Surely you wish to be rid of them, my dear?"

The distress she showed in reaction to that was palpable, and made Cyrus grate his teeth.

"I am rid of them," she responded, but her voice wavered wildly and he knew she was hiding something from him.

He rounded on her, searching her face for the truth. "And you are glad?"

She nodded.

"Prove it," he said. "Take a man down yourself, the one who watches you so eagerly through his spyglass."

Her eyes blazed. "I do not have it in me to kill a man, Cyrus. You know that."

"Prove it to me, and it will make amends for all of this. You are a good shot. I trained you myself."

After a long moment of silent consideration, she reached out, hand shaking, and took the gun from him.

"Rest assured, my dear, if you miss your target, I will take the pistol back and make sure the man never breathes again."

Margaret swayed unsteadily and closed her eyes for a moment.

The captain laughed. "I had not realized you relished a good game, Master Lafayette. This is most entertaining."

Margaret looked from one to the other of them, and Cyrus knew she was shocked. Her intelligent eyes were bright, her hair whipping up in the breeze, making her look every bit the wild witch he had plucked from the Lowlands to keep as his own.

"I will not miss," she replied, and stepped toward the railing, both hands outstretched, holding the weapon. She whispered something beneath her breath. Cyrus had the suspicion she was making magic. However, without a further moment's hesitation, the shot rang out.

Ah, yes, my precious witch is mine, all mine. Cyrus felt a sense of calm descend upon him. He watched as the man who had stood watching her from the rowboat crumpled to the floor, a dark stain spreading across his coat at the shoulder. Cyrus smiled.

Margaret's arms lowered. She turned to face them, offering the captain back the gun as she did so. When she drew closer, she lifted her chin and looked deep into Cyrus's eyes.

"Forgive me," she whispered, and gave a tremulous smile. "I am mightily relieved to be reunited with you." With that, she embraced him. She said something in Gaelic. He barely caught the words, but knew it was a term of affection, of love, of forgiveness.

Nothing mattered now. All he cared about was that she had come back to him, and he believed her. Eyelids lowering, Cyrus savored her warmth, and the fact that she was so willing to be in his arms.

At first Cyrus had bristled with tension, as he if sensed her making magic. Then he fell under her spell. Did he know what she'd done? She looked up at him.

A confused frown marked his forehead. Her magic had indeed worked on him, but he was fighting it all the while. She would have to work harder, but now that the anchors had been lifted and distance was growing between her and Roderick, she could apply her full attention to the task at hand.

Inside, she was reeling. Everything had happened so quickly that she could scarcely take it all in. She was shaking, nauseous and dizzy from what she'd had to do to protect Roderick. The discovery that he and his men had lost their ship to the navy had caused her so much distress that she couldn't keep her thoughts and emotions straight long enough to create the magic to hold Cyrus in check. That had to be her priority—to rouse a whiff more magic to confuse his mind and emotions. That should keep him from taking further action against Roderick and his men. A show of affection toward Cyrus aided her task, although that was even harder to muster and sustain.

"Why did you run away?" he asked. "Was it something Beth said to you?"

Maisie shook her head, not willing to implicate Mama Beth.

Cyrus pursued the subject. "She was a sick woman and her ramblings were borne of jealousy, of fear for her own destiny, that is all."

Was. A cold hand clutched Maisie's heart.

"She knew we'd grown close," he murmured, meandering along, pacified as he was. "She knew my deep affection for you."

"Beth has passed on?"

He gave her a brief nod. Maisie's mind whirred furiously, her grief over Beth and the fact she was still shaking from the action she'd been forced to take moments earlier made it hard for her to concentrate on her magic long enough to quell him.

"Nothing will keep us from being together now. We will be married as soon as we return to London. Together we will be powerful. But I must know why you ran from me."

"I did not run from you." Forcing herself to meet his gaze, she knew she had to reassure him. He would have Roderick and all his men killed if she did not dissuade him. The fact she had shot Roderick herself was not enough. "I will explain."

With one hand clasped around her jaw, Cyrus defied her to look away. His eyes narrowed, his lips curling. "You will never run again, that is certain. I will make sure of it." His tone was sinister and possessive, and his gaze dropped to her bosom. "Once we are wed you will be mine completely."

It was obvious to Maisie how deep his feelings ran. Much deeper than she had even suspected. His desire—both for her power and for her as a woman—had grown more obvious these past months, but never had she felt the depth of his lust for her. The look in his eyes was clear. He wanted her as a lover, as a wife.

It terrified her to even contemplate. She didn't want him. Never had and never would. It pained her, too, because it felt so wrong of him, so misguided. She felt cheated by his trickery. Just as she had been when she'd begun to realize he wanted her power to serve his own ends. It had disturbed her greatly, but the latest revelation in his plans was even more shocking to her, and there was no denying it now. Beth had been right. He feared losing her and he planned to own her in every way. It felt like betrayal. Well, they had betrayed each other, in that case, but she must keep his attention on her until Roderick was safely gone.

She forced the words out. "I had to return to my beginnings to see the place I was born, in order for my magic to blossom fully. It came upon me as a yearning so strong and so sudden, it had to be. On a whim I went down to the dockyard and asked about passage to Scotland. I was dizzy with the desire to see the place again when I was offered the chance."

His eyes narrowed. "You took your most precious things."

"I had taken to carrying them with me."

Cyrus frowned. Pulling on her deepest resources, she wove more magic in his soul. The look in his eyes became vague. Hopeful that he would not realize, she set about influencing him. Once she'd whispered the enchantment beneath her breath, bending his will to hers, she willed him blind to her influence on his thoughts.

After several long moments he nodded. "If it's that important to you, I will request that the captain land us in a Scottish port, instead of taking us back to London."

Relief flooded her. "Oh, Cyrus. Thank you."

He cocked his head, looking at her as if he wasn't quite sure about it, then departed from her side in order to instigate her request.

Desperate to make some kind of amends with Roderick's men before Cyrus took her below deck, she struggled to know what to do for the best. It stunned her to think they had lost the *Libertas* because of her. And now Roderick would hate her for shooting at him. She could only hope that one day she would be able to explain, and that he would be able to forgive her for all that she'd put him through.

What would he do now? Roderick had been bound for Dundee, to meet with the partner with whom he owned the ship *Libertas,* this Gregor Ramsay. Presumably they would still have to go to meet him, ship or no ship. In which case they would be following the navy, which was now turning north on Cyrus's request. She couldn't be sure Roderick would follow, but she could try to assist.

Heart beating wildly, she looked to the skies. Murmuring fast and low, she beckoned the power of the wind and the warmth of the sun to aid Roderick's onward journey, wherever he might be bound. "I'm sorry, my good-hearted lover," she whispered as the wind lifted, "for all the misfortune I brought your way."

Then she put a protection spell on him just for good measure.

"That bloody Jezebel shot you!" Brady gesticulated wildly, standing upright in the boat next to Roderick, who was slumped in the bottom. "That bitch."

Despite the pain and disbelief he felt, Roderick was unaccountably angered by the man's insult.

"We should have strung her up ourselves," Brady added.

Clyde laughed loudly, which made every man jack of them turn to query his strange reaction. "She saved your life is what she did." He gave a shrug and another laugh. "If she hadn't taken the gun from that man's hand, you'd be dead already."

That silenced them all.

"What the..." Roderick tried to rise up on his elbow, but pain shot through his shoulder. "Sit down, Brady," he shouted, "or you'll capsize the lot of us. We are heavy with men."

"Aye," Clyde commented, "sit down, for that would not look good on our headstones. 'The seamen who lie here all drowned because they couldn't handle a rowboat.'"

"Don't be ridiculous," Brady snapped, clearly losing his composure after the turn of events. "If we drown we wouldn't have headstones."

Roderick cursed, loudly. He went to speak, but gave up the will when he found he was being undressed. His coat was pulled off by one man and his shirt torn open by another. Pressure was applied to his wound with the bunched cotton of his shirt. For a moment the pain threatened to wipe him out, then it eased. He laid his head back and tried to make sense of what Clyde had said. One of the men was attempting to examine his shoulder, but Roderick felt stubbornly fixed on ignoring the gunshot wound—and whence it had come. That wasn't going to be possible. Puzzled by Clyde's comments, he had to quiz him on it. "What do you mean, she saved my life?"

"She gladly took the weapon," Brady interrupted. "We all saw it with our own eyes."

"Aye, but I'd be willing to wager the other man would have chosen a target somewhere much less forgiving than your shoulder, and it would be a burial at sea we'd be arranging now, not a rest-and-repair task, with the captain alive and well."

One man dipped his dirk in the salt water, then plucked at Roderick's wound. "Barely scraped the skin," the sailor announced. "Your coat and shirt have suffered more."

Roderick closed his eyes and gritted his teeth. The pain from the exploratory poking he was being subjected to didn't stop his mind from running with questions. Had Maisie turned the gun on him to save him from a lethal shot? Could she have wounded him on purpose, to protect him and his shipmen?

He couldn't be sure and never would be, not unless he heard the truth of it from her own lips. But that was not about to happen.

Once his shoulder had been bandaged and his shirt and coat returned, Roderick stared across the water as the four ships sailed away, roundly putting distance between the rowboats packed with men from the *Libertas,* streaking away from them with Maisie aboard. Roderick barely felt the pain of the injury she'd given him. He plucked the spyglass from his pocket and scoured the deck of the navy ship, but could see no sign of her. "They are headed out to sea and back to London."

As soon as he'd said it, the lead ship abruptly changed course again.

"One ship is now heading north, Captain," someone shouted from one of the other rowboats.

Roderick frowned. A change of plan? Why did he care? He didn't trust them not to turn on him, take down his men with cannon. Nothing to do with the woman, Maisie from Scotland.

"They did us a good turn, Roderick," Brady insisted. "We wanted rid of her."

Deep down, Roderick knew he was right. They were better off without her. She had caused dangerous friction between him and his men, and she'd taken vengeance on him for her imprisonment. Still, he watched the navy vessels and couldn't bring himself to respond, instead wondering where they were headed. The only harbor large enough to receive them in the estuary was Dundee.

Clyde laughed low in his chest. "I wonder if they are aware they are carrying a witch."

"So you admit she's a witch?" quizzed Brady, apparently still angered by Clyde's earlier comments.

"Oh, yes, she is definitely a witch." Clyde paused, clearly enjoying the audience, for the other two rowboats full of *Libertas* men clung close to theirs despite the fact they bobbed about on the brisk sea, the men eager to hear the discussion. "Does that mean she had bad intentions? Maybe not. She's from the Highlands, where many good healers hail from."

"It's true what Clyde said," a voice declared from the second boat.

Roderick had to twist his neck—an uncomfortable maneuver, given that his shoulder was so tightly bound—to seek out who had spoken. It was Adam, the young Dutchman who she had healed.

When all eyes turned upon him, Adam brandished his hand. "She is a good person. She healed me, and I'm glad of it. If I had the chance, I would thank her by offering her my loyalty for life."

"You see?" Brady declared. "She has enchanted you all so much you are blind to it. None of you see the danger now, despite the fact we are adrift without our ship because of her, and she has shot our captain. It is the work of the devil, for she has enslaved you all!"

Roderick could see he was going have to take charge of this and focus them on staying afloat, despite his injury. "Brady, be quiet."

When Brady gave him a questioning look, Roderick nodded. "We must think on our next move."

It was madness to think of anything else right now. Yet he couldn't get the image of Maisie out of his head. It was a mercy that she had missed his vitals. Again the thought made him pause. Could Clyde be right, that she was saving him from a fatal shot? Roderick shook his head slightly, convincing himself it was only foolish lust that made him hanker after her. Wanting one woman this much was no good for a ship's captain. "We head for Dundee, as planned. We owe it to Gregor to be there, if no other reason."

Other reasons crowded his head, and his heart.

"They have the *Libertas* in tow now, Captain, and they are definitely headed into the estuary."

"As are we." He and his men would meet with Gregor

Ramsay as arranged many months before. But Roderick could not shake the curiosity he felt about whether the navy vessel that carried Maisie and the man she called her master were now bound there, too.

"Gregor Ramsay will not be happy about this," Brady commented. "God help our sorry souls if he is there to see the *Libertas* dock in Dundee with the navy standard aloft."

"No," Roderick replied, "he will find out because we'll be the ones telling the tale over a flagon of rum, well away from the British navy."

His obligation to his fellow shipman, Gregor Ramsay, was his priority now, but he had the wild notion that he could regain charge of the *Libertas*. Once they were sure the navy men were not aware that they followed, they could head safely for Dundee, take back the ship, then await word from Gregor.

Why do I even think it's possible? Roderick wondered.

It was a dream born of frustration.

A silence fell over them, all men watching the navy ships, *Libertas* in tow, fade into the distance. Brady shifted and set about putting the oars into position. As he did, the sea fell still and the sun broke through the clouds.

It was uncanny, but the wind lifted again a moment later and the boats bobbed and drifted north.

"Imagine that, the weather is on our side," Clyde said with a chuckle. "Luck is clearly with our captain, for he is still alive, and now the weather is aiding our journey after the *Libertas*."

Roderick knew what Clyde was trying to say, but he couldn't believe it, despite the evidence he'd witnessed the night before. Could it be Maisie's doing?

Brady quickly regained his position and shouted across to the other two boats, commanding them to take up their oars. Men hastened to the task.

Roderick climbed onto a seat, dragging himself up.

The wind truly was on their side.

"Captain?" Clyde asked, awaiting instruction when he saw Roderick's attention sharpen.

"Take turns with the rowing, fresh men on the task every half hour."

"In which direction, Captain?" Clyde asked with a grin.

"Onward to Dundee." He glanced at the coast, recalling their position before the ambush. "We are well beyond Saint Andrews. The mouth of the Tay estuary is almost within sight. Follow the shoreline. We'll cling to the southern bank until we reach Newport. If this wind at our back holds we'll be there by late afternoon. Then we cross to the northern bank."

"You have a plan?"

"Aye. We'll enter Dundee harbor under cover of darkness."

"And then?"

"And then we take back what they have stolen from us."

chapter Twenty-One

Roderick and his men rowed into Dundee harbor well after midnight, when the cloud coverage shielded them from moonlight that would otherwise expose them to the men who kept watch over the ships at night. It was, however, the harbor that Roderick knew best in the whole world, for he had played down there as a lad and dreamed of sailing out to sea on one of the ships he saw. That knowledge of the harbor was proving invaluable for this endeavor and made the task of negotiating a stealthy approach relatively straightforward.

They secured the rowboats by tying them one to the other beneath a wooden jetty. Their plans had been made on the way across the Tay, and from the moment they set foot on land Roderick issued commands in low whistles or by signaling with his hands.

Brady went on ahead to estimate the number of navy men who'd been left to guard the *Libertas*. One of their own crew stayed behind with the rowboats in case they needed them to make a swift departure. If all went well, he and the skiffs would be fetched up after they regained charge of the *Libertas*. The other men followed Roderick's lead in small clusters as they made their way along the dockyards until they found the *Libertas*.

When he caught sight of it, Roderick's thoughts went immediately to Maisie. He should have been relieved to find his ship, but instead found himself thinking of her, and his blood pumped a little faster. In a stolen moment of wry contemplation, he acknowledged his sorry state. Apparently he would never be rid of dreams and desires when it came to Maisie from Scotland.

They hung back until Brady rejoined them. "No more than six men on deck, one on the jetty side."

Roderick nodded at Gilhooly, who'd been given the most important task of all, that of causing a distraction. It was his specialty. He often went ahead of them when they docked in London to lure the excise men away on false missions.

Gilhooly nodded and pulled a flask of rum from his pocket. Uncorking it, he took a long swig, then sprinkled some on his coat before meandering off down the jetty toward the stern of the ship.

A few moments later Roderick heard his drunken carousing as he bellowed up at the rail. "You up there, fetch out the captain of the *Libertas,* for he owes me wages. I was told the ship had returned and I want my purse now."

By the sound of it he was making a good show, because there was a lot of noisy stumbling and what might even have been a dislodged barrel rolling across the jetty.

Roderick signaled his men, then jerked his head, indicating they should follow. As they approached the ship he saw that lanterns were being held aloft and predictably being carried to the stern, where Gilhooly had been told to draw them.

Roderick led the way and clambered up the net that hung down from the bow of the ship, wondering briefly at how his wounded shoulder did not give out. He could hear the navy men shouting back at Gilhooly and telling him to go away, for the captain was not available, nor would he be.

That is where you are mistaken, Roderick thought to himself as he vaulted quietly over the railing onto the deck.

Moving as quickly as he could, he waved the other men up. Once they were crouched behind him, he ducked down and crossed the deck. Using the masts and the shadows they managed to conceal their approach until they came up behind the navy watchmen. Roderick counted five leaning over the railing, lanterns held aloft. The naval officer who was stationed on the jetty below was now in a full-blown argument with Gilhooly. The men observing from the ship were conversing with each other and laughing.

Roderick looked back over his shoulder. He had two dozen men in position, grouped to take one man down each. They were under strict instructions to do as little lasting damage as possible, for Roderick didn't want the navy to add that to his list of misdemeanors. He was already going to have to rename the ship and register it over again in Holland, in order for them to disappear away to the distant seas. But he knew he could trust his men to handle it well. He raised his hand, nodded, and they went in.

The confrontation was swift and easily managed, Roderick and his crew having the benefit of surprise. When one of the navy men dropped his lantern, it splashed into the waters below, and a shout rang up from the jetty. It was short-lived, for Gilhooly knew precisely when to turn on the officer at his side. With the exception of a few muffled exclamations of rage, Roderick and his men took down their opponents in seconds.

Clyde seemed to have more of a struggle with his quarry for Roderick heard the scuffle. It seemed they exchanged a few words in anger, but Clyde insisted he could deal with it when others stepped in.

Young Adam appeared with lengths of rope from the storeroom, and they bound the men hand and foot, gagged them with their own neckerchiefs and began to haul them across the deck to the hatch.

"Into the hold, Captain?"

"Aye. Take them with you. We'll release them when we set sail from the agreed meeting point along the coast, beyond Broughty Castle. I'd prefer to let them loose in Dundee, but I don't want them to raise the alarm before we fetch Gregor."

While the crew busied themselves securing the navy watchmen below, Roderick did a quick pass through the ship. No one else was aboard. To his amusement, he found that their secret cargo of French wine had not yet been discovered.

When the men assembled on deck, he gave the final instructions. "Bring up the anchor as soon as I am dockside."

"I will stay with you, Captain," Clyde said.

Roderick was surprised. The old man hated to be on land. But Roderick knew better than to argue with him. The sooner the ship pulled up anchor and left the harbor, the better. It was also several hours until dawn, when Roderick could make contact with Gregor Ramsay, and the company would be appreciated. Then he thought he saw a mischievous twinkle in the old man's eye.

Trick of the moonlight, no more, he assumed.

Once they were back on shore, Clyde ran on ahead to alert the shipman who'd stayed with the rowboats to rejoin the ship. Then Clyde and Roderick disappeared into the streets of Dundee in search of a mug of ale and a comfortable seat until dawn broke and the notary's office opened.

In the early morning light the two of them made their way to the notary's office. The streets were no longer deserted. Carts were being wheeled to the marketplace, and Roderick and Clyde moved alongside them as much as possible, hoping their presence would not be noticed by anyone who might recognize them or know of their troubles with the navy.

Even though Roderick had to lurk about like a thief after stealing back his own ship, it was good to have his feet back on Scottish soil. It made him think of forgotten times, of his parents—both long gone to their graves—and of the smell of the bracken as he'd roamed the far hills as a child, hunting with his father. Roderick had to admit there was no place on earth where his feet felt as right as this, on Scottish ground.

They kept their hats pulled down low on their brows as they made their way to the notary's office. It was there they'd agreed Gregor Ramsay would leave word of his whereabouts. On the one hand Roderick hoped that Gregor was ready to depart, and quickly. On the other, he hoped that his partner hadn't witnessed the sorry sight of the *Libertas* sailing into Dundee with a navy flag hoisted aloft.

Once the bookkeeper arrived and unlocked the door, Roderick nodded at Clyde. "You'll wait outside?"

"Aye, I'll keep watch."

Roderick had been expecting to be told the name of nearby lodgings. Instead, the bookkeeper handed him a letter written in Gregor's own hand.

It was with some curiosity that Roderick opened it. Perhaps Gregor was requesting they wait a few days, which would be a problem because the navy would be on their trail soon enough. Frowning, he read the letter.

Roderick,

I hope that you and the men of the Libertas *have fared well. If you are reading this, it means you did not receive the word I sent to France to notify you that I will not be rejoining the* Libertas *at this time. As you know, I suspected my task in Fife could take longer than the six months we had agreed. That was not the case. The task took very little time indeed to reach its natural conclusion. However, my life took on a very different direction shortly after I parted ways with you.*

As you have so often pointed out to me, I needed to be more honest with myself and seek the truth, not revenge. I am not so clear-minded as you. It was in my search for justice that I discovered what I believed to be my true path. And you were correct when you joked it would be a lass that would change my manner of thinking on family matters.

We are headed to the Highlands, and if my calculations are correct and you have returned to Dundee by the agreed date in September, I will shortly be pledging myself to my bride. I would have done it weeks ago, but she insisted that we spend four seasons together in order to see if we were truly well matched. It is a Highland tradition amongst some of the clans. She is a stubborn sort, but I argued it down to two seasons and we will be wed before the old festival of Samhain, so you will see how well matched I think we are.

We have broken our journey north and lodge in rooms in Inverness. I've taken this opportunity to write you this second letter. Soon we will head onward to the far reach of the Highlands, to a village called Fingal, where my woman's clan hails from. She has many kin there and we'll be able to build a croft of our own. Finally, I will be able to honor my father—Hugh Ramsay—in a way he would have admired, by establishing a good smallholding for my family, just as he tried to do for me. I will be wed and settled before winter comes, all being well. Raise a glass to cheer us on our way, old friend. Drink to me and my bride, Jessie Taskill.

Gregor

On his first reading of the letter Roderick was mighty amused at the information contained within. Gregor Ramsay had lost his heart to a woman, and he planned to make his home on dry land! Much like himself, Gregor had been entirely set against such a course, but apparently he'd changed his tune rapidly after spending a few days in Scotland.

Did it affect every man that way? Roderick wondered.

Not only did Gregor's news startle and amuse him, but Roderick was astonished to find that his cohort was many, many miles from here in the far north. He had to read the letter again to be sure he'd got it right.

By the second reading the laughter on his lips faded as

his attention was caught by the woman's name. *Taskill. Jessie Taskill.* He clutched the letter tightly, reading the name over and over.

Maisie had confided her family name to him. It had to be her sister. Hadn't she mentioned a twin, and talked about returning to the Highlands to find her? It had to be one and the same.

Memories crowded in on him, other odd things that Maisie had said. She'd quizzed him about carrying another woman aboard the *Libertas,* stating that she felt an odd connection with the name Gregor Ramsay. If that was true, was it her witchcraft that had made her sense the link between him and Gregor, and his new bride? Roderick marveled at the very idea.

Whatever the cause, he knew there was destiny in it. He also knew that Maisie had to find her kin. Regardless of his own needs, his sense of justice and honesty demanded that he supply her with this vital piece of information she had spent her life longing for.

Foreign emotions erupted within Roderick. He needed to find her, to tell her. To see her. How the hell would he ever find her again, though? Futile, fledgling hopes were quickly shattered when he considered that problem.

Thanking the bookkeeper, he took his leave.

"Are we to wait for Ramsay?" Clyde asked when he emerged.

Roderick forced himself to slow his pace when he noticed the old man struggling to keep up with him, having trouble managing his limp on dry land. Clyde was born to be aboard ship. Some men had sworn allegiance to the sea and would never give it up for a woman. Others could be swayed. Gregor had. Could he be swayed, as well? Roderick wondered.

He shook his head. His immediate concern was to find Maisie and tell her about her sister's whereabouts, not because he must know if she wanted him or not. At least, that's what he convinced himself of in his frustration.

"Gregor Ramsay will not be rejoining us. He's decided to wed and stay on dry land."

Clyde nearly keeled over in shock.

"And you must be off to the ship, for I have business to attend to that will keep me in Dundee for at least a day."

The old man drew to a halt.

Roderick kept walking, but then stopped. The demand for an explanation was beating against his back as surely as if Clyde had been pounding his fists there. Roderick turned back. "Women, they are nothing but trouble," he declared.

Clyde pondered a moment, then broke into a wide, toothless grin. "I knew you would see sense and go after the lass. You can't let a woman like that roam free. She's born to be with you."

"You've changed your tune."

"Just because I am wary doesn't mean I cannot see the truth. That Jezebel is a courageous woman, and a clever one." He narrowed his eyes. "And if I am not mistaken she has looked after you well."

"You talk in riddles." Roderick didn't want to hear any of it. He felt a duty to alert Maisie to her sister's whereabouts, but that was all he was going to allow himself to feel.

Clyde chortled. "I see your shoulder does not bother you

so much this morning." He nodded at Roderick's coat, darkly stained with dried blood.

Roderick was about to respond when he realized Clyde had a point. Gingerly, he rotated his shoulder and found it perfectly mended.

The old man reached over, poked about inside Roderick's coat and tugged back his shirt. "No blood upon the bandage, she healed you while you rested in the rowboat. You were too busy thinking about the *Libertas* to even notice."

His eyes twinkled.

Roderick grasped his clothing and pulled it back, tearing off the makeshift bandage that had been applied to him in the rowboat. There was not a mark upon him. And yes, now that he thought on it his shoulder had not even bothered him while he climbed the nets onto the ship the night before. She'd healed him, just as earlier she'd healed Adam, and from a distance, too. It shocked Roderick to the marrow. He'd seen her magic that night in the hold of the ship, but this made his heartbeat falter. "Witchcraft."

"Aye, but it is not so frightening when the witch is fighting in your corner."

Roderick peered at the old man. Clyde might talk in riddles, yet quite frequently he talked sense, too. Could it really be true, that she had taken the gun in order to save him, knowing that she could heal him?

His mood shifted, a weight lifting from him. He couldn't assume it was true, but he must seek her out with the information he had for her, and get to the truth of it. It was his way.

"Go and fetch her back. It was you she wanted to be with.

I caught her looking at you all the while when she was above deck, and you the same, like two young sweethearts."

Roderick stared at Clyde in dismay. He'd always known the old man was a watchful, canny sort, but hadn't realized that he himself had been scrutinized alongside Maisie.

"Captain, she went quietly only because I told her your life would be spared if she did."

Roderick was startled anew. If that was true, and he had no reason to doubt Clyde, ever, it changed everything. "How can I go fetch her," he declared, feeling even more frustrated than he had been before, "when I do not know where she is?"

"She and the man they called her guardian were taken to the naval garrison."

Her guardian was with her. That blackened Roderick's mood. He was even more astonished that Clyde knew so much. "How do you know that?"

"I forced it out of my quarry last night, before I lumped him on the head." He gave a wide grin. "I pulled off his hat and wig, put my dirk behind his ear and told him I'd spare his ears if he told me what I wanted to know."

"Why did you do that and put yourself at risk?"

"Because I knew the question was in your head and would remain stuck there. It was my duty to ask it."

"I'm grateful."

"So now you have no excuse."

"I can find her and assure myself she is safe, but there is no hope in this mistaken notion you have of sweethearts.... And she is fully able to defend herself if she pleases, we all know that." Roderick paced up and down, frustrated. The fact that he could go to her only addled his head more. "She's destined for the Highlands and I'm a seafaring man."

Clyde lifted his shoulders, eyes twinkling.

Roderick stared at him, and then something in him gave way. He nodded. "Go to the ship, ready the men for departure. I will find her."

"And you'll bring her back with you?"

Again he felt thwarted. "If I did, the crew would have her walk the plank."

"Leave the men to me. It is me who muddled their thoughts, and can put them straight." Clyde gripped Roderick's arm. "Bring her back with you. She is meant to be with you aboard the *Libertas*."

He shook his head. "She seeks her kin in the Highlands, but if she needs me, and the men are agreeable to it, we will take her there before we head for Holland."

Clyde nodded. "I'll go to the ship. Leave the men to me. They were already coming round. Brady is the only one fixed in his mind. You fetch your Jezebel, and be quick about it."

I must be mad, Roderick reflected as he shook hands with Clyde and then hurried through the streets to the garrison.

When he got there, he knew with certainty that he was mad. It was a fortress, with soldiers standing all around. Lowering his head, Roderick passed them by, boldly daring them to call him out. There was a whispered discussion going on amongst them, news of a disappearing ship in the night making them uneasy, no doubt.

As he skirted the building he could find no entrance that was unguarded, but luck was on his side when he came upon a delivery cart where three men were unloading barrels.

He observed the action from a ways off, and as the third lifted a barrel onto his shoulder and headed into the garrison, Roderick strode to the cart and lifted a barrel in turn. Shielding his face from view with his arm, he fell in line behind the three men and entered the building.

chapter Twenty-Two

Controlling Cyrus turned out to be much easier than Maisie had hoped. He was responsive to her whispered enchantments; he had an open mind to witchcraft, which made it easier for her to sway him and guide his thoughts. It was a relief to see the wickedness in him subdued. After the years where he had kept her grateful and needy, and had so often caused her to feel uncomfortable in his presence, Maisie felt there was justice in controlling him for just these few hours, before she escaped his special noose of companionship.

If she did not focus on him entirely, however, Cyrus became disagreeable. It was as if he sensed he wasn't in control, but couldn't understand why. His mood at those times wasn't pleasant. That was the situation now, while they sat over breakfast, and her thoughts had been whisked away to Roderick Cameron once again.

They were provided lodgings overnight in the naval garrison in Dundee. Mercifully, the chamber Maisie was given had a bolt on the door. She slept only fitfully and out of pure exhaustion, then awoke at dawn to troubled thoughts and with an aching heart.

That morning, a servant brought her a clean gown gifted to her by the wife of one of the officers. It was a simple design, but fitted her well. There were also clean undergarments and stockings. Warm water was provided for bathing, and when Maisie studied herself in the looking glass, she decided that, all things considered, her appearance was not too disgraceful. Shadows under her eyes were the only outward signs that she'd been split from the man who had so quickly come to hold a high place in her heart. Now that her allegiance was with Roderick—whom she might never see again—she found it harder with each passing moment to even look at Cyrus.

As if he knew that was the case, Cyrus had stationed her opposite him at the table, where warm mead, bread and cheese had been served. Maisie glanced at her surroundings, a room of some grandeur with a long oak table for feasting. A window high up at the end of the room caught the light and poured it over the table. Weapons and shields were mounted here and there on the walls. Their breakfast had been served on a smaller, less ostentatious table to one side, and Maisie attempted to get some of the food down while she assessed Cyrus's state of mind. It wasn't good. Once her attention drifted and she did not sway him to her way of thinking, he became uneasy.

"I still cannot believe you were so reckless," he stated.

Maisie noticed then how bitter and arrogant his tone was. Despite his romantic overtures toward her, it indicated he still viewed her as a wayward witch-child who needed to be watched over, a child who had no mind of her own and would be grateful for his protection.

That had been the case, previously, but Maisie Taskill had matured greatly over the past days, and she'd been shown that even a powerful man, a leader of other men, could speak to her with respect—and adore her as a woman. How she ached for him, her seafaring lover. And the more Cyrus repeated the naval captain's question and asked her if she had been defiled, the more it led her dangerously close to declaring she had been defiled in all manner of ways and enjoyed every one of them.

The need to speak her mind was growing acute.

"You should have talked to me about your desire to return to Scotland," Cyrus continued. "It is a dangerous undertaking. Your heritage could so easily bring you to justice without me there to guard you...." His pause was deliberate, to make her afraid and keep her that way. "But I would have conceded, if it kept you content."

She was valuable to him. The lengths he had gone to in order to recapture her had proved that. During the hours since she had been reunited with her master, she'd forced herself to believe that he was humoring her, allowing her to spend time in Scotland before returning to London with her in tow. Nevertheless, Maisie could barely stomach the thought of spending a full day with him while they talked about hunting for her kin, kin that he had lied to her about. She'd acted repentant in order to be sure Roderick and his men had the best chance of escape, but she knew in her heart she couldn't maintain that for much longer. All she wanted to do was vanish before his eyes. Soon, she would do just that. Steal away and find her way north.

The cautious approach would have been to apologize and sweeten him. Maisie didn't feel like being cautious. She pushed the food away. "I have often mentioned it."

"You didn't, however, mention your intention to pursue it alone, to put yourself at risk in the hands of lawless men."

What could she say? Cyrus would never be able to think of her in the same way again, and yet he seemed fixed on keeping her. When she looked deep into his eyes, she knew that he still wanted her, still pretended to love her. The dark bitterness she saw there chilled her. He meant to make her suffer for her transgression. Punishment would be ongoing.

She would turn her magic on him and pacify him. She would have to when she tried to leave him again. But right then she had a need for the truth to be unveiled. There was nothing else for it; she would have to voice her feelings on the matter. "Cyrus, I am grateful to you, but as a guardian. I cannot be your lover."

The tension in the room thickened, sapping the space of air.

The look in his eyes turned darker still, his temper growing.

"You will warm to the idea, given time." He attempted to smile at her. Given his black mood, it only made him look more sinister.

Maisie knotted her fingers together in her lap, determined to press on. She shook her head. "Cyrus, it can never be. Even if the nature of my affection for you altered, I cannot forget the things you've done. You have molded me and used me to further your own cause, and that has become more apparent to me over the years." She dared not mention him poisoning Mama Beth.

"I have protected you and nurtured your craft!" His eyes were bright with fury.

Maisie felt it, and wondered if he'd blinded himself to the dark nature of his deeds, believing his actions to be just and deserved. She couldn't let him think that, had to show him the error of his ways or he would never change. "What about Gilbert Ridley and the courtesan who ruined his life? It was the very same woman I enamored him with. It was the love spell you encouraged me to do when I was still a child, wasn't it?"

Cyrus looked astonished.

Did he think she would forget? "Don't be surprised. You've educated me well and you tamed my fey ways. I've grown into a more observant woman than I might otherwise have been. How could I not notice things about you, the man closest to me, my master and my keeper? Did you really think I wouldn't question your motives, once I was old enough to address them?"

Cyrus had paled, as if his fury had been dampened by the truth. "Gilbert Ridley had wronged me in the past. He deserved what he got."

"But you cannot play with people's lives that way, Cyrus. Just because someone has wronged us doesn't give us the right to destroy them."

He frowned heavily. His movements were erratic, his eyes flashing as he tried to address her comments. "You don't know the extent of it. He humiliated me amongst my peers."

"But you knew that my magic, my heritage, was to be used for good. You twisted me into something I shouldn't be. I would never have done those things if you hadn't duped me."

"You were eager to explore your magic." His voice had grown quiet, and his desperate tone revealed that his argument was crumbling.

"And you took advantage of that. I could never stay with a man who did such things."

He buckled visibly, his elbows on the table, his head in his hands. "Margaret, please. We can discuss these matters together, when you are my wife."

Maisie was incredulous. The burning question that remained in her mind was something she would have to know or forever be haunted by it. "Cyrus, did you poison Beth?"

His head shot up and he looked at her with astonishment. His eyes shifted left and right, and she wondered whether she would even be able to tell if he was giving her the truth. She wouldn't rest until she knew.

"Who told you that?"

"Did you poison her or not?"

"Pray tell me what made you think such a thing?"

Still he avoided her question. "You were observed putting something in her broth."

Lips pressed together determinedly, he glared at her. When he eventually did speak, it was through gritted teeth. "It was a tincture of mandrake root to aid her rest even while she was in pain."

"Mandrake?" Maisie was aghast. Mandrake was exceedingly dangerous in large doses. Nor was he a true healer, one such as she, who had come from a long line of gifted Highlanders.

Cyrus struck his fist on the table, rattling the dishes. "You are not the only one who learned about healing herbs and potions when we studied together. The physician told me her organs were weak and she might suffer at the end."

He knew enough to cover his tracks. A large and fatal dose could be hidden by his good intention to ease her pain.

"You seem overly concerned with your wife's quick end." Maisie fired the accusation at him.

"Beth lingered too long." His voice was oily as he tried to justify murdering his wife. "It wasn't good for her. It wasn't good for any of us." His mouth twisted. He couldn't hide it, his true intentions, his wicked nature.

It was all the confirmation Maisie needed. "You could have asked me to do that, if your real purpose was to make her more comfortable. I begged you to let me help her, and you wouldn't allow it."

"Don't be foolish. I didn't want us to be at her bedside together! You are the future, my future. She is gone from us now and I am glad of it."

There it was. He'd been driven by his desire for Maisie, his obsession with what could be. Even now, since she had pulled away, he was still struggling to maintain his hold on her, talking of their future together.

How sad it was that Beth had gone to her grave knowing the worst of her husband. She knew he desired his ward instead, and she no longer trusted him. Maisie felt intense sorrow and guilt, knowing it was her arrival in their lives that had brought such a terrible situation to pass.

Before she had a chance to say another word the door burst open.

A serving girl tottered into the room. The look on her face was fearful and her cheeks were flushed as if with fever. Maisie quickly surmised something was badly amiss.

A low command was issued from beyond her, and the girl entered the room fully. She was all atremble, and it was little wonder, for there was a man at her back directing her, a cutlass raised in his hand and pointed between her shoulder blades.

Roderick.

Maisie shot to her feet, one hand covering her mouth to stifle the cry of disbelief that rose to her lips. It was really him. His hair was wild and his coat stained dark where she had wounded him, but she was grateful to see he was fully healed, moving easily, as if he had not been wounded at all. Her chest swelled with longing, with joy and pride.

Cyrus turned in his seat, but not quickly enough to gain the measure of the situation.

Urging the servant on, Roderick slammed the door behind them and then pushed her to one side, warning her with a glance to stay there and be quiet. In the blink of an eye he was at Cyrus's back instead.

Cyrus had been rising to his feet, but Roderick pushed him back down onto his seat. With one hand he gripped him by the hair, pulling his head back, then rested his cutlass across the base of his throat.

Light from the window glinted on the polished blade.

The arrival of an assailant seemed to bring Cyrus to his senses, and he gripped the arms of his chair and narrowed his eyes as he looked up at the man who held a sharp blade to his gullet.

"Make no move, and I might let you live," Roderick instructed.

Cyrus gave a twisted smile, staring directly up at him. "If you knew the power that could be unleashed in this room, you would turn on your heel and flee this place."

"Oh, I know the power, for I have witnessed it in her myself." Roderick looked across at her meaningfully.

Their eyes locked. Maisie wondered if he had come for retribution, but the deep affection she saw in his eyes assured her that wasn't the case. Emotion welled in her. The way he looked at her, as adoring and possessive as ever—despite the trouble she had brought upon him and his men—made her feel as if her knees might give way. She'd thought him forever lost to her, feared she would surely never see him again, yet here he was. Then he smiled at her, and she felt as if she was alight with joy.

"Then you should be more wary," Cyrus responded angrily, but clearly unsure what was going on.

"Silence," Roderick ordered, leaning over Cyrus to enforce his command. "I have come because I have something to tell the lady. You would be wise to let me deliver the message before you irritate me further. I am not in the best of humor." He lifted his head and looked at her again, maintaining his death grip on Cyrus.

He had something to say to her? Maisie waited with bated breath.

"I know where your sister, Jessie, is. I will happily escort you to her."

It was not what she'd expected or hoped he would say, but his words nevertheless astonished and delighted her. "How do you know?"

"She is with Gregor Ramsay, the man I told you about." He gave Cyrus a glance, and Maisie saw that he didn't want to state their whereabouts, not while Cyrus listened. "I received word from Gregor this very morning."

Her mind raced back over what he'd said to her about his partner, and she felt suddenly enlightened. "That's why I sensed my sister, the connection, aboard the ship. Now I understand it."

"Margaret," Cyrus barked, addressing her with a stern stare. "Take action and get rid of this lawless heathen. He is trying to dupe you. Your sister might not even be alive. He is luring you with promises he cannot keep."

"The lady knows that I do not offer her promises that I will not do everything in my power to keep."

It was true. Even when his men turned against him, he'd planned a way to deliver her safely onto Scottish soil. Maisie felt light-headed, thrilled by his comment and the way he looked at her as he delivered it in that gruff, determined way of his. He did not hate her for what she had brought upon them. Never had she been more thankful for anything. It gave her strength.

Moving slowly, she stepped out from the table, one eye on the door.

The serving girl had moved closer to it, cowering by the hinges. How long did they have before the men who guarded this place were told of an intruder's presence? Would she be able to hold them back by magic, should they come for Roderick?

"Cyrus, I have made clear how we stand with one another, and you must accept that I do not intend to stay with you."

"Never!"

She stared at him, aching from the pain and disloyalty that Mama Beth had experienced. "You called this man a heathen. Many would call *me* a heathen, but you told me that did not matter. It does matter. It always will matter."

"It doesn't matter to me."

"Oh, but it does, for it is my *heathen* craft you wanted, and all that would be unveiled when you claimed me as your lover."

"Margaret—"

"You have played with the truth, and you have used me to gain power and prestige."

Roderick cursed beneath his breath and tightened his grip on Cyrus. Maisie realized she would have to be cautious, for now that Roderick was sure of Cyrus's identity, he looked on him with revulsion and anger. "Say the word and I will put an end to him," he growled.

"No!"

Roderick did not relinquish his grip on Cyrus's hair, but grinned. "Can I at least hit him?"

Maisie sighed. Men, it seemed, relished injuring their opponent in some way even after they had claimed the woman.

Cyrus shifted uneasily, struggling to maintain eye contact with her while pinned to his seat by a lethal weapon. "Get rid of him, and I assure you, you will come to understand how much you mean to me."

It was he who looked betrayed now, he who looked pained and aggrieved and heartbroken. He did love her, twisted though it was.

"I cannot," she responded, and braced herself to tell him why. "I cannot, because this man is my lover, and I care for him deeply."

Roderick's mouth curled, and he looked across at her proudly. "And that is why I found myself healed."

She nodded.

The moment was broken by the sound of Cyrus kicking out at the table before him.

Across the room, the servant reached for the door handle, dragged the door open and took flight.

For a moment Maisie thought Cyrus would slit his own neck, for he twisted and bucked against the blade of the cutlass as he tried to break free of Roderick's grasp.

Roderick cursed, glanced back at the open door, drawn by the sound of the serving girl's departure.

Cyrus broke free. He flitted to the far wall and lifted down a sword from the mounted display. "You gave yourself to this oaf?" he shouted, as he approached Roderick, sword at the ready.

"I gave myself to an honest man."

"A mistake I will obliterate from our lives forever." He lunged in Roderick's direction, weapon lifted.

"Roderick, be careful, for he is a skilled swordsman."

Roderick looked Cyrus up and down with some doubt, then stepped forward, defended and quickly returned.

Maisie watched, aghast. Their movements were fast, each man driven by his own, very different, belief in justice. Their blades flashed in the morning sunlight that cut through the room from the far window, the clash of steel on steel a symphony of sound that assaulted her senses, magnifying the terror she felt. If Roderick were to perish now, her life would be over, for he was everything to her.

"If you intend to challenge me, sire, you should perhaps recognize your limitations." Roderick wielded his cutlass again, easily deflecting the more refined blade Cyrus used.

Through her terror Maisie saw that he was scarcely working at all, while Cyrus—overwrought and with panic in his eyes—was determined there would be bloodshed.

They traded thrusts and parries, their blades ringing.

Over and again her heart leaped.

Then Roderick turned his back on Cyrus and Maisie cried out, fearing for his life. But with a quick maneuver, his cutlass shot out as he spun around. Cyrus, who was moving at full pelt to stab his opponent's back, was impaled on Roderick's lethal blade.

Maisie's breath stalled. With a darting glance, she tried to make sense of it. It had happened so quickly, but then she saw it. Roderick turned away to lure him, and Cyrus, in his frenzy, had impaled himself on his opponent's blade.

When Roderick pulled his weapon free, Cyrus staggered backward and fell to the ground, his body awkwardly splayed on the hearth rug. His limbs vibrated and shook, and he cried out, his words garbled.

Maisie crossed to his side.

His breath gurgled in his throat, blood bubbling at the corner of his mouth. When she knelt beside him, she saw his eyes had faded. His lips moved, mouthing her name silently. Even in death, he could not let her go. There could be no other way. Even if she ran and ran, he would always pursue her.

But now he was almost gone. As much as she was relieved that it was over, it wasn't in her nature to have him leave in this way, in immense pain. Fingers to her lips, she drew the magical words from deep inside, then blew them on their way. As her words touched Cyrus, his body slumped. The death rattle of his last breath rang into the silence, and Cyrus Lafayette was at peace.

Roderick stared down at the slumped body of his ill-fated opponent, intrigued. "Come, we had better depart this place and quickly, for the servant girl fled a few moments ago."

Maisie nodded. He picked up his weapon with one hand and reached for her with the other. Maisie ran into his arms.

He quickly led her out of the room and into the corridor beyond. How good it felt to be pressed to his side once more, and to feel his strong arm embracing her. His body, now so familiar to her, felt like a haven.

"You came for me," she whispered, and glanced up at him as they hastened away. She could still scarcely believe it was true.

"I had a good excuse. I had a message to pass along."

"Is that the only reason?"

"No."

How she loved the honest emotion she saw in his eyes, and how she would have missed it if she'd never seen him again. He'd not only made her passionate and strong, he'd warmed her spirit and set her free.

"Now use your magic well, my lady. We must hasten out

of here and make our way along the coast, to where the *Libertas* is safely hidden in a cove beyond Broughty Castle. And we must leave no tracks when we go."

"You regained the ship?"

"Of course we did, because we were aided by magical weather." He looked at her affectionately. "We rowed into Dundee when it was dark, and found the ship had been left under a skeleton watch. It seemed very easy to get it back, in fact. I wondered if I was in possession of a lucky charm."

"You believe the magic and you do not fear me?" She clutched at his coat.

"From nearly the first time it was mentioned I could not dismiss it. However, I'd rather we were on the same side."

"We have always been on the same side, lover of mine. Once you had bedded me our destinies became entwined, because it became a matter of the heart."

He touched her lips with one finger, smiling all the while. "I'm glad we are finally agreed on something."

Maisie could not argue with that. "The men will not be angry?"

"Clyde has gone ahead to prepare them for your return. He will win them over. Brady will be a tough nut to crack, but I will ensure your safety, don't fret. Now let us be on our way," he added, "for we must reunite you with your kin."

Maisie nodded and followed his lead, ready to create havoc with her magic if necessary, to aid their escape. But as they hurried along the long corridors of the garrison, she wondered on his words. Was that all he wanted—to reunite her with her kin? If so, did he do so out of a sense of duty, or love?

Maisie wanted to know, but for now it was enough to

find her hand in his, and to be close at his side again. She happily followed her lover, grateful for whatever time they might still have together.

chapter Twenty-Three

The late-September winds on the North Sea were fierce but magically generous to them, hastening their passage north along the coast of Scotland. Roderick didn't ask, but he knew it was Maisie's doing.

Now that she'd been accepted by someone other than her guardian, she didn't hide her fey nature as much as she had. Moonlight glittered strangely in her eyes and her magic was all around. As surely as an eerie sea mist it enveloped him, drawing him into her voluptuous spell. Roderick didn't fight it or reason with it anymore, because she was everything he wanted, and if she would have him, he would protect and fight for her until his dying breath.

Clyde had surely worked his own sort of magic, because the men nodded and welcomed her aboard when the two of them rejoined the ship. The older men adopted a grudging, wary acceptance of her. The younger lads, such as Adam, were more curious, and their eyes glittered with excitement over whispered exchanges. Sometimes Roderick would hear them discussing her in pairs, comparing notes on what they thought had happened and what had occurred by magic. That made him chuckle. None crossed her, and few had words with him on the matter. Brady was the least accepting, inevitably so, and he glowered at Roderick as he went about his duties.

When Roderick spoke with him, Brady defended his view. "How can you be sure she will not turn, once she has safely reached her destination?"

"She will not turn on us. Believe me, if she wished to harm us it would've happened long before now. She has not hurt one of us, despite the sorry conditions that were forced upon her."

Brady pursed his lips, clearly unwilling to concede, even though there was a touch of regret in his eyes.

"She uses her natural powers judiciously and does not mean to hurt anyone."

"That may be, but I cannot bring myself to trust her."

"I know that, and I cannot change your mind on the matter. But you trust me, and I will make sure you return to your family in fine health and with a pocket heavy with coins."

The first mate grumbled beneath his breath.

Roderick took the opportunity to raise a question. "Brady, there is something I must ask you. If I were to leave the ship awhile, would you be prepared to take on the captainship?"

Startled, Brady peered at him. Eventually, he replied. "Aye, I would. But what nonsense is this? Surely you do not mean to leave the ship for a woman?"

"I ask you only in theory, but I need to know."

The man gave a wry smile and shook his head. "If it happens and I am needed, I will step in, but I'll tell you this. Dealing with a woman on land is a hard enough task without taking on one such as her!"

Roderick laughed. "I am not certain of my plans, but it sets my mind at rest that you will take my place should it be necessary."

He grasped Brady's shoulder, nodded, and they went about their duties. Planting the thought in the sailor's mind proved to be a useful distraction, but Roderick had done so because he found himself eager to escort Maisie onward to her kin, if she would accept his protection awhile longer. It did the trick, however, giving Brady something else to ponder on, aside from the powerful witch they carried aboard ship. He spent less time keeping track of her whereabouts and more standing at the helm, taking stock, as if preparing himself for what might be. It suited Roderick well.

Meanwhile, he kept the ship within sight of land as much as possible, for he knew it was important to Maisie, who spent hours at the railing, staring at her homeland. Roderick saw that as the reunion with her family approached, she grew more deeply thoughtful. It was a big moment in her life, and he was glad he could help her with it.

He did not quiz her about the man who had taken him on in Dundee, the man she called her guardian. What had been said in that room revealed enough for him to take action, and to know there was just cause. Maisie would tell him more when she was ready. Roderick also had enough sense to know that she had to mourn that person, even though he was a rum lot, an unscrupulous man who'd meant only to use her. She had not offered that man her virginity, and that was good enough for Roderick, for now.

At night, when he held her in his arms, she clung to him and claimed him, requesting his lovemaking in a much more forthright manner than she had before. As if liberated by all that had passed in between, her mood was wild.

It was as if they were stars aligned. Even when the seas grew restless. Every toss and roll of the ship only brought them closer together, every move either of them made in tune with the other. It seemed as if there was a link between them and the restless skies above. It was her, he knew it was. She was like a channel through which he communicated with the wild oceans he had tried for all these years to master. But now it was her he wanted to master.

Her power, her witchcraft, was manifest at these times. She glowed, her eyes alight with passion, her body moving against his as if she were a wild creature and knew no rules about decorum and restraint. Roderick reveled in that, proud of her lusty ways. They were driven, fueled by their deep passion for one another.

Neither of them, it seemed, could get enough. Roderick stayed hard after she found her release, and she rolled him over and rode him, their naked bodies misted with sweat as they shared every morsel of pleasure. How radiant she was, how confident in this, the thing she'd known least of when they met. It made him proud to see her so liberated.

He sat up and stroked her breasts, sliding his hands over the hot, damp skin beneath the pale globes, while she rocked back and forth on his length.

The rhythmic clutch of her body on his cock was almost too much for him. "Maisie?"

She nodded. "It's like nothing else I've ever felt. This makes me burn with passion."

Her gaze locked with his and her hands twined around his neck as she squeezed his erection, drawing him off again. He sank his head into her neck, his arms enclosing her, locking them together while they both spilled anew.

When they finally rested, she lifted up on her elbow to look at him. "I did not care for Cyrus, not the way you might think."

"You don't have to tell me."

"But you wanted to know, and I find that I want to explain myself."

"Now that you don't have to?"

She laughed softly. "Yes. I only kept things from you to protect you, not that I did a very good job of it."

"I see that now."

"When my mother was put to death, Cyrus and his wife came and took me away to a better life. His wife wanted a child, and he said he did, too. But Cyrus wanted more than that—a young witch he could train and control. I didn't learn this until very recently, however. To me he was a teacher, someone who protected me and my craft."

"You were with them for a long time?"

"Ten years or thereabouts. I was a child when they came to Scotland looking for an orphan."

"You trusted them at first?"

"Not at first. I was in a terrible state, but Mama Beth was so kind, and Cyrus taught me to appreciate my secret nature.

Then things changed and I discovered that he had only kept me in order to become my suitor, my owner."

"What of his wife?"

Maisie rested her head on his shoulder. Roderick felt he knew the answer even before she said it, because he felt damp tears on his skin.

"She died at his hand, because he wanted me in her place."

Wrapping Maisie closer, Roderick stroked her hair, running his fingers through it before cupping the back of her head as he kissed her. That, he saw, was an immense burden to her, and understandably so.

"What of your childhood?" she said later. "You haven't said much about the time before you were at sea."

"That's because there's not much to tell. I was born in Dundee, an only child. We had very little. My father hunted for rabbits in the hills and sold them at market. I used to play down by the harbor and watch the ships come and go. The sea life called to me."

"Your parents?"

"Long gone. The men of the *Libertas* are the only family I know."

"And me. You have me now."

Do I? Roderick didn't know how to respond to that, so he rocked her gently in his arms, holding her close to him until she eventually dozed, and for a long time after.

On the second day of their voyage north from the Tay estuary, Roderick returned to his quarters to check on her. It seemed he could not go long without seeing her. The threat of imminent separation, no doubt. The very thought of it made him feel thwarted, useless and frustrated. In his heart, a battle was being fought. Love for a woman was forcing him onto a different path. Would she accept him at her side?

When he entered the cabin, she scarcely noticed, for she was poring over the letter from Gregor, reading it once again. She had already read it many times and marveled on it.

"You could recite the words without the page," Roderick said, to announce his presence more than anything.

She lifted her head and looked his way. The frown she'd worn disappeared, and her eyes lit at the sight of him.

That tugged at his heartstrings. How could he bear to be parted from this woman? It was the biggest dilemma of his life. If all he could do was see her safely to her kin and continue on with his responsibilities, then so be it. That steadfast reasoning only made him grumpier. Quickly, he crossed to her side.

"It is why I felt a connection here, because he'd been here before me, before he'd met my twin. It was so vague, but it was there nonetheless." She glanced at the page again and then around the quarters. "I feel it much more clearly now."

"You will always be a mystery to me, Maisie from Scotland, but I no longer question your ways."

His comment softened her expression and she looked at him with great fondness. "If it were not for you I might never have discovered where my sister was. I am forever grateful to you."

Roderick did not want her gratitude, he wanted her. Plain and simple, he felt unaccountably possessive, as if he had a right to own this woman, a woman who clearly could not be owned by anyone. "No, you would have found her, no matter what. I have merely hastened your path in the right direction."

She looked into his eyes, as if searching his soul, and it troubled Roderick so much that he turned away and went to his maps. The one currently laid out depicted in some detail the treacherous craggy coastline and coastal waters along the coast beyond Wick. Several of the older crewmen knew this coastline well, however, and they sailed safely.

A moment later she joined him, standing close to his side and wrapping her arm around his waist as they looked down at the map. "It would have taken me weeks to travel across the land. I have vague memories of our terrible journey south. You have done me a great service. I will never forget your kindness."

It was not kindness. He was driven by the thought that he would never see her again once he put her feet on dry land. Roderick had already had a taste of losing her and he didn't like it.

She had folded up Gregor's letter and set it on the table. "I have to keep reading it, to be sure."

"What is it you need to be sure of?" he asked tentatively. His curiosity was always rife, but he wanted her to open herself to him naturally, as she had started to do.

"All these years, I didn't even know whether my brother and sister were alive. Sometimes I would sense her, but I wasn't sure if it was just wishes and dreams, you know?" She gave him a sidelong glance and a half smile.

Roderick nodded. He did know. It was the way he felt about Maisie. It was as if they, too, were united, even when they were apart. But they had not spoken of it, and with so much at stake and their lives so different, he did not dare to broach the subject unless she did.

"Now I know she is alive, and she is safe with your friend Gregor as her protector."

"Gregor is a fiercely loyal man, especially when it comes to family. He left Fife for the sea because a great tragedy befell his family."

"He and Jessie have much in common, if that is the case." Maisie shook her head. "The letter mentions kin, but it doesn't mention Lennox. I wonder about him." She turned the letter over and looked at it, although her thoughts seemed far away.

"Perhaps your brother will be there, waiting for you?"

"It is possible. He was always chastising our mother for taking us to the Lowlands. He was not as adaptable as Jessie and I. But he was a hotheaded lad, and of the three of us he was the angriest. That has always worried me."

"Many a youth mired in anger grows into a man with purpose." Roderick was thinking of Gregor, whose soul had been in a dark place as a young man when they first met. Now, after doing what he had to do to put the past to rest, it appeared he was happily ensconced with a woman and planning to put down roots and build a croft of his own.

"I hope you're right. I hope that I will find them both there and that they haven't suffered much in the intervening years." She lowered her head and stared down at the letter.

Roderick could not bear to see her look fretful. The lingering questions about her brother and what had happened to them in the intervening years hampered her still.

"We will have you there well before your sister's hand-fasting."

He gave a wry smile, for it still surprised him to think of Gregor Ramsay putting down roots upon the land. If Gregor had, could he do it, too? He looked at Maisie. She would never be tied to a man such as him, not the way he wished. "Unfortunately, my maps do not give me much of an idea how far it is to your village from the coast. Fingal, yes?"

She nodded. "My mother used to say that you could smell the sea in the air, but only when the wind came in the right direction and you were perched on the highest crag. Some of the men went to the coast every once in a while to bring back fresh herring, so it cannot be too far."

"Some of the older men on the ship hail from the Highlands. Clyde will know how far it is, I warrant."

Later, when Roderick called on Clyde, he joined them to study the map. The mood became more wistful still. Roderick had thought calling the old man in on the matter would lighten the moment, but it didn't. Somehow it made it even more weighty and tense.

Clyde stared down at the map, nodding to himself. "I recall the name Fingal, and I think you could be there inside two days. You will need to purchase supplies, but my guess is inside a week."

Roderick frowned. Which was it? Two days or a week? "How long is it since you left?"

"How in God's name would I know?" Clyde said with a wry chuckle. "I cannot count, I do not know my age, and I am not sure when I left."

"Fair point." Roderick smiled at Maisie.

She returned the smile as she studied Clyde. "Why did you leave the Highlands?"

"For work, to find my fortune. Eight bairns my mother had, and I was the last."

"A good enough reason," she replied. "But why have you never gone back?"

Clyde still stared down at the map. "Fear."

Roderick was surprised.

"Fear of what?" Maisie asked.

"It not being how I remembered it. Sometimes the memory is better." He looked at her then. "You're braver than I, for you are making a return. Tell me, why is it that *you* left the Highlands?"

"Our father left us, and our mother followed him. Searching for him was a journey that broke us apart and broke our hearts."

Roderick listened to her tale of sadness and grief. He knew what her mother's quest had brought about, and he understood the sorrow he often saw in Maisie's eyes.

"I think our father turned his back on his clan and the magical ones, because he couldn't live with our mother's strange ways." She knotted her fingers together and glanced at them both quickly. "And who could blame him?"

That was a leading question. Roderick didn't want to say the wrong thing, so he said nothing. Neither did Clyde.

"He headed south to find his fortune. The last word he sent was that he was taking to the sea," she added. "Much like you, seeking a better life and a good wage."

Clyde lifted his head. "What was his name? I knew a man from Fingal once, a long while back."

"Roy, his name was Roy."

Clyde stayed for a silent moment, thoughtful, as he considered his reply. "Aye, I knew a man called Roy from Fingal, and now that I think on what you've said, I believe it was him, your father."

"You knew him?" Maisie's eyes lit with curiosity.

"I'm afraid that your father did not find his fortune at sea, for the sea took him. Perhaps within a year or two he was swept overboard in a heavy storm. I'm sorry to tell you this."

Maisie stared at him with a troubled expression, then shook her head. "I'm glad you told me, for you have solved a question that for many years haunted those of us he left behind."

Clyde nodded. "It is better to know the truth than to wonder endlessly."

"Thank you. I'm so glad you knew of him and remembered what had happened." She turned away and went to sit on the edge of the bed.

Clyde looked at Roderick for guidance.

Roderick nodded at him and the old man left. Roderick joined her sitting on the edge of the bed, took her in his arms and held her.

She wept silently, and clung to him with her forehead pressed against his neck. It only made Roderick ache to know who would hold her this way when she was troubled and he was not there. Then she chuckled.

Looking at her in surprise, he saw that her cheeks and lashes were damp with tears, but she was smiling. "It is for my mother I cried. I remember him, and for all those years we wanted to know what became of him, because we still loved him even though he left us. Yet now it is my mother I feel sorry for, thinking he was having a wild old time at sea. Perhaps it was better that way."

Maisie lifted her head and laughed, and Roderick smiled, too. He didn't quite understand the sentiments, but he was relieved that the burdens seem to have been lifted.

"You have helped me solve many riddles that have plagued my life, Roderick Cameron." Her eyes twinkled and she wiped away the tears that clung to her lashes.

He wanted to do more than help her solve riddles. "I will go with you. I'll take you to Fingal."

Maisie stared at him. "But your ship, your men?"

"Brady is capable enough. He can take charge while I am gone."

She wrapped her hand around Roderick's much larger, callused one. He stared down at it, noticing how different they were. She was a lady, and a witch, a woman he did not fully understand. He was a simple seafaring man with callused hands and rough ways.

"I treasure every moment we have together, but you must not feel obliged to care for me."

"I don't feel obliged. I want to escort you safely until you are with your people again. I promised I would take you to your destination."

"And I said my destination was Dundee, not Fingal."

"I stand by my word. I said I'd see you safely. I cannot let you travel alone, not now, not since we have grown close."

She smiled, but a different emotion shone in her eyes.

It made him want to hold her in his arms for a long time, too long, too tightly. So he shrugged. "Besides, I must speak with Gregor," he said, latching onto that fact. "It is not fair for him to be off marrying a woman without at least one of us there to witness it."

It was a good enough excuse, Roderick assured himself.

Then he looked at her again, and wondered why he needed an excuse to stay by her side.

chapter Twenty-Four

The ship dropped anchor in the bay of Kinlochbervie, the most northerly point on the west coast of Scotland that was accessible by sea, having a sandy beach to row a small boat upon. The coastline all around had been rugged and rocky, and their landing place looked like a haven to Maisie.

She stared at the small cluster of cottages, and beyond, at the land that rose up in front of them, majestic and breathtaking. *Home. The Highlands.* She felt the immensity of the moment unfurling inside her. It left her tremulous with excitement and anticipation, and yet nervous, too. It helped that Roderick was at her side.

Clyde volunteered to row them ashore, and when Roderick climbed out of the boat into the shallow waters, he asked him if he'd like to accompany them and set foot on his homeland. The old man shook his head, adamant that it would be unwise at this point in his life to take such a risk.

Maisie wasn't disappointed, but she understood. If Clyde were to return, it would be to discover that his older brothers and sisters had passed on, and the new bairns would not know him. She felt sure his people would welcome him anyway, but he loved the sea, and he loved what he held in his heart—that part of the Highlands that would always be his, no matter where in the world he was.

He looked at her for a long moment before he said goodbye. "I'm glad to have known you."

"Even though I am a Jezebel?"

"You are far better than every other Jezebel I have encountered." He chortled. The sound was a rare treat.

"I'm honored to have known you, too, Clyde."

He bowed over her hand before she climbed out of the boat to wade the last few feet with Roderick.

When they sat down on the beach to put their stockings and boots back on, it occurred to her that Roderick had not said goodbye, which led her to believe they had already exchanged words, and the shipmen would know when to expect him back.

Shortly after landing, Maisie found herself engaged in conversation with the folk who came out of the cottages to see who it was that had come ashore. Hearing their Highland burr, and exchanging words in Scottish Gaelic, Maisie knew how close to home she really was now. Roderick watched, smiling over at her, as she explained to three of the local women the purpose of their journey.

"I asked," she told him, "and they said we can be in Fingal by tomorrow morning."

Roderick purchased supplies aplenty, cheese and fresh baked bannocks, a skin full of water and one of mead, and a brace of recently caught fish. With detailed directions and descriptions of natural markers on the landscape to look out for, they set off.

As they began to make their way along the narrow path between the peaks and crags, heading inland toward Fingal, Maisie could scarcely believe it. She was not only overcome by the beauty of the place, she recalled it—as if her memories were bringing it alive for her again.

As they went, she pointed out places she recognized from when they would walk about with their mother and their cousins, foraging and harvesting as they went. Roderick was eager to know all about it. He was every bit as fascinated with the landscape as she was, if not more so.

"It is so different to the Lowlands," he commented. "Much more so than I would have expected. We had a good welcome at Kinlochbervie, though."

"Did you not expect the locals to welcome us?"

"I wasn't sure what to expect. I've heard some wild stories about this part of Scotland, and given that Clyde was the Highlander I knew best until I met you, you can see why I hesitate to claim understanding."

She laughed. She noticed that he'd suggested he knew her better than he knew Clyde, who'd been with him for so much longer. It made her hope that was a good sign. She was nervous about what would transpire between them once they arrived in Fingal. Would he turn around after he'd spoken with his friend Gregor, and head back to Kinlochbervie immediately? She hoped not. She was also nervous about what lay ahead for her. The state of her nerves left her adrift in a sea of emotions, and if not for the sensible, solid man at her side, she feared she would have got lost several times over.

As daylight dimmed, Roderick found them a place to rest for the night. In a sheltered spot between two trees the thick grass underfoot made a good bed. The trees leaned together like old friends and were still laden with leaves, providing a thick canopy overhead. He collected soft scrub and ferns to make it warmer and more comfortable.

Then he set about collecting dry branches and kindling for a fire.

Maisie stood by, watching. "You can do this? You can make a shelter, on land?"

"I wasn't always at sea, and my da believed that making a warm bed for the night if you're out hunting was the most basic of skills a man should learn."

He gestured. "Sit yourself down. I'll prepare the fish for roasting once I've got a fire going."

Maisie did so, and watched in silent pleasure as he kindled the fire, then arranged the fishes on a thin branch he scraped down with a dirk, building a trestle to rest the spit upon. After the sky dimmed it was the light of the fire she watched him by. It felt as if they were the only two in the whole world, and she felt content to enjoy that for the evening.

After they had eaten, and he joined her under the trees, they watched the glowing embers of the fire as they rested.

"Will you have to return to the ship once you talk to your friend Gregor?"

Roderick did not answer, just turned his head to look at her, staring into her eyes.

"When do they expect you back, Brady and the men? I mean, how long will they wait for you to return?"

"Are you wanting shot of me?"

"No. You know that is not true. Quite the opposite, in fact."

In the firelight, she saw his expression sharpen. He looked at her longingly.

Maisie's heart swelled in her chest.

"If they get even a hint of the navy being on their trail, I told them they must leave without me."

He was as wary as she was, choosing his words with care, taking his time. It was as if they were stepping cautiously around one another, each afraid to say the wrong thing for the other person.

"But what would you do, if you went back to the bay and they had gone?"

"Live a different life." He gestured around them. "As you can see, I can make shelter. It's a good start, is it not?"

Maisie sighed. "Roderick, do not taunt me so!"

"Taunt you?"

"You jest…and I adore that. I have never been so happy. But sometimes I need to know if your jest has any basis in truth."

"I know." He nodded. "I truly wouldn't mind being on land awhile, but I do not want you to feel as if you are stuck with me."

"Oh, Roderick. I would never feel that way." Her heart ached.

Without hesitation he shifted, moving toward her.

Instinctively, she lay back as he closed in, wanting to feel his heat, his weight, his possession of her.

He crouched over her, like a hunter, but also like a shield. "Never ever?"

She wrapped her hand around the strong column of his neck. "Never ever, ever."

"We will see how you feel once you are reunited with your kin. You can let me go if you want to, or not, if that is your preference."

Maisie kissed him, silencing him, then rolled him onto his back and straddled his hips, holding him down—holding him to the Highlands.

The midmorning mist filled the glen beyond, and Maisie stared across it, remembering this very sight from her child-hood. She breathed in the familiar scents of heather and mixed foliage, and the heady scent of damp, mossy grass and mulch underfoot. They used to run through the mist and up the hill on the other side, chasing one another, the morning dew underfoot only making it more fun.

"We are close to Fingal now."

"That we are."

When she looked at Roderick, she saw that his brow was drawn low as he studied the horizon. Was he still thinking that she wouldn't need him when she found home? "What worries you?"

He turned to look down at her, and broke into a smile. "Nothing at all. I was trying to see clearly. Look there, on the distant crag."

Maisie followed the direction he pointed. Atop the distant ridge a figure sat on a large rock as if watching out, looking in their direction.

Even while he pointed, the figure rose to her feet. It was a woman, shrouded in a heavy shawl. Before she had even thought about it, Maisie knew who it was.

She felt her heart beat faster, echoed as it was in her twin. "Jessie."

"If I had to wager on it, I would say you were right."

Reaching out for his hand, she clung to him, then lifted her free hand and waved.

When her wave was returned, Maisie nodded. "She sensed me coming. She knew."

They watched as the woman turned away for just a moment and shouted back to the glen beyond, waving her arms, alerting others.

In the distance, a bell sounded.

Then the woman grabbed her skirts in both hands, lifting them in order to run in their direction, disappearing quickly into the mist in the valley below.

"She'll come up out of the mists, like a bird flying up from the clouds," Maisie told Roderick, and nodded at the place.

Moments later, Jessie emerged. Grabbing Maisie into her arms, she danced about. "You're here, you're really home."

Maisie laughed breathlessly, remembering that they did that, spun and danced, hand in hand. "Of course I am. I've come in time for your handfasting to this Gregor Ramsay I've heard all about."

Jessie's mouth fell open and she drew to a halt. "You knew?"

Maisie laughed, for it was just as it had been before, as if they had never been apart. "I did, and I will tell you all about it, once we are settled." She gripped her twin's hand. "Is Lennox here?"

"Oh, aye." Jessie laughed. "And he has his own coven. A fine bunch they are, too."

As if to answer her question, a tall man hurtled toward them, running fast, his long hair flying free, his shirt loose from his belt.

"Let me look at you," he said, grasping Maisie by the shoulders. "It's really you." He shook his head, and his eyes shone with tears of relief.

He'd grown into a handsome man, and she felt proud.

"I hunted for you, for you both. Where did you go?"

"I was taken to England. I've been in London until very recently."

"That accounts for the strange manner of speaking you have," Jessie commented. "Like a fine lady you are."

She shook her head. "I am Maisie Taskill from Fingal, and I'm home at last."

When she said that she found herself locked in an embrace with both her siblings. She pressed her head against them, sobbing with relief. But when they drew apart and her brother encouraged them to head back toward the village, Maisie paused and put out her hand for Roderick, drawing him into their fold.

The morning before the festival of Samhain in 1715, Gregor Ramsay and Jessica Taskill handfasted to one another.

Gregor refused to put the autumn season to rest without having her as his wife, for he said there was no holding her, and the new season might tempt her to stray.

Jessie laughed at his notions, but Gregor insisted, anyway. Maisie couldn't have been happier for her twin.

The bond between Gregor and Roderick was a delight, too. It meant that Roderick settled much more quickly than he might otherwise have done. The men worked together, building neighboring crofts. On a nearby hill, Lennox had done the same.

Lennox and his woman, Chloris, planned to make their vows to one another after yuletide. Chloris said she needed the old Christian year to be left behind so that she might break with her past as the year turned over. Lennox agreed to her request, because it meant that they would be hand-fasted before their babe arrived.

The handfastening was done by Glenna, a woman from Lennox's coven, together with the oldest living Taskill, their mother's aunt Seonag.

Seonag was a wise woman, and peered at Jessie and Gregor for a long while before nodding and stating that they were meant to be together.

While her twin was exchanging promises with Gregor, Maisie put her hand in Roderick's.

He nodded. He knew.

She wanted him to stay.

They would wed before the festival of Beltane.

So it was the Taskill siblings became part of their magical landscape again, as they were always meant to be, in tune with the seasons, the elements and the tides.

Lennox, who had a strong coven around him, could never be entirely at rest. In his most somber moments he reminded them that witch hunters, thwarted lovers and souls who believed they had been wronged, might yet still be on their trail. He also told them that they would deal with whatever might come, because they were strong and they were with their kin and their clan.

For in the hidden glens the Taskills were all around, welcoming in those three and the lovers they had brought with them—the lovers who had helped them find one another, and had hastened their path home.

★ ★ ★ ★ ★

Acknowledgments

This book would not have been possible without Cindy Vallar's guidance. Cindy's knowledge of the Age of Sail and her ability to share with others, inspired and informed me, and gave me the tools with which to write a story set aboard the *Libertas*. I am also indebted to the staff of the Maritime Museum in Liverpool for their willingness to answer questions.

My thanks also go to Portia Da Costa, for her friendship, support and encouragement during the writing of this novel.

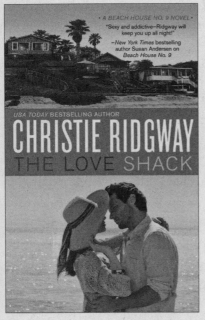

A heart-pounding new romantic suspense from

VIRNA DePAUL

Shades of the past...
Shades of intrigue...

Available wherever books are sold!

Be sure to connect with us at:

Harlequin.com/Newsletters

Facebook.com/HarlequinBooks

Twitter.com/HarlequinBooks

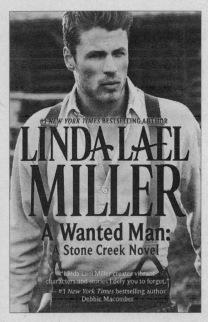

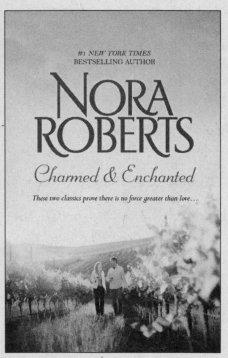